Praise for Stuart R. West's
Corporate Wolf

"Brilliant. Unique horror humor that still ratchets up the tension and manages to shock. Alternately terrifying, hilarious, and ultimately poignant, you owe yourself to read this book."
–Catherine Cavendish, author of *The Haunting of Henderson Close* and *The Devil's Serenade*

"Howling good horror!"
–Russell James, author of *The Playing Card Killer* and *Claws*

"You've heard of the *Wolf of Wallstreet*. Those greedy guys have nothing on the staff of Lerner Corporation. On a company retreat, Shawn Biltmore is attacked by…a bear? Once he returns to work, that's when the wolf hits the fan. Humor mixed with horror is Stuart West's forte. This is another great addition to his wild bunch of books about everything from a haunted mine to a spooky bed-and-breakfast inn."
–Cellophane Queen Book Reviews

And More Praise for the Works of Stuart R. West

Ghosts of Gannaway!

"…the story has some truly scary scenes, it is the slow boil suspense that gets under the skin. I'll be reading more of Stuart R. West!"
–Tom Deady, Bram Stoker Award-winning author of *Haven*

"With *Ghosts of Gannaway*, author Stuart R. West pulls back the skin of 20th Century Americana and extracts a magnificent working-class nightmare. It's the kind of tense, creepy thriller that keeps you frantically turning pages. West's talent and mastery of the craft are undeniably enviable."
–Peter N. Dudar, author of *The Goat Parade*

"Filled with tension, excellent characterization, suspense, ghostly presences, and enough twists and turns to keep you glued to the last page."
–Catherine Cavendish, author of *Cold Revenge* and *The Devil's Serenade*

"Captivating…a ghost story full of surprises."
–Joan C. Curtis, author of *A Painting to Die For*

Twisted Tales from Tornado Alley!

"These tales are top class horror with a smile, which is just as scary as a scowl or a snarl."

–Maynard Sims, author of the DCI Jack Callum series

"West draws upon our worst fears, turns prejudices back on to us, and puts us in situations against all odds as we recoil in horror but rejoice in delight at the intelligence of the writing and aha moments."

–MJ LaBeff, author of the *Last Cold Case* thriller series

"A Midwest fright-fest that will blow you away."

–Russell James, author of *Q Island* and *Dark Inspiration*

"A collection of horrific gems from a unique talent, *Twisted Tales from Tornado Alley* is one to curl up with on a dark night. Just make sure all the lights are on. Oh, and that you know where your cat is."

–Catherine Cavendish, author of *The Devil Inside Her* and *Waking the Ancients*

Dread and Breakfast!

"Like Stephen King and Joe Lansdale had a freaky,
hyperactive baby and it wrote this book!"
–Somer Canon, author of *Vicki Beautiful*

"A fast-paced, uncanny, and hugely entertaining
horror novel!"
–Vanessa Morgan, screenwriter and
author of *Drowned Sorrow*

"A suspenseful, twisty ride! Heart-pounding horror!"
–L.X. Cain, author of *Bloodwalker* and *Soul Cutter*

GODLAND

GODLAND

Stuart R. West

A
Grinning Skull Press
Publication

PO Box 67, Bridgewater, MA 02324

ISBN-13: 978-1-947227-75-0 (paperback)
ISBN: 978-1-947227-76-7 (ebook)

DEDICATION

As always, I'd like to dedicate this book to my two inspiring muses and loves, Cydney and Sarah. And to the McQueen family for their loyal support and constant cheerleading. Finally, this goes out to my late father who survived his own very personal "Godland."

ACKNOWLEDGMENTS

I won't name names (sometimes to protect the innocent!), but thanks to all friends and family who supplied me with childhood tales they'd heard about and/or lived through that helped to fill in some of the background of my nasty little tale. (Not the bloody mayhem, of course.)

I'd also like to shout out thanks to the fine folks at Grinning Skull Press for resurrecting my lean and mean, farm noir, horror thriller. Special thanks go out to the best horror editor in the business, Michael Evans and cover artist supreme, Jeffrey Kosh.

Chapter One

A blast sheared open the night sky. An ear-piercing shriek followed. Bats and birds fled trees, draping a transient veil across the face of the moon. A moan gained in intensity—not quite human, not quite animal—and rumbled across the cornfields like a runaway train.

For those gathered at the small Kansas farm, the long night of survival had begun.

Five Days Earlier

The old dog lay on the steps seeking comfort from the heat. The door flew open. Before the man could kick him into the yard, the dog raced for shelter.

Edwin Lewis Quail stepped out into the sunlight and stretched, painfully thin. Weather-beaten crevices and sun damage marked his roadmap of a face. His cold eyes stood out in stark contrast, like two ice cubes in a Bloody Mary.

He took in a deep breath and coughed. Probably not a healthy cough. But, goddammit, it didn't matter. Things were going to get better now.

Edwin's farm hadn't brought in money for a long time. Too long. His cornfields were dry. The remaining livestock looked sickly and wouldn't fetch much in the town market. The liberals and Democrats blamed something called "global warming" for destroying his crops. Nothing but lies and political propaganda. Edwin knew better. Nobody helped him out; nobody gave a damn. After fifty years of farming, Edwin had given up on waiting for government aid. The government, too busy with its own money-grabbing agendas, forgot about him out here in Godwin, Kansas.

Well, fine and dandy. God put Edwin on this earth for a reason. To take what he could and better his position in life. All up to him.

Edwin squinted into the early morning sunlight, appraising his dying cornfields. All this land—this pretty much now worthless land—had been a struggle to maintain. Nothing he could do to save it. A lost cause. But he had one thing left to do before he put it all behind him.

Like clockwork, the moaning from the room upstairs began. The sound rattled through the windows, permeating Edwin's aching joints. It could wait, though. Edwin intended on enjoying his morning.

For the first time in quite a while, he smiled. A new day was coming. Time for the meek to inherit the earth, as the Good Book says. His laughter grew into a low, guttural growl, born from the pit of his stomach. Soon, he was howling madly at the injustices God had showered down upon him.

The old hound dog crawled into the cornfields, putting as much distance as possible between himself and the beast on the porch.

Lindsay Bellowes unstrapped her backpack and dropped it onto the cafeteria table.

Shannon looked up from poking around today's mystery meal. "Excuse me," said Shannon. "*Some* of us are trying to figure out what we're eating today."

Lindsay sat down across from Shannon. "And *some* of us shouldn't be eating at all."

Shannon knew Lindsay's ways; her constant teasing was a part of their daily routine. Nonetheless, Shannon couldn't help feeling self-conscious about her looks and her weight. She tossed the fork onto the plate and wiped her mouth. Meal over. "Lindsay, are you going to do that thing at the American Royal this year?"

Lindsay grimaced. "I don't think so. It's so redneck city with all the cowboys and creepy old guys. Ewww." Lindsay kicked her feet under the table, fending off imaginary cowboy suitors.

"You know, not everything has to be about cute guys. Besides, you were actually pretty good." Lindsay's mother had always considered herself quite the equestrian, as she'd grown up riding horses. Last year, she pushed Lindsay into a group called The Young Kansas City Cowgirls. The Cowgirls received a spot at the American Royal—an annual Kansas City celebration of everything country, cowboy, and just plain cows—and entertained the audience with showmanship and trick riding.

"Says you," said Lindsay. "But I did look pretty damn cute in my cowgirl outfit, didn't I?" Lindsay jumped out of her seat. She sashayed around the table, fluffing her hair and batting her eyelashes.

"Gag. I would've never been caught dead in that outfit." The outfit had consisted of a short, light blue dress laced with white trim. A Stetson and high-heeled white boots completed the eyesore. "The latest in cowgirl hooker apparel," Shannon added.

"Whatever. You're just mad 'cause you couldn't bring it off."

The girls' high-pitched giggling prompted Miss Swanson to rush over and rap her knuckles on the table.

"That's enough, girls," said Miss Swanson. "Settle down."

"Sorry, Miss Swanson." As soon as Miss Swanson scuttled off to hold court over another table, Shannon and Lindsay broke out in laughter again.

"Hey, can you give me a ride home tonight after play practice?" asked Shannon.

"Cool," said Lindsay. A tall boy with unruly dark hair slouched by them, grinning. "Oh my God, he's so hot!" Lindsay gripped her lunch tray, anchoring herself to the table.

"Who? Gavin? I don't know. He seems like kind of a douche to me. Isn't he a stoner anyway?"

"With a body like that, who cares?" Both girls watched him walk away.

Shannon snuck a glimpse at his bottom, lending credence to Lindsay's assessment. "I think he likes you, Shannon."

Shannon's fair complexion burned crimson. Another thing she hated about herself. Her pixie hairstyle emphasized her blushing cheeks, blonde arrows of hair pointing toward them.

"Lindsay, you think every guy likes me." Shannon appreciated Lindsay's attempts at building her self-confidence. And truth be told, she wasn't totally oblivious to some boys eyeing her on occasion. But her shyness held her back. Lindsay, on the other hand, was blessed with a great figure and a fearlessness in her sexual pursuits. Sometimes Lindsay scared boys away with her aggressiveness. Other times, she didn't. She regaled Shannon with outrageous stories of sexual conquest and brazen behavior. Shannon reacted with appropriate prudish horror. But truthfully? She found herself wondering about sex, jealous of Lindsay in many ways. Shannon paid no attention to her best friend's less-than-stellar reputation. It made her more fascinating. And since sex was a strictly taboo topic with Shannon's mother, Lindsay remained her only lifeline to the mysteries of sex.

Shannon ran her fingertips along her eyeglasses frame. A dimpled corner of her mouth curled up as she pondered making out with bad-boy Gavin.

Lindsay's laughter jolted her from her daydream. "Hello! God, you're such a geek sometimes, Shannon."

Seven years ago, Shannon Wolters met Lindsay in grade school, around the same time Shannon's parents separated. Not the best of times. First, she lost her father, and then she moved with her mother to a different school district. A fresh start but not in a good way. Lindsay had been the first to befriend Shannon. More than a friend, Lindsay was her salvation. Literally. If not for Lindsay, Shannon doubted she would have made it. Girls rarely sustained longtime friendships in high school, but they'd remained best friends for seven years.

For the first time since her dad left, Shannon felt in control of her life. Not much, but it gave her hope. Everything would be all right. An awesome best friend, boys noticing her, good grades. God *must* be smiling upon her.

Peter Brookes sipped his scotch, savoring the smoky, woody aftertaste. He left his leather chair and strolled to the window, gazing out at the nighttime city skyline. His kingdom—New York City.

Hell, he practically owned New York City, or at least most of it. And why not? He'd earned it. His successful stock brokerage firm brought in a lot of capital to New York. Things hadn't always been that way, of course. Twenty years ago, he'd arrived in New York with nothing but an empty wallet and emptier lies on which to fall back. Not even a high school diploma. However, he did possess unlimited charm and a knack for persuasion. The only tools he'd ever needed.

During his initial days at Kobler, Cannon, & Steele, Peter soaked up everything he could from his coworkers. Then he stole their clients. He acted promptly upon several inside trading tips, making hollow promises to the insiders for a percentage of the gains. By planting rumors, lies, and falsified documents, he had several troublesome (to him at least) coworkers fired. He thrived on the competitive spirit of capitalism; it's what made America great.

It had all been so simple. He fought, lied, forged, cheated, and screwed his way to the top of the food chain, stopping only to gather the acquisitions of war from his fallen comrades. Soon, Brookes Financial Consulting Services was born.

Peter had made his first million by the time he was twenty-seven. He had his pick of any woman money could buy. Lackeys showered topnotch cocaine and designer drugs upon him—people who wanted a part of the pie. *His* pie. The one he baked with his own hands, no thanks to the lowly kitchen staff. Peter acquired his fortune utilizing drive, intelligence, and raw talent. Fuck the naysayers who said he was lucky. You take care of yourself; that's all there was to it.

Perhaps Peter owed a little bit of his good fortune to Peter Brookes. The *original* Peter Brookes. "Brookes" hadn't always been Peter's true name. But Peter didn't want to overpraise Brookes's contributions to his meteoric rise. Besides, Brookes wasn't alive to share in his fortune. No, *this* Peter accomplished everything on his own.

Peter took another swig of scotch. He wondered if his new secretary—his current sex toy—had left yet. He buzzed her number. After four rings, he hung up. No matter. He needed to fire her soon anyway. It was always best not to let his affairs linger around the office too long. You needed to cut them loose after a couple of months, before they started growing bothersome. Or worse—before they considered blackmail.

He sighed and called his wife. "Barbara, I'll be home soon. Are the kids still awake?"

"No, they waited up but finally had to go to bed," she said.

Good. "Okay, don't wait for me." He hung up without any further pointless blather. His family drained him. It pleased him that he wouldn't see his two children tonight. They were good enough kids, he supposed, but what more could they possibly offer him? How many times could he feign enjoyment reading those monotonous books or watching films about flying elephants?

Then there was Barbara. Once a damn good-looking trophy wife, the years had caught up with her. He no longer took pride in showing her off at business functions, his tolerance for her fading.

Quite simply, boredom had set in. Even the first love of Peter's life—money—no longer thrilled him. What do you do after you have everything?

His upcoming business trip was just what he needed. It definitely would not be boring. He looked down at the bulging front of his tailored suit pants. "Well, I'll be goddammed!" He smiled and polished off his drink.

With a sigh, Matt Strothers locked the door to his store. All the other businesses in the small strip mall were either vacant or closed for the night. The dull, flat storefronts were ugly, almost painful to look at. The cheap, flat roof appeared ready to fly away at the mention of a tornado. Prefabricated suburbia at its worst.

Above the window, the electric sign flickered off. "Village Video," it should have read. However, several bulbs had burned out long ago; the resultant message now read, "Vil e Video."

Hanging by a thread. Just like his life.

Nineteen years ago, Matt had dreamed of applying his doctorate in film studies to good use. His brief sojourn in Los Angeles made him realize how worthless his degree was. No one wanted to take a chance on an inexperienced film director.

Matt retreated to Kansas City, believing it an opportune place for a *good* video store. Large video chains dominated the marketplace. He harbored a naïve notion that people accepted spoon-fed, popular films because they were unaware of other options. If he could enlighten the moviegoing public, broaden their cinematic horizons, surely his store would be a grass-roots success. After acquiring the financial setup and backing, Matt lived comfortably on his proceeds for a while. The best years.

Matt pulled into his driveway, got out of his car, and looked at the other houses along the street. All of them superficially attractive but incredibly homogenized. Matt worked in suburbia, lived in suburbia, and lived the American Dream. Although it didn't feel so dreamlike now.

Jason, the one good thing in his life these days, greeted him at the front door with a kiss. "Hey, honey. How was work today?"

"Not bad." Matt didn't want to burden Jason with his financial concerns, so he'd been less than forthcoming about where they stood. "What's cookin'? Smells great." Matt tossed his jacket onto the coat tree.

"Chicken cordon bleu." Jason wiped his hands on a kitchen towel. His demeanor was typically upbeat, but Matt noticed suspicion in his eyes. Matt never could fool Jason. "Okay. Now, really... *How* was your day?"

"I had maybe five customers; most of them bored refugee husbands from the shoe store next door." Matt smiled, hoping his joke would outrank financial issues.

"We don't need the video store. I make enough money to support us both. Until you find something you like to do."

Matt couldn't help it. Call it a matter of pride, but he felt Jason relished the fact he made twice the salary Matt did. And that was during the store's prime years. "Best Video won't even take my calls anymore, Jay. Even they're hurting for business. I should've sold the store to them when I had the chance. Now, with downloading, no one goes to video stores any-more."

"Should've, would've, whatever," said Jason. "It doesn't matter. We'll get by."

"I guess." Matt mustered a weak smile. "I suppose we will."

Matt used to believe God had a plan for everybody. At least that's what he had been taught. But if this was God's plan for him, God had lost the blueprints.

Chapter Two

The televangelist blathered on, but Edwin wasn't in a religious mood this morning. Too excited about his future. He looked about his living room. It felt more like a prison. The musty, floral-patterned sofa—the springs long given out—plunged him deep into the worn cushions. A threadbare, burgundy-colored rug lay over the warping floorboards. Gretchen's children figurines, lined up on shelves like so many soldiers, smiled angelically at him. Everything in the room reminded him of Gretchen, from the empty flower vases to the permeating odor of decay. The smell lingered like burned fried chicken.

Nearly eighteen years before, Gretchen had passed on. Her impending death dragged on for almost a year. During that endless period, he had to cook for her, bathe her, and feed her in bed. He grew to despise her. When he finagled her into the bathtub, he couldn't scrub the stink off her. It became a death house. He kept a deathbed vigil, praying to God to give him release and take her.

Doc Collins stopped by on occasion to check on Gretchen. He told Edwin she needed professional medical care.

Edwin just shook his head and laughed. "I don't have any insurance, can't *afford* no insurance. My folks never had any neither, and what was good enough for them is good enough for me."

"What you're doing, Edwin, is *inhumane.*" Collins flipped on his hat and raced for the door.

"You just keep judging me, Doc," Edwin called after him. "The Day of Judgment will be upon us soon, and then we'll see where we end up!"

Edwin always considered himself a righteous man. He lived by the teachings of the Lord. But he couldn't stand others, standing in their ivory towers, casting judgment down upon him.

Edwin pulled himself out of the sofa and turned off the television. He hated the room, the house, the farm, his land. He spent all his life here, toiling in the fields and providing for his family. With nothing to show for it.

He leafed through the ancient travel magazine next to the television. *Florida. That's the dream.* After suffering the cold, harsh Kansas winters for so long, he thought about living his twilight years in the warmth. Fully prepared to leave everything behind. Yes, the bill collectors would come calling, but let his son handle it. After all, Edwin had inherited the farm from his daddy, along with all the outstanding debts, just as several generations had done before him.

Edwin paused on a photograph of a houseboat and grinned. Time to live life on his own terms. No more slaving for other people, making them money. All under God's careful guidance, of course.

The loud groan upstairs shook the windowpanes as if a sudden wind gust struck the house. Cursing, he walked into the kitchen.

Yesterday, Lindsay clued Shannon in on what she'd been up to. She had been texting Gavin, scoping out his feelings for Shannon. At first, Shannon was mortified and super pissed at her best friend. Until she heard the outcome. Gavin had said he'd like to ask Shannon out but didn't want Lindsay to say anything. He wanted there to be some "romantic mystique" left to dating.

She had anticipated all day—perched somewhere between excitement and fear—Gavin's asking her out. So far, it hadn't happened. Her natural cynical outlook prepared her for another disappointment. Yet, he smiled at her in algebra. Like a dork, she quickly averted her gaze, dropping her pencil in the process.

After school, Shannon and Lindsay walked out into the sunlit freedom of the outdoors. An absolutely beautiful spring day. Shannon couldn't have been happier. Or more apprehensive.

When she heard Gavin call out her name, she nearly took a tumble.

"Hey, Shannon! Wait up." He ran down the stairs to catch up with the girls. "Hey, Lindsay, how's it goin'?"

Shannon shot a terrified look toward Lindsay, who seemed to be enjoying this *way* too much. She responded with a suggestive eyebrow wiggle.

"Okay, well, I'll leave you guys to it," said Lindsay, already departing. "My car's in the other lot. See you tomorrow." Shannon wanted to grab Lindsay and pull her in tight like a security blanket. Too late. Lindsay fled the scene faster than a hit-and-run driver. Shannon felt like the victim.

"See ya." Shannon's newfound courage crumpled. Alone and abandoned in a shark-festooned ocean without a life raft.

"Lindsay's pretty cool," said Gavin.

"Yeah, I guess that's what you might call her."

"Are you keeping up with the algebra assignments? The graphing's lost a lot of the other guys."

"Of course, I'm a straight-A student." Discussing grades and school, something in her wheelhouse, put her at ease. "Not that I think it's bad if you're *not* a straight-A student or anything."

"Who says I'm not a straight-A student?"

"Are you?"

"Well, no," he said. "But I've accomplished the art of being a good straight-B student. Just enough studying to keep me out of trouble and not enough to make the honors list." Gavin seemed pleased with himself. *Great, a slacker.*

"Hey, Shannon, I was wondering..." *Here it comes.* Her pulse quickened. She knew her cheeks had blossomed red. *Mood-cheeks.* How she wished for the ability to tan. "Would you like to catch a flick sometime?"

Shannon swallowed audibly, a click emanating from her throat. Gavin's confident swagger dissolved into a meek schoolboy's demeanor. "I mean...

with me?" he added.

Shannon smiled. *Okay, he's not all arrogant bluster.* She found it endearing. "But…aren't you a stoner?" She couldn't believe she had asked it, but the damage was done.

"No, I'm not. Why would you even *ask* that?"

"Well, the people you hang out with… I mean, your friends are all dopers and—"

"Wait, are you going to give me the lecture about how people judge you by the friends you keep?" He grinned, but defensiveness lurked around the edges of his voice. "I get that a lot."

"No, I mean, I just thought—" Shannon waved her hands, hoping to erase her assumption. "Let's just put it this way, Gavin; you surprise me."

"Well, I'd consider that a good thing, wouldn't you?"

"Yes, I guess it is." She twirled a lock of hair around her finger.

"Are *you* a doper?"

"What? *No!*"

Gavin laughed. "There, how does it feel?" His smile widened, the bluster raging back. "Okay, look, I know you're not. Some of my friends are dopers, but I don't join them. And I ask 'em not to do it around me. I don't drink either. And I don't dance on Sundays." He cocked an eyebrow and smirked. "My friends are just…I don't know. Just guys I hang out with who aren't judgmental, stuck up, or materialistic."

"I get that."

"And that's one of the reasons I'd like to get to know you better. I mean, not because you're a doper or not, but because…it's because you're different."

"Different?" Shannon realized she'd suddenly gained the upper hand. An unfamiliar feeling. "You mean you don't want to ask me out because I'm stunningly cute?" *Dance, Gavin, dance! Be my puppet on a string!* She wondered if this was how the popular girls felt when they controlled boys.

"No! I mean…yes," stammered Gavin. "Anyway, what do you say?"

"About what?"

"About going out with me."

"Well, I don't know. It all kinda depends…"

"On what?"

"If you'll change your mind about dancing on Sundays. I cut a mean rug, especially on Sundays."

"Okay, fine," said Gavin, laughing. "How would you like to go dancing this Sunday? I don't know where, but I'll find a place."

"Well, I guess since you're being so accommodating, I'll go out with you." Shannon had no idea she possessed such heretofore-unseen reservoirs of flirtation.

"Great, I'll pick you up at six."

"Wait. My address…" Shannon fished in her purse for a pencil and paper.

"I know where you live. I've known for a while. The Internet is my friend."

"Okay, great." Shannon stared into his brown eyes, wondering what the next step should be. Should she be bold and kiss him? Before she could muster up the nerve, he trotted off.

"Oh hey, Shannon," he yelled while shuffling backward.

"Yeah?"

"I *do*, you know."

"Do what?"

"I do think you're stunningly cute." He said it through cupped hands, capturing the attention of several other students in the parking lot.

Shannon fumbled for words but came up short. She waved at him, then immediately blushed. She felt faint, her knees wobbly. Sixteen years old, and she'd never had a boyfriend. Always considered herself unworthy. Her father left because of her, after all.

Yet, here was a boy—a cute boy—who actually used the term "romantic mystique." And he had asked her out, for whatever reason. This was, by far, the greatest day she'd ever experienced. She found herself looking forward to many, many more great days. Especially with Gavin.

Peter rode up in the ornate elevator. At least twice every day for the last ten years, he had made this same journey. Usually his only time for reflection before the doors opened into the penthouse suite, forcing him to strap on his "family face." He enjoyed the long trip, abhorred when it ended.

After the elevator panel hopscotched to forty-six, the doors clunked open.

"Daddy!" Michael, his oldest child, dropped a robot toy in front of the fireplace and raced toward Peter.

Peter affected a smile—something he'd developed a skill for—and extended his arms. Michael leaped into them.

"Hey, how's my number one boy today?" Peter's lips stretched into a frozen, dead man's rictus. His facial muscles ached.

"Great! Me and Toddy played all day at pre-school!" *The $100,000 tuition pre-school where Michael plays with blocks.* Peter didn't mind the money, not really. It wasn't like he didn't have mountains of it. Still, it infuriated him. The only job Barbara ever had was finding new ways to spend his money.

"That sounds *great* right back at you," said Peter. "Where's your sister and Mommy?"

"Michelle's at a sleepover. And Mommy's in the kitchen getting dinner ready."

Code-speak for yelling at the hired cook about dinner. He crossed the marble floor, depositing Michael onto the sofa.

"Better get your shoes off the sofa before Mommy sees you." Peter held his finger teasingly to his lips.

"But, Daddy, you *put* me here," squealed Michael.

As Peter walked through the living room, his hostility escalated. Barbara sought out the most expensive interior decorators in New York City to furnish the extravagant living room. More hired help maintained the immaculate appearance. Peter had long lost interest in Barbara's only talent—bedroom prowess.

He had met Barbara at a wealthy, prospective client's dinner party fourteen years ago. She entered the banquet room on the arm of one of his competitors. Reason enough to deem her a worthy trophy for the evening. Her beautiful, long neck stretched regally out of her elegant gown. She carried herself majestically and with confidence. And most importantly, she knew how to apply makeup. So many of the women Peter encountered splashed their makeup on liberally, appearing whorish. Yet, Barbara's face was perfect, the subtle eye shadow accenting her gorgeous, oval-shaped brown eyes. Peter decided then she would complete his empire. A stunning woman he could show off, and if necessary, use as a distraction to older businessmen.

Within three hours, Peter had seduced her away from her companion. He had her propped up on the bathroom sink, her hose down around her legs.

"This is the start of our relationship," Peter said. "A very powerful and important relationship." He stared into her smoky eyes.

"What about a 'beautiful relationship'?" she asked.

"That's not part of the plan." Then he took her.

Peter cleared his mind and entered the sterile, white kitchen. "Hello, Barbara." He planted a love-barren kiss on her proffered cheek.

"Hello, Peter." Peter suspected she was just as bored as he was, but she'd never leave him. She had more to lose. He could always get another trophy wife. What could she do? Her once swan-like neck showed wrinkles and the ravages of time. Her eyes were still stunning, but they were now underscored by bags that weighted down her entire appearance. He could no longer wrap his hands around her once-slender waistline. Old and used up.

"How was work, darling?" She afforded him a fleeting glance. Her focus returned to the chef preparing whatever monstrosity she'd picked out for that evening's meal.

"Fine."

"Peter?" Her voice held a glimmer of life. "Tell me again about this trip you're taking." She drummed her long, tapered fingernails against her cheekbone.

"I've told you. I'm meeting a prospective client in Oklahoma City. I'm not sure when it'll be, but soon. I'm just waiting on a call."

"And *why* will you be driving again?" Barbara knew about his affairs but turned a blind eye to them. To her, living a life of privilege trumped a faithful marriage.

But his forthcoming trip was not about an affair. No need to leave town to have sex.

"I've already explained this," said Peter. "I want to take some time off. I need to get away. A long, leisurely drive is what I want." All of which was a lie, of course. If he flew, he suspected airport security would question his travel gear.

"Well, you've never done this before." Barbara turned back toward the chef's progress.

"I just want to experience nature," said Peter. "That's all."

Matt lay awake in bed, his mind racing. His debt overwhelmed him. There were student loans, the mortgage on his store, and the ever-increasing bills from the mental institution. Jason had asked him about going back to his family for help, but that was out of the question. He hadn't talked to them in years and planned on keeping it that way.

He rolled over and studied Jason's face in the moonlight. Jason's full lips gave the appearance of a blissful smile, even in sleep. His dark eyelashes fluttered slightly, small wings sweeping him into dreamland. He reminded Matt of the innocence of youth and not only because he was ten years younger than Matt. He found optimism in every situation. The way kids do.

Matt sat on the edge of the bed, feeling the inevitability of age chasing him. Tired, achy, his bladder full—the new norm. He quietly made his way to the bathroom downstairs.

Jason Rodriguez had first entered Matt's life eight years ago. Two years later, Matt left his wife.

The hardest thing he ever did. Matt, already riddled with grief about his affair with Jason, struggled to come to terms with his latent homosexuality. Staying away from Jason for eight months hadn't changed his desires, no matter how much he fought them. Worse, Matt recognized his wife's struggle with her own depression. She'd grown quiet, unmotivated. Yet, he'd found a compatible companion in Jason, someone he could talk to, share his innermost thoughts with. Emotional walls stood between Matt and his wife. And Matt had been the chief architect, no doubt about it.

Matt told his therapist he didn't want to hurt his wife. The therapist demanded Matt tell her the truth.

"Sit down. I have something I need to tell you," he had said to his wife. He'd taken a few deep breaths, looked heavenward as if for guidance. "I know I've been distant the past year or so…and I want you to know it's not your fault." Her eyes brimmed with tears. "But it's all me. It's *all* me."

"What are you saying, Matt?"

Matt saw how their strained marriage had taken its toll on her. She looked much older than her age.

"I need to take some time off. I'm going to find an apartment…at least for a while. Until I can figure out what's going on with me."

"'What's going on with you?' What's going on with you? What about me, your wife? What about—"

"I'm sorry. I'm truly sorry." Maybe—if he actually *said* it—he could move on with his life. And she, hers. "I think I'm…gay." The words lingered resonantly, hanging over his head with shame.

She'd stared at him, her mouth open, lips quivering. Her pain-anguished eyes had slipped away into slivers of anger. "Get out." Her calm tone had unsettled Matt. Then she repeated it, softly, yet firmly. "Get out."

Over the next eight months, Matt had gone to work and come home every night to his small, one-bedroom apartment. He'd seen no one, had no social life. Holed up in his apartment like a hermit, he had pondered his life. When he had finally felt human again, he called Jason.

Matt stared out the window into the moon-struck streets. Prior to Jason, he'd never experienced a long-lasting, meaningful relationship. He'd been a patterned, repeat "leaver." He hoped he'd never leave Jason but worried he didn't have the capacity for happiness. To have what it took to sustain a lasting relationship.

All his life, Matt had left behind people he cared about. He'd left behind his family—his wife—and he despised himself for those hurt in his wake.

Time to make amends. At least he hoped he could. He needed to contact someone, someone he hadn't seen in some time. And he prayed all would go well.

Chapter Three

Edwin narrowed his eyes, forcing the computer screen into focus. He found more information than necessary. Age, address, school, groups she belonged to, make and year of car. *Everything.* Tucked away into the kitchen nook, the computer gave him the world at his fingertips.

Edwin leaned back and cracked his knuckles. He wouldn't have found his financial benefactor without the computer. Of course, he never thought he'd use a computer, let alone own one. He sure as hell would never have paid for one. But, for once, good fortune smiled down upon him. Or, more likely, God's good graces had steered him clearly onto his path to salvation.

He folded his bony hands and prayed, the blue screen illuminating his leathery face with an icy pallor.

Thank you, God, for allowing the righteous their just rewards.

Then he leered at the girl's photo filling the screen. Hard to believe a little trollop like that could answer his prayers. But God's proof didn't lie.

The year before, Edwin had met Lindsay Bellowes at the American Royal. As he stood next to his penned cattle, he'd had no buyers, not a lick of interest. A group of teenage girls passed by, giggling, braying at the cattle. Gussied up like harlots, their miniskirts barely covered their hindquarters. Disgusted, yet torn. A match scratched against his loins, the flame burning harder. A true-blue American man, after all. The way God made him.

While most of the girls carried on down the aisle, tittering like a bunch of baby chicks, one strayed from the flock. She'd bent over, poked a finger through the chicken wire, her blue skirt riding high up her legs.

Edwin licked his lips and stepped out from the shadows. "Hey, there, missy. You like my cattle?"

"They look kind of, I dunno, hungry…or sad, maybe." She pouted her lips. Edwin watched her move through the hay, carefully avoiding cow patties. *A looker, all right. Full-figured with nice, big breeding hips.*

"What's your name, missy?"

"Um, Lindsay." Her playfulness had disappeared as she tottered from one foot to the other.

"Well, Miss Lindsay, how would you like to come out and visit my farm some time?"

"Yeah, I don't think that's gonna happen." Edwin hitched up his overalls and approached her. He leaned down, close enough to smell her sweet perfume. Edwin hadn't smelled anything that nice in some time.

"Oh, come on now, missy. I could put you to use out at the farm. Give you a good life, too."

"Ew. I've gotta *go*." She ran down the aisle, her skirt bouncing up and down, exposing pink underwear.

"What's your last name, Lindsay?" Edwin hollered after her.

"It's 'In Your Dreams, Pervert'!" Her harsh laughter had blasted Edwin full-on in the chest like buckshot.

His eyes widened with rage. He knotted his hands into fists, slammed them against his legs. She obviously didn't know what a righteous man he was. And the very idea of this whore calling him a *pervert?* Damn near sacrilege. Edwin growled, his voice carrying over the cows and pigs crying for freedom from their pens.

It'd been years since Edwin had a woman around the farm. He felt entitled to everything that entailed, including womanly duties. That's the way God made man and woman. A woman's lot in life is to pleasure the hardworking, dominant man of the house. And for this little slut to insult him and not give him his due respect felt like a downright slap to God's face.

He vowed to get even with the little tramp. For himself and her sinful disrespect to the Almighty.

Later, during the show in the large arena, Edwin had spotted the same little hussy in a group called The Young Kansas City Cowgirls. He checked the program. Sure enough, her name was listed, the only Lindsay in the show. *Lindsay Bellowes.* Edwin had circled her name with a pencil, carefully folded the program, and secured it in his buttoned pocket.

I've got you now, slut. Edwin tapped the computer screen with his fingernail.

The screaming began again, grew louder, twisted down the stairwell. It pierced Edwin's skull.

"Shut up, boy!" Edwin knocked the chair to the linoleum when he bolted up.

He pulled the dinner bucket from below the sink and dumped the remains of his breakfast into it. Grabbing the plank of wood on his way out for protection if he needed it, he made his way to the stairwell. He stared at the door at the top of the stairs. "Shut your yap," he screamed. "I'm comin' already!"

God's burden. He reminded himself he wouldn't have to tend to God's burden very much longer.

Things were about to change. No more poverty, no more backbreaking fieldwork. Edwin had a plan. A damn good plan.

"So, where're we going?" Shannon covertly inched her black skirt down to her knees, or at least as far as she could pull it. Lindsay had insisted Shannon would look "whorishly awesome" in her daring wardrobe choice. Now she regretted it.

"Well, it's Sunday, and I told you I'd take you dancing." Gavin pulled the car into Wild Bill's Cuckoo Burger's drive-in parking lot. No one ever questioned the odd name of the restaurant, just accepted it like an old friend. The drive-in stubbornly embraced a 1950s motif, a quaint relic dropped into the middle of suburban Barton, Kansas. "You know how hard it is to find a dancing venue we can actually get into? I mean, since we're not twenty-one?" Gavin parked the car under the restaurant's awning and cut the ignition.

"Um, sorry, but I've already eaten." She hadn't. But Shannon didn't feel comfortable eating in front of Gavin on their first date in case she got a case of the clumsies.

"That's okay. Get a drink or a milkshake. The sky's the limit for you when it comes to Wild Bill's menu." He snatched off his sunglasses and smiled at her. Shannon wondered if he'd practiced the move.

"Diet cherry lime-ade, please." Shannon frowned at her black stocking-covered legs. Wishing she'd worn jeans, she silently cursed Lindsay.

"Wow, cheap date." Gavin pressed the button. An indecipherable voice blared from the tin box. "Ah, I didn't really get a single word you said, but I'd like two diet cherry lime-ades, please."

Shannon snorted and threw her hand up to cover her mouth.

"I like when you laugh. You don't need to be shy with me."

Shannon blushed and then attempted a speedy recovery. "Well, you ain't heard *nothing* yet." She exploded into raucous laughter. To her ears, she thought she sounded like a donkey.

"You're certainly different, Shannon Wolters."

"Different 'weird' or different 'good'?"

Gavin appeared to weigh his words carefully before answering. "Both." Their laughter attracted the attention of some of the other restaurant patrons.

"Hey, I thought we were going dancing."

"We are." Gavin jumped out of the car and ran to her side. "My lady." He opened her door, bowed, and swept his hand in front of him.

"What? What are we doing?" She had an idea and didn't like it one bit. But she couldn't help smiling through her embarrassment.

"We're dancing!" Some '50s doo-wop crackled out of the speaker overhead. Shannon accepted Gavin's hand and hesitantly stepped out, her black flats scraping over the gravel. She glanced around to see if anyone was watching.

"You've got to be kidding me," whispered Shannon. Gavin gently prodded her to the sidewalk between the parked rows of cars. He pulled her tight against him, swaying back and forth, even though the music called for anything but a slow dance. Embarrassment swept over her, nicely sweetened by a pinch of romantic giddiness. She buried her face in Gavin's chest, wanting this to end, yet wanting it to go on forever.

"I told you we'd go dancing on Sunday," said Gavin.

"Oh, my God! I can't believe we're doing this. People are staring at us."

"Let them stare. They're probably looking at you because you're the prettiest girl here. The Queen of Cuckoo Burger." He thumped his chest once for emphasis. "And I'm the Prince of Shakes."

"So. Are you always this creative? Or are you just stingy?" She raised her head to stare into his eyes.

"Definitely creative. In a penny-pinching sort of way."

Shannon chuckled, holding onto his strong frame. "When can we stop?"

"I don't know. Until they kick us out, maybe? Okay, ready? Hold on!" Suddenly, Gavin dipped her. Her eyes round with shock, Shannon let out a whoop. When Gavin pulled her up, she threw her arms around his neck.

"Don't do that again," she said between breathless laughs.

"Okay, sorry." They twirled across the sidewalk. Lost in the moment, she stretched up on tiptoes and kissed Gavin. His hands cradled the back of her neck, and then he returned her kiss fully. Several cars honked their horns, either out of disapproval or jubilation. Shannon didn't care. Right now, she *was* the Queen of Cuckoo Burger. She might indeed die of embarrassment, but only if this new feeling of love didn't kill her first.

With a snort, Peter Brookes tossed the girl's underwear onto the ruffled hotel bed.

Earlier, when he withdrew $500,000 from the bank, she had been the teller who serviced him. Several hours later, she serviced him again.

"Get dressed and get out." He stared at his shirtless body in the mirror above the dresser. He liked what he saw. With great money came a great, chiseled physique. He could afford the best trainers New York City had to offer. Frankly, there was nothing he couldn't afford. Soon, he planned to test this interesting theory.

"Wait a minute," said the naked girl. Peter couldn't remember her name, not that it mattered. "I'm not ready to leave. Besides, didn't you promise me something?" She smiled seductively at Peter, but it came across as rather pathetic.

"Oh, right." He pulled his wallet from the suit jacket slung over the chair. "Here. Here's five hundred dollars." Peter tossed the crisp bills in her direction, not caring where they landed.

"Peter, you can't treat me like a whore." Her youthful prettiness gave way to a bitchy mask of scorn and self-entitlement. Somewhat like his wife.

"Why, yes I can, because that's exactly what you are. You came here with me because I promised you a watch. I'm not going to give you a watch, but there's enough money there to cover one. And since this is a business transaction, that makes you a whore. Oh, and call me *Mister* Brookes, not Peter. You're my subordinate."

"You bastard!" She slapped her hands onto the bed. Her body trembled with fury, although her fake breasts remained unnaturally still.

"Yes, I very well may be a bastard. But that doesn't change the fact that you're a whore. Now, get your fucking ass—a very *nice* fucking ass—dressed, and leave."

She stormed off to the bathroom. The door slammed shut, rattling the headboard that had shaken for an entirely different reason minutes ago.

These days, Peter remained calm during these encounters. He found this peculiar, a little troublesome. He used to be quite fond of the aftermath.

At first, Peter's sexual liaisons had focused on seducing and conquering. He derived an immediate thrill by landing the hottest girl at the party, meeting, convention, wherever. Blessed with handsome looks, endless charm, and hoards of money, his arsenal was formidable. Some might frown upon this as an unfair advantage, but Peter took it all in stride. Rarely did he experience rejection.

It used to be only about sexual conquest, and Peter had been fine with that. Slowly, the thrill had weakened, though, the blazing flame reduced to wisps of smoke. He had upped the ante, setting his sights upon beautiful *married* women. He'd thought of it as competing in a cutthroat environment, not unlike his day-to-day business encounters. It became a challenge to him when he had a worthwhile male opponent attached.

Once more, the excitement had diminished, so he changed the rules again. It hadn't taken long for Peter to discover the joys of demeaning women. He established mastery at berating a recently seduced woman, mortifying them with a litany of colorfully turned phrases and heady psychological games. He reduced women to blubbering messes, eyeliner running down their faces, his words like knives. Sometimes the women would turn physically hostile. The *ultimate* sensation. Charging at him, fists upraised, ready to inflict bodily harm. Once, a particularly volatile slut had attempted to take a letter opener to him before he disarmed her and threw her, naked, into the hallway.

The bathroom door banged open, jolting Peter.

"You fucker!" Fully dressed and makeup smeared, she looked like a different woman. Everyone wears masks. "I passed up a date with my boyfriend to be with you."

"Lucky him," Peter said, sighing, barely acknowledging her existence. "Oh, by the way, quit wearing so much makeup. You apply it poorly, you use too much, and it makes you look like an even bigger whore." Peter smiled as her sobs receded down the hotel hallway.

It should have been more fun. Once, Peter would have fallen on the bed, laughing, enjoying the lasting memories of his artful cruelty.

But it wasn't enough anymore. He shrugged, winking at his reflection. That was okay, though. Recently, he had upped the ante in his games yet again. *Soon*, he thought. *Soon.*

Matt walked up the sidewalk to the front doors of the Lakawatomie Mental Institution. Sunflowers pushed their way through the broken cement—a cracked sidewalk leading to an institute for people with fractured brains. Yet through these very cracks, life struggled to persevere, begging for a chance at normalcy, at survival.

Matt had been negligent in his visits, mainly because they were too painful. He used to come every month, but it was always such a soul-draining experience that he now visited twice a year, at best.

The tired-looking woman at the reception area met Matt with indifference. "Hi, I'm here to visit Mary Strothers," he said.

The woman finished typing the sentence before she looked up. Seemed like an eternity. "Let me call for a nurse."

A nurse, dressed in an outdated uniform, pushed through the door. The electronic lock secured with a snap behind her. "Hello, Mister Strothers, if you'd like to come with me?" At least this woman attempted a smile, forced though it may have been.

She passed her identification card through a scanner. Once the green light flashed above the door, Matt followed her down the poorly lit corridor. Familiar, anguished cries beckoned from behind the doors they passed.

"How's Mary been doing?" He always asked the question, always dreaded the response. Even though the answer inevitably remained the same, things might change one day. *Hope springs eternal,* as Jay always said.

"She has some days better than others. She's in her room. Would you like to see her there? Or would you like to arrange to see her in the general hall?"

"No, her room's fine." Matt had visited Mary only once in the general hall, something he never wanted to repeat. Other patients had wandered up to them, staring, one man even stroking Matt's hair.

The nurse stopped in front of Mary's room and knocked on the door. Of course, there wouldn't be a reply, but they were sticklers for proper protocol. The nurse once again swiped her card and entered.

Mary sat on the edge of the unmade bed, gazing out the window. Complete chaos had overtaken the room. Clothes strewn everywhere, open dresser drawers, and an overflowing trashcan were the least offensive. An unbearable smell hovered over them like a cloud of cigar smoke. Mary remained immobile, ignoring their presence.

"Mary, look who's here to visit you," said the nurse, nearly singing. "Okay, I'll leave you two to your visit. Let me know if there's anything I can do." Before Matt could respond, the nurse left, leaving the door to the hallway open this time.

"Hi, Mary, it's Matt." Her now prematurely gray hair appeared filthy and unwashed. He caressed her cheek gently and then quickly withdrew his hand. She seemed so fragile; he didn't want to break her. No more than she'd already been broken. "How've you been?"

Silence, nothing new. She had been mostly nonverbal since her initial institutionalization. Occasionally, she babbled nonsense, and sometimes she let loose an agonized scream. The screams bothered Matt most of all. He felt she was close to regaining lucidity at those moments, the howls the tormented results. The times when she remembered her past. Sometimes Matt thought it would be best if she stayed protected within the deep recesses of her mind.

"I'm sorry I haven't been by to visit you much this year, Mary." He sat down next to her. The bed wobbled beneath their combined weight. "I've been busy with the store and…" Matt dropped the pretense. He had more to say, but they were worthless excuses. She probably didn't understand him anyway.

He pulled her toward him. She hung limp as a rag doll in his arms. "Mary, I'm so sorry." Tears streamed down his face. "I'm so sorry you're in here. It's my fault you're here. I never should've left you. I'm sorry." Matt sobbed, gasping for air. Finally, the tears stopped. Mary sat, seemingly unaware of everything.

Matt left to find the nurse. He turned around one last time to look at Mary, hoping for a miraculous breakthrough. "Goodbye, Mary. I promise I'll visit again soon."

He spotted the nurse leaving another patient's room. "Excuse me, nurse?"

The nurse stopped suddenly, her sneakers squeaking on the floor, and turned toward him. "How can I help you?"

"Would you please have someone wash Mary's hair?"

"I'll see what we can do," she replied with a curt smile.

Matt walked down the long hallway, gaining speed as he went. By the time he exited the facility, he had broken into a full sprint toward the comfort of his car.

Chapter Four

Feeding time.

Edwin tiptoed up the stairs and set down the bucket and piece of wood to unlatch the chain lock on the door. He peeked in to make sure Joshua was on his bed, as were the rules. "You havin' a good day, son?"

Joshua muttered a strangled syllable. Edwin interpreted this as "yes."

Edwin picked up the bucket and his makeshift weapon, then pushed open the door. Two-by-fours covered the sole window, natural light unable to penetrate the boundary. The single dangling bulb illuminated fresh fingernail carvings on the walls. A soiled mattress rested on the floor, a shredded quilt next to it. A heap of foul-smelling clothes, mostly overalls, had been tossed in the corner. Joshua's waste bucket occupied the opposite corner of the room, flies buzzing above it.

The three-hundred-pound man-boy sat up on the mattress, wearing nothing but stained underwear. Black hair and a beard matted his face. Edwin stared into what passed for eyes in his son's face—one eye a wet, white eggshell, the other heavily lidded and constantly roving. Joshua's mouth hung open, saliva strands stretching from top to bottom while he moaned.

Sometimes Edwin couldn't believe Joshua was his child, let alone the only loyal one. But frankly, he was the only one who had amounted to a good goddamn. True, God had only given Joshua half a brain, but when he followed orders and didn't suffer one of his fits, he proved to be a damn-good farmhand. These days, Joshua did most of the heavy lifting Edwin used to handle, but he'd been glad to relinquish the duties. Joshua could move hay bales faster than lightning.

"Chow time, boy." He dropped the bucket in front of the mattress. Joshua scrambled across the bed. Edwin fell back a step. The boy could move.

Joshua reached into the bucket with his huge paw. He shoveled the greasy mess into his mouth, then licked the rim of the bucket. Edwin remembered why he quit eating dinner with Joshua at the supper table. His constant drooling repulsed him. And he grew tired of cleaning up after him. One year of cleaning after Gretchen had been more than enough.

Joshua finished his breakfast in seconds. He held the empty pail out to his father, a pleading look in his one good eye.

"Not now, boy," snapped Edwin. "Times are tough, and we don't have much food."

Joshua sat back, rocking on his haunches. A high-pitched squeal rose from his closed mouth.

"Don't start your cryin'. We've got a big day of chores ahead of us." Edwin backed up again, prepared to flee the room if Joshua started one of his tantrums.

The tears stopped flowing. Joshua crossed his arms across his barrel chest, holding himself, swaying slowly.

Edwin reckoned Joshua to be somewhere around sixteen or seventeen years of age. With Gretchen not around to remember birthdays, and Joshua too dumb to remember his own, Edwin pretty much just forgot. Not like it mattered in the long run, anyway.

Edwin had raised Joshua by himself. Gretchen had passed a couple of years before Joshua's birth, so the boy never did benefit from a mother's loving touch. Probably made him tougher, though, a good thing. The boy needed to be tough. Soon—very soon—the farm would be Joshua's. It would be up to him to carry on the proud tradition of the Quail name. At least, Edwin assumed Joshua could procreate.

"Joshua, I've got a surprise for you. You and I are going to the big city. Something real important for you to do there."

Joshua attempted to smile. Edwin wished he wouldn't. His pink and black tongue lolled about like a slug. Ground down teeth gnawed at his flesh, rimming his gums with blood.

"It's the most important chore I'll ever have you do, boy." Edwin's grin spread across his sun-cracked face. "So don't screw it up."

Joshua's loathsome smile grew, his tongue bobbing. He put his hands together with child-like glee. Then he howled toward the ceiling.

"Good boy!"

It didn't take long for Joshua to get ready.

Edwin drove the old Ford truck down the highway, maintaining the speed limit religiously. With its dark blue paint job mottled by large rust spots, Edwin thought the truck resembled one of those hippy vans that were popular in the 70s. But the truck had been reliable for twenty years. More than he could say for his family.

The truck rode out a sudden dip in the highway, the eroding shock absorbers bouncing Edwin and Joshua up and down. Joshua placed his hands merrily together as if enjoying a carnival thrill ride.

Joshua had never been off the farm except for his brief school trial in Karlin. Edwin knew bringing Joshua to Kansas City might be risky. He would stick out like a sore thumb. And he could, at times, be as un-predictable as a rogue elephant. As long as Joshua stayed out of sight, though, the plan would work. He needed the boy's strength and talents to achieve his goals.

Edwin glanced at the carefully positioned bottle, swathed and pro-tected by rags, nestled on the truck's floorboards. The bottle of chloro-form was old, older than the hills, but it hadn't been opened for well on twenty years. Sealed tightly and stored in the cellar alongside Gretchen's preserves, jams, and pickles, it was something Gretchen had used for me-dicinal purposes. Seeing as how Gretchen's fixin's still tasted fine, he had no doubt about the chloroform's potency.

Edwin pulled the truck off an exit about thirty miles from Kansas City. Turning onto a quiet gravel road, he scoured the area. He drove into a muddy thatch, barren of grass and hidden by trees.

"Stay here, boy," he ordered. "I've got to stretch my legs."

He stepped out of the truck. Joshua, taking in every new sight and sound, flattened both palms against the window.

Edwin grabbed a handful of mud and slathered it over his license plate. He repeated this until the number was illegible. He slopped more mud on the back bumper and the tire flaps, creating a semblance of having driven through swampy fields.

After the mud dried, Edwin drove to the local gas station by the highway exit. The wind whipped mercilessly at Edwin, nearly taking his cap with it. At an outdoor payphone, he carefully dialed the number written on the crumpled piece of paper.

"It's time," he said into the phone. "You wanted two days' warning; here it is. You'd best leave now."

Edwin licked his dried lips.

Yes, indeedy. Judgment Day is nigh upon us.

Shannon and Lindsay walked through the school parking lot. Today, school had challenged Shannon for more reasons than one. She couldn't focus. Mrs. Albright, her algebra teacher, had called upon her to answer an equation. She didn't respond immediately, her head in the clouds. To the amusement of the classroom, Mrs. Albright had chastised Shannon about daydreaming. Of course, Shannon felt the blood rush to her cheeks, but it didn't matter, as Gavin turned around and smiled sweetly. The possibilities of where things might go with Gavin seemed endless.

"You didn't really dance at Wild Bill's," exclaimed Lindsay.

"We did!"

"And you…you…were the one who kissed him first?"

"I was."

"Wow. I thought I'd have to lead you through this to the bitter end," said Lindsay. "But my little girl is growing up and showing her inner whorishness." Shannon giggled. They strolled toward Lindsay's yellow Firebird, a gift from her parents when she turned sixteen. Shannon had arranged for Lindsay to give her a ride home today, primarily because it would allow them to talk privately about the date. "So, tell me more. What happened next?"

"Well, we just sort of drove around after that. I wanted to get out of Wild Bill's as fast as possible."

"I'm surprised you didn't do him on one of the tables!"

"Lindsay!" Even though Lindsay's off-color comment tickled her, Shannon feigned shock.

"So, you drove around. Is that all that happened? C'mon, girl."

"We just talked. He's actually a…a pretty deep guy."

"Yeah, deep brown eyes."

"No, I mean, he's smart, funny, sweet, and interesting. He's intoxicating."

"Oh, God. 'Intoxicating.' Gag."

"Okay, maybe that's a little much." Shannon looked down at her feet, old feelings of insecurity resurfacing. "But he's everything I could want in a guy."

"Did he kiss you good night?"

"Hellz yeah!" Shannon recalled how he'd opened her car door, taken her hand, and led her to the front door. Romantically, yet more than a little awkwardly, he took his time positioning himself in front of her. Then he leaned down and kissed her. She wanted to remain within his arms forever, but the porch light had snapped on, and there stood her mother, vigilant behind the curtains. Shannon gently broke their embrace while staring into his eyes.

"Okay, when's the next date?" asked Lindsay.

"Well, we didn't set one." Although she would never admit it to Lindsay, Gavin's noncommittal follow-up had worried her. She considered the possibility Gavin might be stringing her along. No. No more doom and gloom. Finally, she had turned the corner, no peeking back around it. Ever again.

"Uh-oh," said Lindsay.

"What? What is it?"

"Here comes lover-boy."

"Hey," said Gavin.

Shannon whirled on her flats, nearly releasing a small shriek. "Oh God, you scared me!"

Gavin grinned. "Probably not the response I was after."

"No, I mean, you don't scare me all the time, just…" Shannon trailed off.

"It's okay," said Gavin. "Hey, I was wondering if you wanted to get together to study tonight for the test tomorrow?"

"Gavin," said Lindsay, "is this your idea of another cheap date?"

"Lindsay!" To Shannon's relief, Gavin appeared amused, not insulted.

"Well, I can promise another diet limeade afterward." His smile told Shannon he, too, was looking forward to continuing where they'd left off.

"Forget it," said Shannon, giggling. "I don't think I can ever go there again."

"Okay, okay, we'll go somewhere else."

"Deal. Seven?"

"That, I can do."

"Cool." Shannon skipped toward Lindsay's passenger door. On impulse, Shannon stopped and skittered back to Gavin. She placed a fast peck on his lips. Running back to the car, she didn't allow time for embarrassment to set in.

"Woot," called out Lindsay.

"I'll see you tonight," said Gavin, clearly caught off guard.

Shannon looked back briefly at Gavin, wagging her fingers daintily at him. Or as daintily as she could muster. *My God*, thought Shannon, *is he blushing?*

Gavin watched Lindsay's car leave the lot. He noticed an old, rusty, blue Ford pickup following closely behind them. He hadn't seen the truck before, but that didn't necessarily mean anything. Probably just a "project" given to one of the gear-heads for auto mechanics class.

Still, as he watched the girls pull out onto Johnson Drive, he couldn't help but see how the truck sped up and changed lanes when they did. And what was up with all the mud caked onto the back of the truck? It wasn't like there were an awful lot of places to go four-wheeling in Barton, Kansas.

Gavin's smile vanished.

Peter Brookes stared into the dead eyes of the whitetail deer head mounted in his study.

You didn't really put up much of a fight, did you?

Peter shot and killed the deer last fall on an arranged and guided hunt through a 250-acre privately owned woodland about an hour and a half from New York. One of the most disappointing and ultimately frustrating events he'd ever experienced. Everything had been set up for him to succeed. Fully armed, instructed, and guided—the deer may as well have been gift wrapped and tied to a tree. No spontaneity, no room for hunting and tracking skills, no challenge, and definitely no joy. A strange word to use regarding the death of a deer, joy. But it seemed appropriate. Or should've been. When he pulled the trigger on the deer, Peter saw the life go out of the animal and felt a little bit of life leave him as well.

Peter stood, admiring his gun collection. He unlocked the glass cabinet and pulled out his pride and joy. A Holland and Holland Royal Grade .700 NE double rifle that he'd had engraved and set with diamonds. As he stroked it, he knew what it felt like to hold a million dollars in his hand. Damn near what he paid for it, too. He hadn't had the opportunity to use the gun yet, but that was about to change.

A timid knock sounded at the study door. Peter carefully placed his gun back into the cabinet and locked it. "Come in," he called.

The door swung open. Michael, clad in flannel pajamas, ran into the room. "I can't sleep, Daddy. Can you tell me a story?"

Peter slowly exhaled, the grind already setting in. "Can't Mommy tell you a story?"

"She told me to have you do it." Peter felt a small tinge of loathing when his son wiped his nose on his pajama sleeve.

"Did she now?" Peter resignedly sat down in the large leather chair and patted his knee. "Fine. Let's do this then."

Michael raced across the room and hopped into Peter's lap. Peter drummed his fingers on the arm of the chair, mentally composing his tale.

"Once upon a time, there was a man who wanted to be king," began Peter. Michael snuggled in closer to his father. "But he wasn't always a king. He came from a land far, far away, where his parents were monsters who mistreated him every day."

"What'd they do, Daddy?"

"They beat him and made him sleep in ashes and on cold bricks." Peter stared at his son to make sure he understood. "One day, the man woke up and decided to kill his monstrous parents. He set fire to the home and burned his parents alive. Then, the man decided to go to the kingdom of 'Richland,' where he would take over as king."

"Do they vote for the king?"

"Not in Richland. In Richland, it's the strongest and smartest man who becomes king." Michael appeared lost in thought, whether from excitement or horror, Peter couldn't tell. "You don't become king overnight, so the man started small. He took several of the king's servants to the top of a huge tower and threw them over to their deaths. Soon, news got back to the king about the new man in town, so the incumbent…ah…current… king sent soldiers to kill the man. But the man was faster, stronger, and smarter than the soldiers were, and he overcame them, throwing them off the tower as well.

Finally, the man decided to go see the king himself. He pretended to be nice to the king, and just when he had gained the king's confidence, the man cut the king's head off. *Whack!* He claimed his crown, sat on the throne, and became the new King of Richland."

Michael's small lips trembled. His thumb jutted out, seeking solace in his mouth, but he reconsidered. Peter had taught him thumb sucking was unacceptable behavior. "Daddy, was he a good king?"

"Yes. He treated himself well."

"Was he ever punished for killing those people?"

"No. If anything, he was rewarded."

Michael contemplated the tale Peter told him. He stared at the deer head on the wall. "Did you hate that deer, Daddy?"

"No, of course not."

"Why'd you kill it then?" Tears bubbled at the corners of his eyes.

"Because I could. Now, off to bed with you." He watched Michael scamper out of the room.

Peter harbored doubts that he truly loved his son. Callous as it may have sounded, he never deluded himself. For the six years of Michael's life, Peter's feelings for him had never really changed or evolved. Call them stunted feelings. And Peter didn't see a change in the foreseeable future.

Six years ago, when his wife had told him of her pregnancy, her eyes lit up expectantly, waiting for his joyous response. It never came.

Peter stared at her calmly and asked, "What do you intend to do about it?" Her smile melted away. She ran out of the room, sobbing.

Children had never been part of his plans. While there was a certain allure to having an heir carry on one's name, he realized he didn't have the patience for parenting. Before a child reached an age of merit, he'd have to endure too much dull repetition.

When Michael was born, Peter remained at the office throughout his wife's labor. Barbara wanted him to be in the "birthing suite," as she called it. He deemed it an impractical and stupid idea. After all, he had already paid for the most expensive doctors, birthing experts, even a midwife. If they couldn't handle it without him, then he considered it a colossal waste of money and time. Barbara responded in her typical fashion, with much drama and tears.

When Peter finally arrived at the hospital, he stared blankly at his newborn son. Through the viewing window, he watched as his son helplessly writhed about next to other identical babies. The creatures were reddened, wrinkled, little malformations—miniature versions of people. The entire experience of bringing these grotesqueries into the world somewhat saddened him. How could responsible adults give them life and not prepare them for the horrible existences most of them would experience? Of the inhuman suffering and cruelty that they would no doubt be subjected to?

Peter's hand had slid down the glass window, leaving a smudge. Unexpected tears falling down his cheeks had stunned him. The tears hadn't spilled over the happy, joyous birth of his son. Instead, he had mourned his birth.

Did Peter love his son, Michael? Probably not. Did he despise him? Absolutely not. Peter tolerated his son but felt pity for him more than anything.

But wallowing in the past never helped. He'd much rather embrace his exuberant mood.

Then he laughed.

I'll bet that's the last time I have to tell Michael a bedtime story.

He smiled, poured himself a brandy, and tipped it in the direction of the deer head.

Sixteen years ago, the doorbell had rung late one night at Matt's house. Matt generally associated late-night callers with anxiety and dread. This time had been no different.

"I'll get it, honey," he'd told his wife. He pulled on his robe and went downstairs.

Flipping on the porch light, he had peered out the peek-hole but saw nothing. He'd pulled the curtain aside and spotted an idling taxi in the street. Wracking, muffled sobs filtered through the door.

When he opened the door, he saw her. She lay on the front stoop, curled up in a ball like a sleeping dog. Shaking, her bony arms clung tight across her chest. Even given her emaciated appearance, her filthy dress appeared two sizes too small. The hemline of the skirt had been ripped, and it was covered with dirt and, maybe, blood.

It had taken Matt a minute before he recognized her. "Mary?" he asked uncertainly.

"Who is it?" Cheryl had asked from behind him.

"I think it's my sister...Mary." A bout of nausea had swept over him.

Matt had carried her gently into the living room and set her down on the sofa. Cheryl had grimaced and then ran off to retrieve some towels.

Matt had approached the still-waiting taxi driver and knocked on his window. The driver said, "Hey, you owe me forty-three bucks."

"Where did you pick her up?"

"Down at the train station. She didn't say much. Just handed me your address." The cab driver waved a crinkled piece of paper in front of Matt's face as validation. "She said you'd pay the fare."

"Oh, yeah, of course." Matt had fumbled through his bathrobe pockets, even though he knew he had no cash there. "I'll be right back."

"Hey, you know, it's none of my business," he had yelled back at Matt, "but if I were you, I'd get that chick to a hospital. She don't look so good."

Matt had taken the driver's advice, and he and Cheryl rushed her to the Olathe County Hospital.

After a seeming eternity, the ER doctor had returned to talk to Matt and Cheryl. "Are you family?" he asked.

"Yes, she's my sister." Even though he hadn't seen her in years, Matt still cared deeply about Mary. Yet it felt odd calling her his "sister." He thought he'd closed his family book long ago.

"She appears to be in shock," the young doctor had stated. "She's almost near a state of catatonia, but I'm no psychologist. She's been beaten, abused, and underfed. She has pneumonia and a broken arm. Frankly, I'm surprised she's even able to walk. We're going to have to admit her for a while."

"Oh, my God." This sort of trauma seemed alien to Matt's dull, married life in suburbia. It made him realize "boring" was not such a bad lifestyle, after all.

"Do you have any idea who would've done this to her?" the doctor had asked. "I'm going to need to report this to the local police."

"No, of course not," Matt said. But it wasn't the truth—not exactly. A sickening suspicion had filled him with queasiness. "Who would want to hurt Mary? She was the nicest…" Tears filled his eyes as his words lodged in his throat. Especially since he realized he'd spoken about Mary as if she had already passed away.

"Could it be the baby's father?" the doctor had asked.

"What?"

The doctor had consulted his charts. "Mary has recently given birth. You didn't know?" The doctor had held a stern, disbelieving look on his face.

Drenched in a cold sweat, Matt had run into the hospital hallway. He'd barely made it to the bathroom before his stomach unleashed its contents.

After several weeks of psychiatric evaluation, intensive medical care, and lots of bed rest, the hospital had released Mary into Matt and Cheryl's care. The psychiatrist had expressed his skepticism they could provide Mary with the care she needed, but Matt had insisted.

For several months, Cheryl had taken it upon herself to be the primary caregiver while Matt worked at the video store. Mary remained uncommunicative and needed constant attention. If anything, her vocal skills had diminished since the night they found her on their doorstep. At least then she'd been able to string a few words together.

The toil of caring for Mary had worn Cheryl down, obviously so. Cheryl had grown quiet and unhappy and withdrew into herself. After struggling impotently with Mary longer than they should have, they had finally admitted defeat and checked Mary into the Lakawatomie Mental Facility.

The police's perfunctory investigation had yielded no results. Matt had never mentioned his suspicions. He had no proof. But he knew—in his gut, he fully knew—what had happened.

Matt's sick, son-of-a-bitch of a father had raped and impregnated his own daughter.

Chapter Five

Edwin's daughter, Mary, had been the last child to remain in the family home. And Edwin had never known her, not really. There were only so many hours in the day. Working in the fields occupied most of his time when he wasn't sleeping.

Mary had never been much to look at, in Edwin's opinion, but she'd proven her worth around the house after Gretchen passed. She cooked fairly well. Gretchen had taught her everything she needed to know about taking care of the men at the farm. The way it should be.

About a month after Gretchen had moved on to her higher reward, Edwin became agitated. Antsy, almost. It'd been some time since he'd experienced the comforts of a woman. Gretchen, in the last year of her life, hadn't been up to fulfilling her wifely duties.

Late one evening, the chores completed, Edwin found himself literally pacing the floors. Mary had retired to her bedroom, leaving Edwin alone to consider his options. Like a caged animal, he had prowled the room, rubbing his scraggly day's growth of beard. Then he'd knocked gently on Mary's bedroom door.

"Yes?" she responded in her typically timid voice.

"Mary?"

"Yes?" No inflection to her tone. Since her mother's death, Mary had become a hollow shell of a person. She slept little, the telltale signs of dark circles ringing her eyes. She never conversed with Edwin beyond the topics of meals. He'd never seen her laugh, never seen her cry, never seen her do much of anything, truth to tell. Edwin had taken it in stride. Just the way God had made her.

"I need to talk to you," Edwin said.

After a long hesitation, she opened the door. One of Gretchen's long nightgowns rested loosely around Mary's shoulders, the dirty bottom trailing along the floor.

"Now, you've been doing a real good job at taking up your momma's responsibilities, Mary."

She nodded silently, her eyes flitting about the hallway, never meeting his gaze.

"And you know, the Good Book says that it's a woman's place to take care of the men-folk." She stepped back into the room. "It's time you took it upon yourself to fulfill the rest of your momma's...obligations."

Her shoulders had caved in, the oversized nightgown appearing like a large blanket surrounding her thin body. "But...I'm doing everything Momma did," she said meekly.

"Not everything." He walked into the room, closing the door behind him. Edwin grabbed her firmly by the shoulders and pushed her onto the small bed. Mary screamed, burying her face in her hands.

"It's your duty." Edwin smiled, sliding his overalls down to the floor.

Edwin had continued his nocturnal visits for the next seven months. Mary had all but quit speaking, and while not willingly accepting his advances, she had at least quit fighting him. Sure, she still cried and her body tensed, but she lay there as a woman should, accepting her lot in life.

Eventually, Edwin noticed her weight gain. Fury had overtaken him when he suspected her of secretly eating more than her fair ration of food. But he waited until he'd finished his nightly visit before confronting her.

"Mary. You sneaking food for yourself?"

She shook her head, her long, greasy hair matted to her head.

"Well, then, how do you explain the belly you're now showin'?"

She turned her head to the side, shut her eyes, and wailed.

Edwin had placed his hand on her exposed stomach. "Well, I'll be god-damned. You're pregnant." A lop-sided grin had crawled across his face. Edwin laughed while Mary squeezed her eyes shut tighter. "It'd better be a boy. I need the help in the fields. God is once again smiling *down* on me!"

He should have never doubted God's plan. Worries had plagued him about getting the fieldwork done, but help had come in the form of a blessing from above. The Good Book says to be fruitful and multiply. And he had always done his best to live by the written word.

Four months later, Edwin had heard a scream ring out through the open kitchen window. He'd turned the tractor around and raced for the house.

He found Mary on the kitchen floor, a God-awful stench permeating the room, and blood spreading underneath her onto the linoleum. "Get yourself into your bedroom, *now!*"

Mary, defying her father, had remained on the floor, writhing in her own waste. Edwin had managed to drag her to her bedroom. He'd left Mary's room and waited for his new son.

After several hours of Mary's caterwauling, he reluctantly called Doc Collins. *Hated* doing it. The old farmhouse had witnessed the birth of many children without any outside intervention, after all. But with his new son's health possibly at risk, he had finally relented. Besides, his weakling daughter didn't appear up to the challenge of delivering the baby on her own.

Doc Collins had arrived less than thirty minutes later.

"Mary's giving birth, Edwin?" Collins asked him. Edwin had felt the man's untrusting eyes sizing him up.

"Ayup, that's right."

"Who's the father, if you don't mind my askin'?"

"I do mind," Edwin spat. "I *do* mind your askin'!"

Doc Collins stared at Edwin in stony silence while opening his bag. He followed Mary's screams down the hallway. Before opening the bedroom door, Collins had looked back again, favoring Edwin with a not-so-subtle headshake.

The doctor came out fifteen minutes later, his hands covered in blood. He looked snow-white in his black suit. Inside the room, Mary's screams continued. "Edwin," he said, his voice trembling, "we need to get Mary to a hospital…there may be some complications—"

"Ain't gonna happen, Doc. Can't afford it, and I told you before, I don't have any insurance. Can't afford any—"

"But…" began the doctor before he lapsed into silence. Then he went back into the room. Thirty minutes later, a blessed hush fell over the house. Edwin waited in the living room, anxious for his new arrival. Finally, he heard a strange, moist gurgling. He raced for Mary's room. Pushing the door open, he saw Doc Collins sitting on the edge of the bed, holding the swaddled infant. Mary lay in the bed, now quiet, her eyes closed.

"Edwin," Doc Collins whispered, "the boy ain't *right*." Averting his gaze, Collins held the baby toward Edwin. The baby's crying sounded different from any Edwin had ever heard: deeper, more strained. He grabbed the baby out of the doctor's hands and yanked back the blanket. Edwin gasped. An *abomination*, no other word for it. The baby's face looked gray as ashes. One eye was completely bone-white; the other fixed Edwin with a brown, liquid-like glare. The thing's mouth opened and shut like a gutted catfish, squeezing out unnatural sounds. And it was larger, fatter—*more muscular?*— than two babies put together.

"What…what's wrong with it, Doc?"

"I'm not sure." Collins had taken out a handkerchief from his pocket and dabbed his forehead. "I've…never seen anything quite like it. I mean, it's breathing and doing everything else a newborn should do. But…*look* at it."

Edwin forced another glimpse. He nudged the baby's balled-up fist with his thumb. The baby lashed out, grabbed his thumb, and squeezed it hard. Edwin's eyes opened wide.

He created a strong baby. A *very* strong baby.

Nothing wrong with my baby.

He held the farmhand God had delivered unto him.

"He's fine, Doc," said Edwin, his voice swelling with pride.

Doc Collins shook his head. "No, Edwin. No, it's *not*. You need to get this baby and Mary to the Karlin hospital as soon as you can—"

"I already told you, Doc. That ain't gonna happen."

"Mary's lost a lot of blood. She needs to be seen."

"The Lord *provides*. There've been many babies born here in this house.

We don't need any outside help."

Collins shot up and brushed past Edwin without saying a word. After he slammed the kitchen door behind him, he called out, "I'll be back to check on them later."

Edwin cradled his new godsent son in his arms. "Joshua," he whispered. "You shall be named Joshua." The baby spat up dark liquid that dripped down onto Edwin's chest. He didn't mind, though. The Lord had once again answered his prayers.

Edwin heard Mary moan. He laid down the mewling baby next to her and went outside to continue his chores.

Two weeks later, Mary was gone. Edwin had driven into town for some feed. Upon returning, he checked her room and saw Joshua lying on the bed, alone, rolling across the rumpled blankets. Her emptied closet was the only farewell note she left. He slumped down onto the bed beside his son. What did he know about raising a boy by himself? The last two weeks had been hard enough, even with Mary's help. If you could call it "help." Some help. All she did was cry, stopping on occasion to scream. Between the non-stop howling of his daughter and son, he fell asleep every night with his pillow wrapped tightly around his head.

Now, for the first time ever, Edwin had to fend for himself. With the Good Lord's guidance, though, he'd make it through this trial, hard as it would be. One of God's toughest tests for him yet.

Edwin kept Joshua in Mary's room, mainly to muffle the endless crying. He fed Joshua straight milk from the cows. No sense wasting money on that baby formula nonsense. Didn't take long for him to graduate to adult food, either. Healthy appetite on that boy.

At times, though, Edwin had a hard time keeping up with Joshua. As the boy grew older, bigger, and stronger, so did his penchant for getting into trouble. Edwin locked him upstairs in the attic while he tilled the fields. Edwin took him outside a few times—testing the water, so to speak—but the results were disastrous. Once Joshua throttled a hen to death; Edwin had found the boy in the henhouse, covered in blood and feathers, flapping the dead hen's wings like a broken toy.

Walking came early for Joshua, though, earlier than for most infants.

Soon, Edwin trained him in the simplest of chores, redirecting the boy's violent tendencies toward productive work. The boy just needed to burn off nervous energy like a pent-up 'coon dog. Edwin's life grew easier as the boy assumed more responsibilities. And, by God, the boy may have been a half-idiot, but he had a definite affinity for farm work. Between Edwin's brains and Joshua's speed and strength, they made a formidable farming team. Before all the cash flow and economy problems started, that was.

Now Edwin counted on his son's strength for an entirely different matter.

Edwin and Joshua arrived at Barton High School at about 2:00 p.m. that hazy afternoon. Plenty of time before school let out. After driving up and down the parking lot's full aisles, Edwin spotted the yellow Firebird and double-checked the license plate.

Edwin found an empty spot close by and parked. He slumped down in his seat, pulling his hat's bill lower. After hushing Joshua, he instructed him to do the same.

"*Dammit,* boy, we're here for work, not a joy ride to the big city." Joshua grinned stupidly, happier than a pig in slop. "Just do what I say." Edwin loosened the chloroform bottle's cap and prepared the rag.

"Stay in the truck, boy." Edwin took a quick glimpse around the parking lot. Seeing no one, he hopped out and went to the back of the truck. He loosened the hitch-knots on one side of the black tarp. Snagging a quick peek underneath, he took stock of his equipment: rope, extra rags, and chains, just in case he needed them.

From a distance, he heard the school bell ring out. Jumping back into the truck, Edwin checked his watch. Three o'clock on the nose. Students exited the large brick building in droves, making their way toward the parking lot.

Look at all these kids, born with a silver spoon in their mouths, never having to do an honest day's work in their lives. Their rich daddies buy them cars and slutty clothes so they can tool around town, fornicating like rabbits, no doubt.

Soon, Edwin caught sight of his prey. Lindsay Bellowes, decked out in a too-short skirt and black harlot stockings, true to her slut ways.

"That's the one we want, Joshua," Edwin said, gesturing toward the girl. He splashed chloroform onto the rag. When Joshua stuck out his ham-hock hand, Edwin quickly knocked it down.

"Hold on, boy!" A smaller girl with short, blonde hair and glasses accompanied Lindsay Bellowes. Soon, a tall boy with hippy hair joined them. A wrinkle in his plan. He hadn't counted on the parking lot being so crowded, and he didn't think his target would have company.

"Change of plans, boy." He impatiently slapped his thigh with the damp rag. "I gotta think of something else."

Joshua squealed. Edwin told him to shut his mouth.

Look at those jezebels! Making over that boy with their wanton eyes, flashing their legs in their scanty outfits, batting their whorish eyelashes. Ready to eat him up.

Things had changed since Edwin's school days. Sure, he'd only made it to sixth grade in the one-room shack not far from his farm. And there had only been two girls in his class, one of whom he ended up marrying. But never would he have acted so forward with those girls. Not one bit.

Edwin watched aghast as the shorter girl ran up to the boy and kissed him in public. He shook his head disgustedly, rolled down the window, and spat onto the pavement.

Joshua watched the kiss between the boy and girl. He leaned forward, straining his heavy-lidded eyes open, and then yelped with delight. *Or lust more than likely,* Edwin thought.

"Okay, boy, here we go," he said as the girls got into their car. "We'll follow them hussies. Then, after Miss Lindsay Bellowes drops the other one off, we'll grab her. Just do as I say." Edwin hissed her name out with bitter venom, over-enunciating every syllable. He felt a sharp jab to his gut, recalling how disrespectfully she had treated him at the American Royal last year.

The yellow car pulled out of the parking lot. Edwin slipped his Ford into gear and followed. Recklessly, the Firebird swerved out onto a busier four-lane street. Edwin carefully obeyed the laws of the street without losing sight of his target. Once he safely entered the crowded street, he made a proper lane change and sped up. But not too closely behind them.

The sun-cracked tarp flapped in the wind behind them as Edwin picked up speed. He hoped it wouldn't be too noticeable, but it couldn't be helped.

The tarp should've been tied down by now, with Miss Lindsay Bellowes resting uncomfortably beneath it. On her way to meet her fate.

Joshua's excitable behavior over the trampy teenage girls' shameless behavior hadn't escaped Edwin's attention. Best to admonish the boy properly and right up front.

"Now, Joshua, I know you have boy urges." He spoke slowly and clearly. "But I want you to keep this girl safe. I don't want you acting on your animal instincts. Do you follow me, boy?" Edwin risked a momentary glance in Joshua's direction to make certain he held his full attention.

Joshua clapped his hands lightly. Could mean anything.

Edwin followed the sluts for another fifteen minutes, quickly losing patience. Their wasteful joyride could go on for hours. He checked the gas gauge, hoping he wouldn't have to stop to refill.

Finally, the girls exited off the four-lane street and turned into a suburban neighborhood. After winding their way through endless streets lined with towering trees, the yellow car slowed in front of a two-story, white house. Edwin checked the street sign.

Dammit, he thought, *Oak Street. That's where Miss Lindsay Bellowes lives. She ain't gonna drop the other slut off at all.*

Edwin idled the truck slowly, stopping catty-corner and behind the Firebird. He kept his gaze locked on the car's passengers. "Get ready, boy." He re-doused the rag with chloroform and handed it to Joshua.

Much to Edwin's aggravation, the girls sat in the car, talking. He looked over the neighborhood. Quiet and very few cars parked in the driveways along the street. *Perfect.*

It hadn't been Edwin's intention to be involved in this part of the plan. Ideally, he wanted Joshua to grab the girl and throw her under the truck tarp. However, with the addition of the other slut, he'd have to dirty his hands. A two-man job, but simple enough.

Reaching under the bench seat, he pulled out a tire iron. He snatched a piece of paper out of the glove box.

"Well, boy, looks like we're gonna get both girls," said Edwin. Not an unpleasant thought, to be honest. He might just save Miss Lindsay Bellowes for himself. And maybe he would let Joshua indulge his urges when he finished with her. Maybe—just maybe—he could get twice the amount of money. A two-for-one sale. Yes, indeed. Much better than he hoped for.

Finally, the two girls exited the car.

"Come on, boy," Edwin whispered. "Stay in the truck 'til I grab the driver. Then you get the other one. And make sure both their purses get tossed back in their car." Edwin knew every spoiled little girl had a cellular phone nowadays. He didn't need the phones traveling with them. He'd thought of everything—a foolproof plan.

Edwin opened the truck's door. The rusty hinges groaned, catching the two girls' attention. Their heads swiveled, their expressions puzzled. Both girls stood silently by their open car doors.

"Excuse me, young ladies," called Edwin. Waving the paper in front of him, he concealed the tire iron behind his back. He trotted to the driver's side to confront Miss Lindsay Bellowes.

"Yes?" asked the blonde girl. Edwin detected fear on her face. His loins tingled.

"I believe I'm lost. I'm trying to find my aunt who resides in these here parts." He thrust the paper toward Miss Lindsay Bellowes. "Could you take a look and maybe give me some directions?"

Lindsay Bellowes eyed Edwin with suspicion while she reached for the paper. Edwin grabbed her arm, spun her around, and then forced her onto the car's front seat. He raised the tire iron above his head and brought it down hard—but not too hard—onto the back of the girl's head. Years of experience taught Edwin the difference between a blow to stun and a killing blow to a beast. He pulled the iron back again in case he needed to repeat it.

The other girl screamed. Edwin looked over the car roof. Joshua ran up behind the blonde girl and clamped the rag over her mouth. Her legs kicked at the air as Joshua picked her up. One arm, having escaped Joshua's bear hug, flailed about in every direction. He carried the girl back to the truck as she struggled in his ironclad embrace.

A groan came from the front car seat. The girl stirred. He reached under her face, forcing his hand over her mouth. He raised the iron for another blow. A sharp stinging sensation tore through his hand. A bite. He brought the iron down on her head, this time harder. She slipped into unconsciousness. A purse sat on the front seat, another on the floor on the passenger's side, just where Edwin wanted them. He took a cleansing breath and looked to see how Joshua was faring.

Joshua lay on the pavement by the truck, cradling his manhood. Ten feet away, the girl raced to the nearest neighbor's house, screaming like a banshee.

"Get your ass up and get her, *now*," Edwin screamed. Joshua shook off his pain and clawed his way to his feet.

The little blonde was just a-wailing and pounding on someone's door as Joshua staggered toward her.

Edwin grabbed Miss Lindsay Bellowes around the waist. Blood dripped from her brown hair. Lighter than a hay bale, he tossed her over his shoulder and headed toward the back of the truck. Efficiently pulling the tarp back with one hand, he pitched her into the pickup like a bale of hay. Leaning against the truck bed, he caught his breath and wiped his brow.

Edwin looked for Joshua and the blonde tramp, but they were nowhere in sight.

Lindsay gasped then dipped out of sight.

Shannon stood still, unable to comprehend what she had just seen. Something in her brain clicked, a wake-up warning, hot and urgent. The wiry old man had pushed Lindsay back into her car. Shannon screamed. A muscular arm encircled her waist and lifted her. She kicked her feet. She pulled at the rag covering her mouth, but the man's grip held firm. Repeatedly hammering back with her fists, one solid blow landed on her assailant's crotch.

With a groan, Shannon's attacker dropped her. She whirled around to confront him. A hideous, giant of a man lay curled up in the street. His long, matted hair cracked like a whip as his head snapped back and forth. Shannon looked into what passed for his eyes, one dead, the other rolling. Less than human, something out of a nightmare. She kicked him in the crotch.

Shannon looked at the old man, hunched over Lindsay in the car. Relief swelled in her when she saw Lindsay's hands flailing in the air. Shannon had to act fast, but she couldn't do it alone.

She raced past the howling behemoth to the sidewalk, staying out of arm's reach. Ahead of her, the front door of the house jumped and shook in her vision. *Almost there.*

She heard the old man yell, "Get your ass up and go get her, *now!*" She banged up against the front door, pounding on it. The doorknob didn't turn. She risked a glance behind her. The man was up and loping toward her like a wounded bear. For his size, he moved fast.

Shannon abandoned the door and bolted through the front yard. The man-beast lunged at her, his fingertips grazing her shirt. Momentum took him to the ground with a thud. Hurtling down the street, shrieking, Shannon prayed to draw someone's attention.

Anyone…please, God…

Heavy breathing and footfalls plodded along behind her. Growing louder, gaining…

Shannon turned between two houses. A chain link fence barred her path. Without slowing, she leaped. Her hands came down upon the top of the fence as her legs followed. She hit the ground running, repeated the vault at the back fence. Looking over her shoulder, she saw the man struggling to mount the fence.

Shannon froze in the middle of the next street over. She pirouetted, hoping to spot someone. She wanted to scream but kept her trembling lips closed. It would do no good. The neighborhood appeared dead.

She pressed her knotted-up fists against her hipbones to steady them. Took several deep breaths. Down the street, a garage door stood open. *Civilization.*

From a distance, a fence rattled. Then a grunt, deep and beastly. He had cleared the fence and was coming for her.

She raced toward the open garage, her tennis shoes falling silently, impotently upon the street.

Breathless, Shannon entered the garage. She dropped behind a recycling bin. The stench of rotten fruit and meat made her gag. To avoid retching, she clamped a hand over her mouth. She peeked around the bin. The man pounded down the street, heavy feet sending reverberating echoes through the empty neighborhood. He passed her, head swiveling in all directions.

She waited, finally daring to breathe. If she closed the garage door, he would hear it. She tried the door to the house. *Locked.* She rapped on the door lightly, probably not weighty enough. *No answer.* A soft mewling sound reached her ears, which she mistook for a kitten before realizing it was coming from deep within her chest. Some horrible sound poised between sobbing and quiet hysteria.

She studied her surroundings. A hammer hung on the wall beside a pile of snow shovels and leaf rakes. She gripped it with shaking hands, holding it firmly. Against the back wall, a refrigerator sat wedged into the corner. If she could edge it out, she could squeeze behind it. She peered out the door. The man stood in the street directly in front of the garage but looking away.

Carefully, she shimmied the heavy refrigerator forward, bit by bit, praying the noise wouldn't attract her monstrous pursuer. Just enough room to slide behind it. The hot coils on the back burned her chest. Shaking uncontrollably, she nearly dropped the hammer. Sweat dripped down her forehead.

Footsteps shuffled across the driveway. Closer. They stopped. A quiet hiss, building. *Sniffing?* Then a snort, huge and phlegm-filled. Rhythmic, high-pitched grunts. *My God, is he laughing?*

A thought tore through Shannon's mind, a horrifying notion. *He's playing with me. Mouse to his cat.*

She heard him enter the garage. His feet swept lazily across the floor. A small snap of a fallen leaf stepped upon. *Then silence.*

The refrigerator kicked on, hummed. A locomotive raced through Shannon's heart. She squeezed the hammer, her grip tenuous at best in her sweaty palm.

Thick, dirty, fingers appeared around the corner of the refrigerator. With frightening speed, the beast shoved it away. And there the horrible man stood, looming in front of her, a ghastly smile across his bearded face. He beat his chest, bellowing in victory.

Shannon slammed the hammer into the beast's face. He stumbled back, but just a couple of steps. Wiping the blood away, he licked his hand, smiled again. Shannon screamed, her only possible response.

The man snapped a thick hand over her mouth. With his other hand, he pinched her wrists together and carried her out of the garage. An old pick-up truck pulled to a screeching halt in front of them.

"Goddammit, boy!" The old man hopped down from the driver's seat. He peeled back a tarp covering the back of the truck. The large man tossed Shannon into the truck bed. Her cheek bit metal, a hollow, hopeless *thump*. The older man quickly secured her mouth with tape and tied her hands behind her back. Something nudged against her, something warm. Shannon turned and saw Lindsay, unconscious. A bloody rag encircled her head. The tarp rolled over them. Shannon sobbed as the last sliver of daylight vanished.

Yesterday, Peter had received the call he'd been waiting for. He checked the caller ID. *Unknown.* Still, he didn't want to get his hopes up.

"Peter Brookes."

"It's time." The craggy voice sounded like it gave birth from the middle of a windstorm. "You wanted two days' warning; here it is. You'd best leave now."

"I'll be there the day after tomorrow."

At long last, the day is here.

Peter had already put half of the twenty-four-hour drive behind him. He had originally planned on two twelve-hour stretches, but he felt so invigorated that he pushed himself into the night. Looking out at the endless plains and flatlands, he felt a blistering contempt. He hadn't been back to the Midwest in a long time. Sure as hell didn't miss it, either. He never did understand why anyone would actually choose to live here. Nothing but hicks, rednecks, and dirt.

Peter turned up the stereo to distract himself from the surrounding Midwest misery. Show tunes, his music of choice. Actually, caffeine and the soundtrack to *Camelot* had been his only sustenance since he left New York. He realized if his business competition ever discovered his fondness for show tunes, they would ridicule him mercilessly. Maybe even see it as a weakness. Well, so what? Everyone was allowed their vices, no need for embarrassment. Besides, it was the only thing he'd held onto from his childhood. Everything else he had been more than happy to jettison.

With an excruciatingly long haul ahead, Peter had nothing but time to reflect on how this exciting opportunity had originated. "Unexpected" didn't do it justice.

Less than a month ago, he had received the first phone call.

"Peter Brookes."

"Is this the famous high-finance wizard, Peter Brookes?"

Peter's throat dried up at the sound of the voice, a voice he thought he'd never hear again. He leaned back in his chair and exhaled slowly.

"Yes, it is. Who's this?" Although he already knew.

"The rich and mighty Peter Brookes? But it's really Peter Quail now, ain't it?"

"Hello, Father," said Peter quietly. His heart sank lower than his self-esteem. The old bastard had a knack for doing that to him. "How'd you find me?"

Edwin Quail burst out laughing, ratcheting it up into a coughing fit. "Well, I saw your picture in a magazine. Didn't take much to track you down after that."

"What do you want?"

"Well, how is that for a fine how-do-you-do to your father after all these years? You left home when you were just a boy without as much as a thank you very much, and you don't think you can show me a little respect now?"

"What do you *want?*"

"Well, if that's the way it's gotta be, then fine. I want money."

"That's too bad. You're not getting anything from me." Fury incensed Peter. The son-of-a-bitch felt entitled to what Peter had made on his own after sharing nothing with him but beatings and humiliation.

"I brought you into this world. I gave you everything. You wouldn't be where you are now if it weren't for me!"

The sheer outrageousness of his statement floored Peter. "All you ever gave me were beatings and barely enough food to survive. I'm finished here." Peter hated losing control of his emotions. Hadn't done it for years. Funny how "family" can bring back bad habits.

"Wait," yelled Edwin. "How about if I give you something? Something you'd like?"

"What could you possibly give me?" Morbid curiosity settled in, gnawing at Peter's bones.

"I read that you like to hunt."

"Yes…"

"I'll supply you with the best hunt you could ever imagine." His father's voice turned quiet, cagey.

"I'm listening."

"I'll give you a human hunt," said Edwin.

Peter considered the words carefully. He thought about the ramifications. It sounded too good to be true.

"Call me back on my cell phone." Peter quickly rattled off the numbers and hung up. He made a mental note to fire his assistant since she allowed the call to go through. His hands shook. Not out of fear or anxiety, but from *excitement*.

Fate can be a funny arbiter at doling out fortune. But Peter certainly put more faith in "fate" than he did God—the absent deity Edwin used to rail on about. Most certainly, Peter's golden opportunity arose from that phone call. But honestly, hadn't fate planted the seeds years ago? When "Peter Brookes" was born from the loins of fate and his own nurturing wiles?

His career hadn't started in New York City. The first stop had been Los Angeles, when he still went by Peter Quail. As he stepped off the bus, the urgency of the people and the pace of the city immediately enthralled him. A thriving, living entity, a long way from Godwin, Kansas. Utilizing the last of his meager savings, Peter checked into a cheap motel. Then he hailed a taxi to a better part of town and bought a suit. With no immediate plans in place, he knew he needed to look the part.

On a whim, he joined a line of people standing in front of a nightclub. An hour and a half later, he pushed his way through the throng of scantily clad women and suited men toward the bar.

"Scotch." Peter had never tasted scotch before. Had just read about "the sophisticated man's drink."

The bartender nodded. "Ten dollars."

"*What?*" Over the loud bass line of the throbbing music, he thought he misunderstood the bartender.

The bartender repeated the cost. Peter stood up, shaking his head. He plucked one of the remaining large bills from his wallet and tossed it onto the counter. Laughter rang out next to him.

A man sat at the bar, possibly in his mid-twenties. Even though loud, boorish, and beet-red, his bearing emanated wealth. Elegantly dressed in a three-piece suit, he continued tossing money onto the bar like Halloween candy. A whorish-looking blonde woman, tight dress barely covering her crotch, clung to his shoulder. He gestured for Peter to come over.

"Just get off the bus, kid?" The man couldn't have been much older than Peter was.

"Actually, yes." The man roared again, this time the slut joining him. Peter smiled, trying not to appear overwhelmed like the fresh-faced, country yokel circumstance had made him.

"Have a seat." He jabbed his finger toward where another woman sat. The woman huffed and left. "Name's Peter Brookes." He shook Peter's hand with startling strength.

"My name's Peter, too." When Peter sat down, another scotch was already waiting for him. "I can't afford this."

Brookes sighed. "Stick with me, kid. We've got a long night ahead of us."

They sat at the bar for hours, an endless parade of women and men dropping by for introductions and free drinks. Brookes was a stockbroker, very profitable by his own telling. After making a name for himself in Los Angeles, Brookes recently accepted a job in New York City. The company hired him sight unseen due to his accomplishments. Once Brookes finished boasting, the topic of Peter's career surfaced. Peter lied, told him he had gone to Harvard and studied to become a stockbroker. Brookes stared at Peter dumbfounded before lapsing into laughter. His way of handling everything.

Brookes took him home that night to his apartment. More like a mansion. Sleek, glistening furniture looked like something out of a European's wet dream. Open, airy rooms vaulted to a twelve-foot-high ceiling. Art and statues of a decidedly erotic nature demanded appreciation.

They partied into the night. People came, drank, snorted lines of cocaine, then left. Peter soon found out they were everyday party sycophants.

Several of the partygoers caught Peter's eye. Quiet, intimidating, and black, Peter thought these men didn't fit in with the rest of L.A.'s beautiful people. Money and drugs exchanged hands. Peter's first crash course in fast and dangerous living, Los Angeles style.

Brookes took Peter in as a temporary houseguest. Peter never really understood why, either. Maybe fate had intervened for the first time—and it was about damn time, too.

In two weeks, Brookes was set to leave for New York, prepared for financial domination. He quit his current job but left plenty of time to party.

Peter's education continued. Nights filled with debauchery, days occupied by finance and business knowledge. Brookes seemed only too happy to share his shark-like experience.

"Rule Number One: Most of stock brokering is cutthroat ruthlessness," Brookes bellowed, his face hovering over several lines of cocaine.

After a week and a half, the party stopped. So did Brookes's heart. One morning Peter found Brookes slumped over on his sofa, his sunglasses dangling from one ear.

Peter pushed Brookes's body over, sat down next to him. He thought of his options. Of course, the smart thing to do would be to call the police. But with the amount of drugs around, he could easily be implicated in Brookes's death. Besides, Brookes wasn't married, was an only child, both parents deceased, no *true* friends to speak of. He wouldn't be missed.

Peter had a better idea.

Finding the number in Brookes's cell phone, Peter dialed. "Hi, this is…Peter. Peter Brookes's friend? I have a problem…"

As expected, Brookes's drug dealer knew a guy. Several guys, in fact. The dealer told Peter it would cost him. Big time. Peter reassured him money wouldn't be an issue. He knew where Brookes kept his paper fortune. Brookes couldn't use it now anyway.

Several hours later, a "clean-up" man arrived. Not at all what Peter expected. Short, bespectacled, quiet, pushing fifty or older; the perfect cliché of an accountant. He dragged Brookes into the bathtub and tended to business. Saws buzzed. Grunts drifted out from the bathroom. Peter tackled the scotch. The man didn't say a word until he left, struggling with two large suitcases. "The papers will be ready in two days," were his parting words.

Peter didn't know how they did it. He didn't want to know. But they supplied him with a driver's license and other essential papers. Apparently fingerprints weren't a problem either. Peter gathered up the rest of Brookes's certification, licensing documents, and the remaining cash. He boarded the airplane to New York as Peter Brookes. No one mourned the death of Peter Quail. Frankly, no one knew about it.

Until now...

Peter adjusted the stereo and pumped caffeine into his system. A motel's lights flashed ahead. He slowed his Lincoln Town Car but then quickly discarded the notion. He sped on to his destination, singing, happier than he'd been in some time.

Jason stood in front of Matt, his eyes wide with worry.

"What's wrong?" Matt set his wine glass down, prepared for the worst. Nothing ever bothered Jay.

"There's a police detective here, Matt. He wants to talk to you."

Matt's nerves jangled. Police made him edgy. Surely, it's a mistake. "What's he want?"

"He didn't say."

Matt brushed by Jason as he moved toward the front door. A bald, man with glasses stood in the doorway, holding a notepad.

"Matt Strothers?" His caterpillar-like eyebrows lifted.

"That's right. And you are?"

"I'm Detective Brian Sidarski with the Barton Police Department." He offered his hand to Matt.

"What's this about, Detective?"

"I'm afraid I need to tell you that your daughter…" he paused while checking his notepad, "Shannon Wolters…is missing."

Matt fell back against the wall, jarring the hanging mirror. Matt hadn't seen his daughter in eight years. It wasn't like he'd had a choice in the matter. Cheryl, his ex-wife, had made it impossible. She found a homophobic, sympathetic judge who took away Matt's visitation rights, even slapped him with a restraining order. But Matt had been thinking about Shannon a lot lately. Recently, she'd turned sixteen. He'd thought a lot about attempting to see her. If she was willing to see him after all this time.

"Maybe we'd better sit down?" offered the detective.

Matt nodded and led the detective into the living room.

"What makes you think she's missing?" Matt's mind raced, unable to grasp the situation. He hoped—*prayed*—for a logical explanation. Surely, God wouldn't be so cruel as to take his daughter from him when he was so close to seeing her again. But a growing knot of despair in his stomach told him differently. Unhappy endings seemed to be the norm in his life these days.

"Here's what we know," said the detective. "Shannon Wolters, along with her friend, Lindsay Bellowes, were last seen after school—Barton High—driving off together. We found Miss Bellowes's car in front of her house with the doors open. I'm afraid there was blood matching Miss Bellowes's blood type found on the front seat."

"Oh, *God*. And they're both missing?"

"That's correct. Neighbors reported hearing some screaming in the neighborhood earlier, but they thought it was kids playing." The detective sighed and shook his head. "Now, Mister Strothers, I don't want to worry you unnecessarily. The blood *could* be from a simple cut. There wasn't a large amount."

"Were they…kidnapped?"

Detective Sidarski took his time before answering. "We really don't know at this time. Are you able to account for your whereabouts today between three and four p.m.?"

"Wait, you don't think *I* did this?"

"Well, your ex-wife certainly thinks it's likely."

"For God's sake! Cheryl's been on the warpath with me since I left her. Of course, I didn't do it. I was working at my video shop all day."

"That would be Village Video? In Olathe?"

"Yes."

"Can any of your customers corroborate this?"

Matt thought for a moment. There hadn't been many customers. But a few of the regulars could back him up. "Yeah, I think so. If necessary, I can call them."

"Mister Strothers, I understand you had your name legally changed when you were nineteen? From…Quail?"

Matt felt his world spiraling madly out of control. He didn't like where this was headed. "That's right. I took my mother's surname. As did my sister."

"Why'd you do it? Change your name?"

"Because I hated my father. What does this have to do with my daughter, Detective?"

"Probably nothing." Sidarski tossed off a casual shrug. "I just like to know who I'm dealing with. And, your sister, Mary Strothers…"

"Yes?"

"She'd been sexually abused. It looks like during your divorce proceedings, your ex-wife accused you of doing it."

Matt shot to his feet, his fists clenched. "That's all bullshit! Cheryl said those things to gain leverage in keeping me away from my daughter." Jason gripped Matt's arm, attempting to calm him—the last thing Matt wanted right now. He felt a need to work through his anger; his life, such as it was, was bubbling to a boiling point.

"There's no need to get angry, Mister Strothers. All of this is probably unrelated." Sidarski gave Matt a firm look, condescending and full of judgment. "I'm just trying to understand everything in case it can help us find your daughter."

"I did not take my daughter."

After a lengthy silence, Sidarski said, "I believe you, Mister Strothers.

Please get me the names of your customers by tomorrow, if you would." He stood up and strolled back to the hallway, business as usual.

"Detective, what do you think happened?" asked Matt, his voice cracking. "Do you think she's alive?"

"I'd like to believe she is, Mister Strothers. As for what happened, they're both good girls, so I doubt they're out joy riding or what have you. Since both purses were left behind, money and credit cards still intact, it doesn't look like a robbery. Unfortunately, I think they've been abducted."

Matt sat down again and shut his eyes. "Who would do this?"

"That's what we're trying to find out. I'll do my best to keep you posted. Should you hear anything, do contact me." He dropped a business card onto the living room table. "Oh, one last thing, Mister Strothers. A boy at their school—Gavin Hensen—said he saw an old Ford pick-up truck following the girls after they left the parking lot. He described it as dark blue with large, orange rust spots on the body. Probably about twenty years or so old. Do you know anyone who has a vehicle like this?"

Matt sat in stunned silence. Yes, he did indeed know someone with a truck like that. But surely there were lots of old trucks matching this description. Even his sick bastard of a father wouldn't go this far. Would he? *Could* he?

"Mister Strothers?" asked the detective. "Do you know of anyone who owns a vehicle like this?"

"No, I don't think so."

Matt made the decision, there and then, to return to Godland.

Chapter Six

That little girl sure was a persevering young thing. She'd been cater-wauling from the truck bed for the last two hours. *A tighter, stronger gag might shut her up,* Edwin thought.

He exited the highway at Cantor and followed a small dirt road for several miles. Parking in a heavily wooded area, he flipped back the tarp. Miss Lindsay Bellowes groaned, a good sign. He didn't want to risk any of his cash reward by supplying damaged goods.

When Edwin loosened the rag from the blonde girl's mouth, she snapped at him.

"Why, you little vixen," said Edwin, grinning. He slapped her. It felt good to be in control. Been some time since he'd felt that way. "That'll teach you to try and bite me. You and your friend both need to learn some re-spect." He secured a new rag over her mouth and bound her hands to her feet.

Too bad Edwin couldn't use the chloroform to shut the girl's pie-hole. But it had lost its potency and hadn't worked earlier. No matter, no how. By the grace of God, everything would work out.

"Let's go, boy."

Joshua smiled, rocking on the truck bench.

Edwin studied the map of Kansas, charting the rest of their journey.

On the way down, he 'd taken I-35 the entire route. Now, smaller back-road highways suited his needs better. It would take an extra hour, but it would be well worth it. *No sense in borrowing trouble*, as his momma used to say.

After another fifty miles, the blonde girl finally stopped screaming. Best thing for her. She would need all the strength and energy she could muster later.

And he needed his energy to spend Peter's money.

It had been a heaven-sent miracle as to how Edwin located Peter, no doubt about it. Several months ago, on a day like any other, Edwin sat astride his tractor in the cornfields. He spotted a discarded magazine in the ditch. Thinking nothing of it at first, something called to Edwin, a celestial voice from the heavens. He thumbed through the sporting magazine. When he saw the photo of Peter, he had damn near keeled over. A short interview with him lay buried in a hunting article. They quoted Peter saying, "Killing a deer is the thrill of a lifetime," or some such snooty nonsense. No surprise there. As a child, Peter always volunteered to slaughter the livestock, gleefully relishing the task. Back when he showed promise.

The month before, when Edwin called his ingrate of a son, he had planned to ask for money. Nothing more. Edwin had, after all, raised him, fed him, and taught him everything he knew. But the little bastard showed no gratitude.

After Peter rudely rejected Edwin's request, divine inspiration struck. Edwin played to the boy's sadistic nature. When he suggested a human hunt, Edwin knew his son would take the bait.

Just a matter of hours now…

Dusk set in. Edwin drove through Puckett, Kansas, an eyesore of a ghost town. A once-prosperous mining town, God saw fit to punish Puckett's folks by ravaging it to the ground with a tornado. Driving past what remained of the abandoned houses and ransacked stores, Edwin shook his head in disgust. He didn't know what the townspeople's sins had been, couldn't even imagine. God's punishment was just, though. Edwin drove past the last dilapidated building—tellingly, a funeral home—and entered the flatlands.

Red flashing lights appeared in his rear-view mirror, followed by a heart-squeezing *whoop*. Joshua whipped around, whimpering at the sight.

"Shut up, boy; you're not helping matters none." Edwin pulled onto the graveled shoulder. As he watched in his mirror, a tall, lanky figure exited the police car. The man ambled toward them, straightening his hat. Joshua, squirming in his seat, moaned again. "I said shut up, boy!" Edwin listened carefully for any noise from the truck bed. Just the typical *tics* from the engine settling. The girls remained quiet.

He rolled down his window in anticipation of the officer. As an afterthought, he reached under his seat, snagging his hunting knife and sliding it underneath his thigh.

"Good evening, sir." A young fellow, nothing more than a pup, with a deputy's badge pinned on his shirt.

"Good evening, officer. I believe I was doing the speed limit."

The deputy glanced over at Joshua and produced a slight but visible grimace. "The reason I pulled you over is you have mud covering your license plate. If your plate's not visible, it's a ticketable offense. Are you aware of this?"

"Why, no, sir. I didn't know it was covered up." Edwin squeezed the steering wheel tight, holding on for dear, sweet life.

"How'd you get the mud on there if you don't mind my asking?" The officer smiled. *Encouraging.*

"Well, I took the boy out hunting today." Edwin inclined his head toward Joshua. "I thought I'd show him how to do it." The deputy, both hands on the windowsill, leaned in slightly. He studied the contents of the truck, but mostly Joshua. Edwin gave the policeman a knowing wink, the kind that said "feel my burden," and added in a low voice, "You see, the boy ain't right."

"I see." The deputy cleared his throat, obviously uncomfortable. "Where'd you go hunting?"

"Back at Devon, down the road a ways."

"Any luck?"

"We got us a couple rabbits, not much."

"And I assume you have a hunting permit?"

"Oh, yes, sir. It's around here somewhere." Edwin fumbled through his shirt and pants pockets, knowing full well he had no such permit.

"That's all right. Tell you what. When you get to the next town, pull over, and clean the mud off your plate. Do that for me?"

"Yes, sir."

"Y'all have a nice night and drive carefully." He straightened and turned. Edwin let out a quiet sigh of relief.

A brief but loud *thump* arose from the truck bed. Edwin's heart fluttered like an irate bird. He craned his head, daring a look back. The deputy stood at the back of the truck, staring at the cracked tarp tied across it.

"Sir?" called the deputy. "*Sir!* Please step out of the truck!" With one hand on the tarp, he held the other over his holstered pistol.

"Be ready to help me," Edwin whispered to Joshua. Joshua stared vacantly, then nodded. Edwin cupped the knife in his right hand and hopped out of the truck.

"What's the matter, officer?" Edwin attempted to smile, but his twitching lips didn't cooperate.

"What's in the truck bed?"

"Just the rabbits…some hunting equipment." Edwin approached the officer slowly. He waved to announce his harmlessness.

Another hollow thump. Edwin felt it all the way up to his rotting teeth.

"Maybe one of them rabbits ain't dead," said Edwin, forcing a chuckle.

The deputy took a few steps back. "Open it. Now, please."

Edwin hesitated. The officer glared at him, his fingers unsnapping his holster.

"Sure, not a problem." Edwin walked toward the truck bed. Facing the truck, he carefully slid the knife into his belt above his crotch. The deputy moved in closer behind him. Edwin fiddled with the knots, feigning awkwardness. "I'm sorry, officer, but…arthritis…old age and all." Edwin wiggled his fingers in the air. "What say you give me a hand?"

The officer paused, and then stepped toward the tarp. He tugged at the rope.

Edwin yanked the hunting knife out of his belt. He lunged at the deputy, jamming it into his throat. Blood gushed, the torrential spray soaking Edwin. Edwin pulled the knife out, quickly slashing it across the deputy's throat. Geysers of blood blurred Edwin's vision. He heard the policeman shuffle back. Clearing one eye with the back of his hand, Edwin watched the deputy grasp his throat, trying to stall his life force from leaving.

"Joshua! Help me, boy!" Edwin dragged a shirtsleeve across his face, wiping away the remaining blood.

Joshua bounded out of the truck. He threw himself against the deputy, his weight carrying them both down onto the pavement.

"Grab his gun, boy, his gun!"

Joshua jumped to his feet, pleased with himself, and brandished the gun in the air like a newfound toy.

"Pick him up and put him in the bed," ordered Edwin. He could see clearly enough now to unhitch the tarp. The girls stared at him underneath the moonlight, their eyes round with horror. He slapped the blonde girl again because he knew—he just *knew*—she made him kill the county deputy.

After a while, Shannon gave up screaming through the rag, a futile effort. The sound of other traffic had long ceased. The ropes held tight, cutting into her wrists. Barely able to move, she listened for Lindsay's breathing. Lindsay had to be alive. It helped knowing she wasn't alone.

She couldn't understand anything. A waking nightmare, nothing made sense. Her mother had no money, and Lindsay's family didn't either, so that ruled out kidnapping. She shut her eyes tight, struggling to bring order to her new world. She thought of Gavin, how she might never see him again. She had never experienced anything like romance before. She prayed it wouldn't end just as it had begun.

Shannon bit down on the inside of her cheeks, bringing painful awareness to the forefront. Time to get her head straight. Stop thinking about Gavin. Only one thing mattered. *Survival.*

It all happened so fast. From being the Queen of Cuckoo Burger to being chased through the streets by some inhuman...*monster.* The only way to describe her pursuer. She had worked with special needs people in the past on a voluntary basis; she thought she'd seen it all. But this man didn't even look human.

The truck rolled to a stop. She waited, hyperventilating through her nose, the sound deafening in her ears. She heard several voices. She recognized the old man, but the other... *Someone new?* She squirmed, inch by inch, repositioning her back against the truck's side. Lack of circulation numbed her hands, useless leaden weights. Ignoring the prickling sensation, she flapped her hands up against the truck's side. *Thump.* The conversation outside stopped. She hit the truck again, this time harder. A voice distinctly called out, "Sir!" Shannon's heart jumped, throbbing with hope and fear. The truck door creaked open. More voices spoke, almost jovial sounding. The ropes binding the tarp tugged. The old man cried out, "Joshua!" She listened to what sounded like scuffling and a struggle.

The tarp tore back. The old man's face was dark and wet, his eyes starkly white in contrast. Covered in blood. His slap bit into her cheek. She closed her eyes, waiting for another strike. A heavy weight fell on her. Something large. Before the tarp enveloped her in darkness again, she nudged her shoulders against the object. She shifted the weight away, wedging it against the truck's side. She rolled over and stared into the panicked eyes of a man. His lips quivered, gasping for air. Blood trickled out of several gashes in his throat.

Shannon screamed, the sound muffled yet explosive in her head. Lindsay, now awake, did the same. The tarp rolled back over, shutting out the light. Mercifully so. She wouldn't have to watch the man next to her die slowly.

The deputy's blood seeped underneath her, soaking her back. Before she passed out, she felt warm liquid splashing against her ear. A good night kiss.

The sounds of the tarp rolling away jolted her back into consciousness. She stared into the sky, noting the position of the full moon. She'd been out for at least two hours.

She avoided looking at the man next to her. His death gasps had stilled, his life fled. Cold and wet, the chill of the spring night wracked her body with shivers. Suddenly, the big man's head poked into view. He stared at Shannon with dead eyes. His mouth gaped open, exposing broken shards of teeth. Drool dripped down onto Shannon's face.

"Just pick him up and don't dither around," yelled the now-familiar voice.

The behemoth grabbed the dead man and hefted him out. Shannon caught a glimpse of a police badge. And the police radio attached to his shoulder—a tease—so close, yet so far.

"Carry him out as far past the field as you can, boy," ordered the man. "And try and bury him in that wooded area."

Oh my God! If they killed a cop, they're capable of anything.

By the light of the moon, Shannon saw Lindsay clearly. The skin around her eyes was puffy from crying. Shannon said through the rag, her words barely audible, "Are you all right?" After a long pause, Lindsay nodded her head.

Thank God. A very small gift in their hopeless situation, but one Shannon embraced.

Peter made better time than he thought possible. At this rate, he'd arrive at his destination earlier than planned. Even though he hadn't slept in over twenty-four hours, he felt alive, exuberant. Yet, every time he anticipated the hunt, his excitement dwindled by the inevitability of seeing his father.

Peter had grown up on the farm in Godwin, Kansas. His father called their town "*Godland,* Kansas." He said, "God blessed our land as something special, something fertile, where the soil grows great wonders to feed the American people." "Hell on Earth" seemed more accurate.

Peter never had a say in working on his father's farm—forced into it at the age of three. Along with his older brother, Matt, they toiled in the fields for up to twelve hours a day. Sunburned and blistered hands were their only rewards. Clothed in their father's hand-me-downs, they ate just enough to survive. He and his brother shared a bed in a small bedroom. Peter used to pull the mattress to the floor while his brother slept on the box spring. They never let their father know. He would've found some reason to disapprove.

Edwin hadn't wanted them to attend school at first. Thanks to the intervention of Peter's mother, though, Edwin grudgingly relented. They rode the bus into Karlin every day, eeking out their high school education. They barely managed that. No time for homework. Seven hours of school, followed by another seven hours in the field, forced Peter to drop out in his junior year.

Worst of all were the beatings, though. The old bastard hit him and his brother raw with a belt, buckle end up. Their father lashed them across their backs, their legs, everywhere he could reach. In his youthful naïveté, Peter couldn't understand it.

One time, he asked his father, "Why?"

"Because it's divine retribution," said Edwin. "God put me on this green earth to raise you boys into becoming the best, most God-fearing men you can be." If that's what God wished for, Peter despised God. But he grew to fear his father. Not God.

"But mostly, I beat you boys because I *can*." Peter never forgot his father's gleeful grin, full of both mirth and malice.

Oddly enough, Peter found solace in the most unlikely of manners. Watching his father slaughter the livestock, he wondered what it'd be like. He asked his father if he could try. His father smiled, proud of him for the first time, and put him to work.

The first time Peter approached one of the pigs with the killing knife, his stomach cramped up. He stared at the pig for the longest time, hoping to be man enough to follow through. His father, watching from the fence, taunted him. Called him "sissy" and other such names. Finally, he harangued Peter into the awful chore. Peter drew back the knife and dragged it across the pig's throat. Much easier than he thought it'd be. The pig released a mortifying death squeal, pitched higher than a whistle. Blood splashed onto his work boots. He smiled at his father.

Peter found a way to make it work for him. A secret scenario only he knew about. When Peter pulled the knife across the pig's throat, he imagined his father's neck under the knife. From that day on, he volunteered for the slaughtering, deriving what vicarious pleasures he could.

But when Peter turned eighteen, he'd finally had enough.

He remembered taking his older brother, Matt, aside. "Mattie, I'm leaving. And you should do the same."

"Where will you go?" asked Matt. "What will you do?" Long ago, Peter realized his brother resigned himself to living out this awful existence. He didn't understand things could be better. Believing in the bile their father spewed, Matt stupidly accepted "life" on the farm as God's plan.

"I don't know what I'll do," replied Peter. "But anything's better than this. If this is why God put me on this earth, He can go straight to hell!"

Matt's jaw dropped. "Peter, you don't really mean that." He placed his hand on Peter's shoulder as if trying to get him to retract his blasphemous statement.

"No, I really do. And Dad can go to hell, too. I'm sure that's where he came from."

Peter saw the planted seed of doubt spring to life in Matt's eyes. Just a small seed, but a promising start.

"I mean it, Matt," continued Peter. "Leave now. Take Mary with you if you can." Peter tossed some clothes and other essentials into a paper sack. "Goodbye, Mattie."

Peter stopped by the kitchen on his way out, just long enough to steal twenty dollars from his mother's purse, then hitched his way to Kansas City—vowing never to come back.

Yet, sometimes things changed, and he was now only hours away from rolling back into Godwin, Kansas. The return of the prodigal son.

Something nagged at Peter, though. After his current business endeavor with his father concluded, could he count on never hearing from the old shit again? Or would the bastard be a constant nuisance, asking for more money? The thought of Edwin blackmailing him weighed heavily on him. Peter might have to readjust some of the details in their business dealing.

The memory of slashing his first pig's throat brought a grin to his face. The ear-piercing squeal echoed in his mind like a recollection of a nostalgic, sunny day.

Jason didn't want him to go. He didn't understand Matt's driving *need* to go.

Once Jason finally realized Matt wouldn't back down, he reluctantly agreed. Only under the stipulation that if he didn't return within twenty-four hours, Jason would call Detective Sidarski.

Of course, Matt knew better than to tell Jason his father was absolutely insane. Peter, always the wiser brother, realized this many years before Matt did. Once Matt embraced this harsh reality, it helped him come to terms with his father's abusive behavior. At least he understood it better.

The saying goes, "The apple doesn't fall far from the tree." That adage had always troubled Matt. He wondered if he carried the "evil gene" his father possessed. Would he wake one morning, deciding to be a bastard the rest of his life? Had his father *always* been evil? *Yes.* At least as far as Matt could remember.

Matt looked out the window at the endless flatlands, his only companion on his journey. Those and his ruminations.

His thoughts kept returning to his sister, Mary…

During his senior year, on a particularly sweltering day, Matt felt sick on the school bus. The air conditioning had apparently given out. Windows were down, making matters worse. Dust and heat blew in, cooking them inside the ambulatory oven on wheels. As the bus sped down the gravel roads, Matt's stomach churned like a butter mill.

As always, the other kids on the bus shunned them. Matt was okay with that. Chores occupied every waking moment at home, so the bus rides were Matt's only opportunity to spend time with Mary.

"Are you okay, Matt?" asked Mary. She wore one of their mother's dresses, the only wardrobe allowed her. The dress, looking like something out of the forties, was a gaudy, floral-patterned affair. With the corners pinned up and fabric draping down in large folds, Mary practically swam in it.

"I think so. Why?"

Mary placed two fingers to her lips to suppress a chuckle. Matt loved seeing this side of his sister. When she smiled, her entire demeanor changed. "You look kind of sick," she said.

"Oh, it's nothing. Must've been something I ate." He did feel sick. But as her older brother, he wanted to shield her from anything upsetting. His duty as a man.

"If you say so." She looked out at the dust billowing across the road.

"Matt?"

"Hm?"

"How do you think Peter's doing?"

Since Peter had dropped out of high school, he had grown even more withdrawn, more sullen. Sometimes he scared Matt; other times, he saddened him. "I think he's doing about as good as can be expected. What do you think?"

Lines creased her forehead, too many for a teenager. "I'm worried about him."

"Why?"

"He's…different."

"Different from what?"

"Different from you, I guess…" she trailed off. Matt always trusted his sister's judgment, but she really didn't know Peter very well. Not like he did.

"Well, I would hope we're different."

"You know what I mean, Matt."

"Not really. What do you mean?"

"I guess… I think he might be…" Mary dropped her voice to a cautious whisper. "…dangerous, maybe?"

Matt knew Peter had been through some hard times. He'd never heard the full story, as Peter never talked about himself much, but the scuttlebutt around school was Peter had asked out a cheerleader. She rejected him, laughed at him. Sure, Peter walked around in a bitter cloud of sullenness. But *dangerous?* "He's not dangerous, Mary."

"He frightens me sometimes."

"Has he done something to you?"

"No. It's not that."

"Then what *is* it?"

Mary looked at Matt, her bottom lip quivering. "He reminds me of Father." The other students hushed their conversations, straining to listen in on theirs.

Matt didn't see it. Yet, he realized the trait could be dormant. An extremely violent man, their father's mood changed at the drop of a hat.

Matt hoped the behavior wasn't hereditary. He didn't want to become that man. "He's not like Father."

"I don't know…" Close to tears, Mary noticed the sudden onlookers. She sank down in her seat, hunching her shoulders to ward off unwanted eyes. "I've seen the way he looks at the animals, sometimes. The way his eyes seem…glazed over, maybe?"

"Mary, is that why you don't talk to Peter much?"

"I guess so. And, you know, because that's the way Momma and Daddy want it. The way it's supposed to be."

"Mary, that's not Peter's fault."

"I know."

"And even if Peter does take after Father, that's not his fault, either."

"I know. The Good Book says the sins of the father are to be repeated by their sons, though." Matt's shoulders sunk. Maybe Peter was right. Their father used the Bible for his own means, a method of brainwashing, with Mary being his newest victim.

"Mary—" He didn't want to deflate her beliefs, so he stopped. Struggling with his own beliefs was hard enough.

Mary waved her hands through the air. "I don't want to talk about this anymore, Matt." Her abrupt change amazed him. Her eyes lit up, the smile returned, the lines on her forehead faded.

"Okay."

"Here! I almost forgot." Mary burrowed through her notebook. She pulled out a piece of construction paper, green and yellow flower cutouts pasted upon it. "I made this for you today in art class."

Matt studied the gift. On the underside, the thickness of the glue weighed down the paper. A flower frame surrounded a drawing of a boy and girl holding hands. The drawing's realism took Matt aback. He immediately recognized the subjects.

"This is really good! I never knew you could draw like this."

"You like it?" Her eyes danced, full of hope.

"I do. I really do. You should consider becoming an artist."

A hint of a frown crossed her face. "I don't think that's going to happen. Father—"

Before she crashed back down to earth, Matt forged on to keep her aloft. "*Forget* about Father."

Mary fought the battle to laugh and lost. "Matt!"

"I mean it, Mary. It's really, really good. Forget about being a farmer's wife. You should be an artist. No. Wait. An…*artiste!*" Matt affected a comically stereotypical Frenchman's accent. "It *eez*…to die for!" He kissed his fingers, tossing them in the air with a flourish.

Mary roared with laughter. "Matt…shhh. Quiet down. Everyone's looking."

"Let them look, Mademoiselle. You are *L'Artiste Extraordinaire!*"

Finally, their laughter died down. They slumped down against the weathered bus seat.

"Matt?"

"Yeah?"

"You know, you're my favorite." She rolled her head against the seat to look at Matt.

"I know. You're my favorite, too."

"I love you, Matt."

"Love you, too." Matt grabbed her hand. They held hands for the rest of the agonizing bus ride home.

Matt's last good memory of childhood.

Visions of what his bastard father did to Mary overwhelmed him. Matt shuddered and rolled up the car window.

Did his father take Shannon? And, if so, why? A sudden wave of nausea soured his stomach. He didn't want to think it, but he had to. Edwin had raped his own daughter… so…*what if…?* Matt lurched forward, cupping a hand over his mouth.

He had been a sideline player in his own life for too long now. Long overdue to take charge. *Just please don't let it be too late.*

Strange. Matt swore he'd never visit his father again. He hadn't seen Shannon in years, much to his shame. Yet, here he was on his way toward a rendezvous with his father—and perhaps his daughter.

Peter would call it "fate." His father would preach about "God's plan."

Maybe it *was* God's plan for Matt to return to Godwin, Kansas. To save his daughter.

He floored the accelerator.

Chapter Seven

Since the death of the lawman, Joshua had remained uncustomarily quiet. Swaying back and forth on the truck seat, cradling one giant knee underneath his chin, he gazed out the window in silence. Edwin took great pains in explaining that sometimes, in God's righteous war, there were bound to be casualties. The boy just didn't get it.

Edwin pulled into the little town of Shelton and turned onto a narrow strip of a dirt road. Having done some trading here in the past, he was familiar with the area. Out past Ned Shepherd's farm lay an expansive plot of land going to waste. The landowner had up and died. Now the bank wanted to sell it. Vacant for going on two years now, a wooded area sat deep behind the barren wheat fields. Perfect for Edwin's—and God's—needs.

He didn't think to bring a shovel. Hardly thought it necessary. But the boy could dig a shallow grave with his hands. Wasn't much he couldn't do, really, as long as it didn't require any brain power. Edwin instructed Joshua to bury the body in the woods.

Joshua stared blankly at Edwin and then finally nodded. He lifted the body out of the truck with nary a peep from the girls. Edwin smiled, picking his teeth with his fingernail. The lawman had been nothing but a road bump; nothing he couldn't overcome on his road to reward.

After about forty-five minutes, Joshua returned to the truck, panting.

Sweat dripped from his hair and beard. Dirt and scratches covered his arms. "I'm right proud of you, boy," said Edwin. Joshua opened his black hole of a mouth, muttering. "Yep, real proud!"

Two hours later, they exited onto the gravel road leading to the farm. Edwin knew the fifteen-mile jaunt by heart. He drove at breakneck speed. Since no police officers ever came around these parts, it seemed like a good opportunity to make up for lost time.

He sped past the long-vacated, one-room schoolhouse where he had met his wife. The shack's roof had fallen in. Nothing but hay bales held up the walls. Those and fading memories. He rolled back his shoulders and jutted his chin out. *No need to dwell on the past.*

Finally, he pulled into his driveway. It felt good to be back in Godland.

The truck door opened with a scraping sound born of rust. Edwin stepped out into the cool night air, stretched, and cracked his back. His work was finished. Now it was all about the future.

Gravel pinged against the bottom of the truck, a hailstorm shooting up from hell. The truck crawled to a stop. Shannon breathed deeply, preparing herself.

The tarp pulled away with a slash and a *snap*. Shannon squinted into the scant illumination provided by the moon. The beastly man loomed over her, eclipsing the moon. He reached in, and grabbing Shannon around the waist, he heaved her onto his broad shoulders. Shannon's nose filled with the sour stench of perspiration and other smells she couldn't identify. She didn't try too hard.

He carried her around the side of a white house. Old shutters sagged like a stroke victim's face, and paint peeled off the shingles like blisters. Shannon, her head bobbing up and down on the man's back, took a mental inventory of her surroundings. They passed a long shed, the tin roof only partially attached. The man stopped in front of two splintered wooden doors in the ground. A mound of cement—a fabricated anthill—sat nestled between the shed and doors.

The doors opened with a rusty-sounding groan. The giant took Shannon down narrow concrete stairs. Her claustrophobia grew as she watched the night sky's light vanish. Dirt walls closed in on her. Lowered into the ground, buried alive. She squirmed, kicked, screamed through her gag. The man stroked her back gently as if calming a fever-ridden child. Then a scrabbling sound, a key in a lock. Another door groaned open. Inside, the air felt stagnant, yet cool. A sole light bulb dangling on a string spread out a circle of light. Wooden shelves stocked with dusty jars lined the dirt walls.

The man lowered her onto a filthy blanket. He left, leaving the door open behind him. Shannon struggled to get to her feet, but the ropes binding her wouldn't loosen enough.

The man re-entered, this time with Lindsay hoisted over his shoulder. When the man dropped her to the dirt, Lindsay scooted close to Shannon. He left again, ducking beneath the doorframe. Then he locked the door behind him. The *clack* sounded like a mousetrap snapping on its prey.

Only able to communicate through their eyes, the girls stared at one another, desperate.

Minutes later, the man re-entered, holding a knife and bucket. He shambled toward them, a misshapen, giant baby learning to walk.

He picked up Shannon with one hand, turning her to face the wall. Shannon whispered the Lord's Prayer, anticipating her final moment of life.

Murdered underground and no one will ever know.

Instead, the man cut the ropes between her hands and feet. He repeated this with Lindsay. Then he yanked the rag from Shannon's mouth. Shannon stretched her legs, never taking her eyes off the beast. A tingling sensation grew through her legs, circulation slowly returning. The man loosened Lindsay's gag with a surprisingly soft touch.

He prodded the bucket toward Shannon, his misshapen fingers gesturing with a backhanded motion. His mouth contorted, the corners working to form a semblance of a smile.

Shannon hesitated before accepting the gift. The bucket shook in her hands, liquid slopping over the side. She sniffed the contents of the bucket. No odor. A small sip, and she tasted lukewarm water. She tilted the bucket back and drank. A relieving salve to her parched throat. The man yelped unintelligibly, shaking his head like a wet dog.

Lindsay drank next. Then the man stepped into the small ring of light. Seeing him clearly for the first time, Lindsay dropped the bucket to the dirt floor. And she screamed.

Startled, the man fell back, groaning. With his eyes closed, he pulled at his hair, his fingers entangled in dark mats. He ran out the door, slamming it behind him.

"Oh my God, Shannon! What the hell is he? Where are we? What's going on?"

"Lindsay! Lindsay, calm down! Just talk to me. We have to be here for one another." Shannon's tears erupted again, an involuntary response. "I don't know what's going on." She leaned her shoulder against her friend. "Please. Let's both try and stay strong…until we can find a way out."

The girls, racked with spasms, pressed gently against one another. Speechless, their tears eventually ran dry.

"Lindsay, we will find a way out of this," whispered Shannon. "We will. Just stay strong and stay with me. We'll get out of here." Strong words, yet hollow. Shannon didn't believe them for a minute. But she had to remain strong for her friend's benefit. Their only defense. "I promise you… we'll get out of this."

The door swung open again, startling the girls. The old man strutted in, a proud rooster in a hen house. Not at all the same lost, doddering man they first encountered today.

"Hello, young ladies." His grin cracked his face like a worn leather belt. "Now, y'all go ahead and scream your fool heads off." He cackled, a sound like breaking glass. "Ain't no one 'round for ten to fifteen miles to hear you. So just go ahead and scream. Scream for all you're worth." His bony fingers formed into a hook, baiting them. "Go on! Get it out of your system."

The man's eyes flitted back and forth between them. His tongue explored his lips. Shannon remained quiet, damned determinedly so.

"No?" said the man finally. "That's fine then. But you girls best behave yourselves, y'hear? You ain't going anywhere 'til it's time."

"Time for what? What do you want with us?"

"You'll find out in good time. Patience is a virtue. If I were you, I'd try and get some rest. You're gonna need it." He turned to leave, hesitated, then swiveled in his boots. "By the way, young ladies, welcome to Godland." His laughter bounced off the low, wood-reinforced ceiling. He tapped the dangling light bulb, sending it swinging back and forth. Shadows bobbed across the man's face. He locked the door behind him, his laughter receding into the night.

The girls sat in stunned silence, listening. They heard distant sounds of pigs squealing and cows lowing. A bird cawing. Something screeching. A long way from the sounds of suburbia. The middle of nowhere.

"Shannon?" whispered Lindsay.

"Yeah?"

She patted her pocket. "I have my cell phone."

With only two hours to go, Peter's phone rang.

"Hello?"

"It's me. I have the goods." There was an upbeat vitality to his father's tone, an alien sound.

"Very good. I'll arrive within two hours."

The long pause prompted Peter to believe the call had dropped. Finally, "You're early!"

"Deal with it." Peter remained calm. He wanted nothing more than a strictly business relationship with Edwin.

"Well, then, I reckon we oughta move it up to tonight, even if it is gettin' on late."

"I'm ready." For the last twenty hours, Peter's stops had been minimal. Nothing mattered but the hunt. He hadn't needed—nor desired—sleep. The ultimate trophy awaited him.

"Oh, one more thing, Peter. I got a surprise for you."

"I'm listening."

"I got double what you want."

"We'll discuss that when I get there." All phone communication had to remain ambiguous. Yet, he couldn't help but smile. He knew what his father meant. Just knew it. The resultant excitement pricked at his skin, buzzed through his body.

"But it's going to mean more money."

"I told you, we'll discuss the details when I arrive." Peter hated the power his father still wielded over him, hated that he allowed it to happen.

"I'm going to need more, boy."

"You'll get what's coming to you in full." He hung up. Moisture dampened his back, his shirt adhering to the seat. He rolled down the window but quickly put it back up due to the overwhelming stench of cow manure.

Over the last twenty years, Peter had learned how to master a calm and measured demeanor. If you didn't wear your heart on your sleeve, your enemies never saw you coming. All his emotions, his anger—his stark hatred—he had left behind him in Godwin, Kansas. He'd had no more use for them, had simply outgrown them.

Now, everything came flooding back again. Memories. Feelings of helplessness and despair, rendering him vulnerable and careless. Unpredictable, even. Not the best way to enter a hunt, especially with the stakes so high.

He remembered the last time he had hunted in Godwin, Kansas, twenty-three years ago. With his brother, Mattie. Even though Matt was a year older, Matt had always acted like the younger brother. Peter had felt obligated to take care of Matt, exposing him to the ways of the world. At times, he'd even tried to protect Matt from their abusive father, unsuccessful as he had been.

When they were in their mid-teens, Edwin had taught Peter how to hunt. If you could call it a learning experience. His father had pushed him into the woods behind the farm, bullying him into shooting deer and other wildlife. Once, he had cracked Peter across the head with the butt of his hunting rifle for shedding tears over killing his first deer.

Matt had never gone on their hunting trips. Peter suspected Matt had wanted to spend as little time with their father as possible. One day, Peter saddled Matt up with a rifle and dragged him into the woods. Reluctantly, Matt agreed to go. Learning their father had gone into town for business sold the deal for him.

"There, Mattie," Peter whispered, pulling back the brush. "There's your target." A deer leaned over a small creek, drinking. "Take your shot. Remember what I told you. Squeeze the trigger, don't pull it."

"Peter, I really don't want to do this."

"Come on. You have to become a man someday."

Matt lowered the gun and glared at Peter, anger burning in his eyes. A strange pride blossomed in Peter. Maybe Matt had some backbone after all.

In one swift movement, Matt raised his rifle and shot. The shells slammed into the backend of the deer. It went down, bleating horrifically. Attempting to rise by the force of its front hooves, the wounded animal flopped back to the ground. Blood matted the deer's backside, spread across its coat. A deep red contaminated its natural white and fawn coloring. Its entire body shuddered as it helplessly scrabbled its hooves across the fallen leaves. Matt's cheeks flushed, his eyes brimming with tears.

"Are you happy now?" yelled Matt. "Let's go home!" Matt's rage sent a flock of starlings flittering throughout the treetops into the sky.

"You have to finish the job." Peter grabbed the barrel of Matt's gun and nudged it toward the deer.

"Fine." Matt stomped through the brush down toward the injured deer. The rifle shook in his hands as he held it inches away from the deer's head. Then he lowered the gun. "Peter...I *can't* do it."

Peter glowered at his pathetic mess of a brother. He loved him. Yet, at that moment, he despised Matt for his weakness.

"All right." Peter reached into his belt and withdrew a knife. He straddled the deer, pulling its head up by the antlers. He dragged the blade across the deer's throat slowly, unleashing a steady stream of crimson blood. "And that's how it's done." Peter looked at his brother, shrugged his shoulders. And nearly laughed at his brother's obvious discomfort.

"How...how could you do that, Peter?"

"After a while, Matt, killing's no big deal." Peter wiped the knife blade on his overalls. "And because I *can*." Even though Peter enjoyed the moment immensely, it still troubled him that he had quoted his father. It had just come naturally.

That had been Peter's last hunt in Godwin. And he'd wager money that Matt never hunted again.

Now, the hunt was about to begin again. The biggest hunt of his existence. The circle of life.

As he sped down the dark small-town highways, Matt remembered the last time he made this trip. It had been under very unpleasant circumstances.

Nineteen years before, Mary had called him out of the blue. Their mother had died. Matt met the news with a shameful hostility. He wanted to mourn her, but truthfully, he'd never been very close to her. In fact, he felt he hadn't known her at all. Not really. She had invested all of her time in Mary, keeping her close and working under her wing in the kitchen. In retrospect, Matt realized his mother had done that to keep Mary away from their father. At least Mary hadn't suffered the physical abuse he and Peter had. Or so he had thought at the time.

Matt contemplated not returning for the funeral, but he couldn't stay away. He owed it to his mother's memory. And he wanted to check on Mary.

When he pulled up to the farmhouse, he was relieved to see his father's blue pick-up truck gone. Taking a deep breath, Matt knocked.

"Matt?" At the doorway, Mary squinted into the sunlight, shielding her face with her hand.

"Mary." Dark circles ringed her eyes, her hair now unkempt and prematurely gray. The ragged hemline of her dress, which Matt remembered her wearing twenty years ago, dragged the kitchen floor. When he embraced her, he feared he would crush her skeletal frame. "How are you, Mary?"

"Matt," she repeated. She pulled away, crying. Matt stepped into the kitchen. With a gentle touch, he brushed her face.

Gravel scattered across the driveway outside. Matt glimpsed out the window and braced himself. The pick-up truck coughed to a stop, smoke still spewing from the tailpipe.

"Well, well," Edwin said upon entering. "Look what we have here." His voice dripped with contempt. "Ingrate little bastard only comes home when someone dies." Pushing past Matt and Mary, he barely afforded them a glance. He banged a small box down onto the kitchen table.

"Hello, Dad." An uncontrollable urge to run back to his car and drive away struck Matt. But he needed to stand his ground. He wouldn't let his father intimidate him after all these years. "How have you been?"

"Don't much matter none, now does it?" He kicked a kitchen chair out from the table. "You don't give a good goddamn." He sat down, stretched his legs out, intentionally blocking Matt's path.

The familiar odors of the house engulfed Matt. He recalled the flowery scents, his mother's various perfumes and powders and tissues. The smell of an older woman's purse. Now, an additional stench permeated the air— rot and decay. It was more than spoiled food; the house reeked of death. Death's holding house.

"And I see you're the same caring, loving father you always were," said Matt quietly. He steadied his hands at his sides. He didn't want the old bastard to see his fear.

His father glowered at him with cold gray eyes, keen as knives. A grin spread, his teeth as yellow as the corn he harvested. "Don't tell me little Matthew's found his balls. Well, now, don't *that* take the cake?"

Matt ignored his comments. No sense in another unnecessary fight. He'd spent too many of his childhood years wasted in that exercise in futility. "When's the funeral service?"

"Funeral service? Funeral service? There ain't gonna be no funeral service, boy." Grabbing the box, Edwin thrust it at Matt. "I can't afford no funeral service. If you want a funeral service, *you* pay for it. Here. It's bad enough I had to pay for her to be cremated."

"She was my *mother.* She deserves a service of some sort."

"Well, Mister Big City, you gonna foot the bill?"

"Yes, if I have to."

His father inched closer, his shoulders bunching up like mountaintops. "Well, I'll show you what I'm gonna do!" He tore off his cap and tossed it on the table. After he snatched the ashes from Matt, he stormed outside. A metallic banging fought for dominance over the old man's cursing.

"Matt, don't get him upset." Mary appeared terrified. Her already pale color turned ashen, the color of sickness. "Please."

"Mary, has he hurt you? Does he beat you?"

Mary's entire body quaked, a seismic effect. Even though she said nothing, her physical response told Matt everything he needed to know.

"Mary, I think it's time you came to live with us in Kansas City. Just until you get a place of your own. Cheryl won't mind."

Matt saw a fleeting spark ignite in her eyes. It didn't last long. Despair dampened the flame. "I…can't, Matt. I can't."

"Why, Mary? Surely, not for him. You don't owe that man anything."

"Mother taught me where my place is, and it's here." Mary lifted a weak hand, passed it over the kitchen. "It may be hell, but it's all I have."

The old man bashed through the kitchen door, slamming it against the wall. Dirty plates rattled on the countertop.

"Okay, come on, let's go." He held a piece of PVC tubing, the ending of it enclosed with duct tape. "Come on, damn it!"

Matt and Mary glanced nervously at one another. Mary glued her chin to her chest, presumably to hide her tears.

"Where to?" Frayed nerves rode Matt's spine up to his brain. He had no desire to follow his father anywhere because the result was bound to be unpleasant.

"You wanted your damn funeral service. Well, that's what we're going to do." He motioned for them to follow him with a crooked and calloused finger.

"We'd better go, Matt," said Mary quietly.

Matt grabbed Mary's hand and pulled her close behind him. They followed the old man into the yard and toward the large oak tree by the south side of the house. Matt's father dropped the PVC tube into a shallow hole at the foot of the tree. He kicked a small pile of dirt onto it.

"There's your goddamn funeral service." He licked his lips, the same manner he'd been doing for years. Matt despised it. Even though he caught himself doing it from time to time. "Hope you're happy now. You wanna say some words?"

"You're an awful bastard. You're sick! That was your wife."

"That's how she would've wanted it, boy. She was born here, lived here, and now is returned to Godland." Raising his head to the sky, he howled, dancing a bow-legged jig.

Matt grabbed Mary's shoulders and turned her to face him. "Mary, you've got to come with me now. Can't you see he's crazy?" He pulled her with him toward his car.

A powerful blow landed on Matt's back. Stunned, he whirled, still holding tightly onto Mary's hand. Mary's feet lifted off the ground as light as she was.

Edwin stood, shovel poised for another attack. "You let her go now, boy." He shook the shovel up and down, rusty steel a blurr in Matt's face. "She ain't goin' nowhere. I need her here."

Any doubts Matt harbored about his father's mental state dissipated like wisps of smoke. He knew he was deranged, absolutely so. Matt slowly released Mary, feeling her slipping away into the abyss of insanity his father called "Godland."

"Mary, please come with me." While keeping his gaze firmly locked onto his father, Matt attempted one last, desperate plea. "Please, Mary."

"Matt, I…can't. *I can't.*"

"Get on outta here, boy. And don't come back. Put your tail between your legs and scamper away again, you little coward. You little worthless shit."

Matt felt as helpless as the child he had been in Godland. He couldn't force Mary to leave. He backed toward his car, lending credibility to Edwin's labeling him a "coward." He tumbled into the car, his back blistering with pain. Then he rolled down the window. "Mary, you have my address. Please, forget him and come to Kansas City. *Anytime.* Please. For God's sake, Mary."

Edwin scrambled toward Matt's car, fast for a man his age. He brought the shovel's blade down upon the hood with a loud *clank*. "I said to get the hell outta here, boy!" He raced toward Matt's window, pulling back the shovel again.

Matt floored the pedal, gravel spitting up as he fishtailed down the driveway. He stopped at the road, stealing one last glance at Mary. Just as when he left home twenty years ago, Mary stood alone, tears streaming down her face, one fragile hand waving goodbye.

Edwin beat at the driveway with the shovel, screaming at real and imagined demons.

The memories of Matt's last visit home wracked him with sobs. He rolled down the window and inhaled the fresh air.

That last encounter had been bad enough. He had failed at saving his sister. And he had no idea what to expect now. But he sure as hell wouldn't allow his daughter to become another one of his father's victims.

Matt traveled on into the Kansas flatlands, a newfound determination propelling him to drive faster.

Chapter Eight

Edwin carried Joshua's lunch bucket down the steps, his son shambling closely behind him. He thought it best to give the girls some food, energy for the upcoming night. Leftover remnants scraped off plates from the sink. Probably better treatment than they deserved, but even pigs need to eat.

He stared at the girls cowering in the corner, enjoying the sight.

"All right, then. Iffen I give you gals something to eat, you better not take advantage of my kindness and try anything stupid. You understand me?"

The girls met him with silence.

"I said, '*You understand me?*'"

The girls nodded, heads shaking faster than a hummingbird's wings.

"Okay, that's more like it. Here's your slop." He dropped the bucket to the dirt. Part of a fried egg bounced over the rim, sickly yellow and greasy. "You'd best eat. You're going to need your liveliness."

The blonde girl reached in, pulling out a half piece of toast. Edwin grinned as she tore it in half and handed part of it to her friend.

"What...what do you want from us?" she asked. "We don't have any money." She nibbled on the toast while eyeing Edwin.

"Money? No, I don't want your money." Even though Edwin knew Joshua didn't understand why he laughed, the boy joined him in his merriment, clapping his hands. Every moment was "playtime" for the boy.

"What do you want then?"

"You'll find out in good time. Now, as I told you, if you feel like scream-ing and carrying on, be my guest, but it ain't gonna do you no good, 'cept for wearing out your strength. And don't even think of escaping, 'cause there's no way you'll get through the door. It's padlocked."

"Please let us go," said Miss Lindsay Bellowes.

"Why, sure, little lady. I'm plannin' on lettin' you go. That's the whole idea." Edwin saw hope rise in Lindsay's eyes. He couldn't wait to dash it.

The blonde girl remained skeptical. "When?"

"When I say so, missy, when I say so. Now get some rest." When Miss Lindsay Bellowes leaned forward to look into the bucket, the light fell upon her womanly curves. A fully grown woman's breasts wasted upon a teen-age tramp. A voluptuous body. The blonde one, on the other hand, looked a little too scrawny for his tastes.

He locked the door, leading Joshua back to the farmhouse. Stretching out at the kitchen table, he drew a hand down his sunken cheeks. He hadn't experienced the warmth of a woman's body in years. Maybe before he put the girls out for the hunt, he might find time for a little bit of companionship.

When he smiled, his idiot son mimicked his grin.

As soon as the door closed, Shannon whispered, "Lindsay, try your phone."

Lindsay cracked her fingers back and forth, then fished into her pocket for the phone. Her hands trembled so much, she could barely hit the correct buttons on the keypad.

"No! There's no signal." Lindsay sagged back against the dirt wall, the phone falling beside her. Shannon snatched the phone, hoping Lindsay had made a mistake. No bars. Lindsay buried her head between her knees, all hope having flown the coop again.

"Lindsay!" Shannon draped her arm around her friend's shoulders. "Keep it together. We will get out of this. When they let us out of this cellar, maybe we can get a phone signal. Just don't let them see the phone, okay? Maybe we can ask to use the bathroom or something."

"He did say they'd let us go, right?"

"Yeah, that's what he said." Shannon didn't believe the old man, not for a second. But she needed Lindsay to keep hope alive. For her benefit as much as Lindsay's. "But I think we need to find a way to get out on our own. Just in case." Shannon stood. With a small leap, she kicked a leg into the dirt wall. Tunneling out seemed like a ludicrous idea, but she wasn't going to roll over and die down here. No matter what.

Lindsay watched her friend's efforts with calm resignation. "Shannon? What *is* he? The big one, I mean?"

Short of breath, Shannon said, "I'm…not really sure. Obviously, he's challenged in some way, but I've never seen anything like him before."

"He's disgusting. Oh my God, what if they want us to mate with him?" Lindsay shot to her feet.

"That's *not* going to happen. He seems to be the nicer of the two. He actually caressed me at one point."

"Gross! I can't…I won't touch him."

"After all the guys you let grope you?" Shannon dredged up a smile. "Some of *them* were pretty gross."

The girls shared a quick, unexpected laugh before falling into a hug. Shannon broke the embrace before the sobbing ratcheted up again. "Okay, crying's not going to help us."

Shannon looked around the cellar. She pulled two jars off a shelf. Mold ate at the contents behind the dirt-covered glass.

"Lindsay, listen at the door and tell me if you hear them coming."

Lindsay crossed the room, positioning herself next to the door. Shannon took off her shirt and wrapped it around one jar. With her foot, she wedged the other jar into the cellar's corner. Gave it a swift kick, securing it against the wall. She brought the bundle down on top of the jar, then repeated the motion. It made little sound, this she knew, but she still shot Lindsay a panicked look in case they'd been overheard. Lindsay nodded, giving her the okay to continue. She raised the wrapped jar high above her head and brought it down again with a grunt. She felt the jar give, a barely audible *crack*. Unfolding the shirt, she carefully plucked out several of the larger shards. She waved Lindsay over and handed one to her.

"Be careful. Put it in your pocket and use it if you have to."

Lindsay grabbed the makeshift weapon and carefully slid it into her jeans pocket. Lindsay wore her typical "painted-on" jeans, always her preferred wardrobe choice. The phone and piece of glass bulged obviously. A dead give-away.

"Lindsay, try and keep your hands in front of your jeans when they come back, okay?"

"Okay."

"All right. So we have a little something to fight back with. It's not much, but it might help." Shannon scooped up the rest of the broken glass and hid it behind the other jars on the shelf. She put her shirt back on, a few new tears in the garment where the glass cut through.

"Now, as I said earlier," continued Shannon, "the large guy—Joshua, I heard the old man call him—is the nicer of the two. I think he sees this as some kind of game. When he chased me earlier today, I think he was having fun."

Lindsay's mouth twisted down into a grimace.

"Yeah, I know, he's gross and scary. But we may be able to use him somehow."

Lindsay groaned, shaking her head in disgust.

"Lindsay, all I'm saying is be nice to him. Maybe we can talk him into let-ting us go. But remember, he's really strong, and he's really fast. He's danger-ous. Don't forget that. Okay?" Shannon placed her hand on Lindsay's cheek. "Okay?"

"All right." Her voice sounded tiny in the hollows of the cellar, nothing more than a child's squeak.

"We're going to fight. And we're going to live."

Jesus, look at this shithole.

Peter drove onto the winding stretch of gravel road leading to the farm.

It was even worse than he remembered it. Farming buildings were falling apart, the fields dying from drought, and the overwhelming country stench was as prevalent as ever. Peter grew up with the smell; at the time, he'd thought it the natural odor of the earth. Nothing but cow shit—and now it seemed so foreign. Hard to believe he'd forgotten it. It's funny what memories one can bury sometimes.

Peter slowed down, not wanting to incur any gravel damage to his Town Car.

His thoughts wandered to his brother, Matt. Even though he hadn't spoken to Matt in years, at one time, he was probably the closest thing to a friend he had. He didn't despise Matt as he did the rest of his family. He had simply outgrown him. It became apparent his brother would never change his ways. Always the victim, never taking charge of his life. Just another link to the miserable past he was better off putting behind him.

Years ago—once Peter set up roots in New York—he dropped Matt a postcard with his business number. More out of pity—maybe a tiny bit of misplaced responsibility—than anything. He told Matt to give him a call if he ever needed anything. In typical Matt behavior, it didn't take him long to ask for a loan. Needing some start-up capital, he said, for the preposterous idea of opening his own video store. Peter scoffed at first, but really, it shouldn't have surprised him. Matt meant well but never set his goals high enough. He dreamed small and lived smaller. Matt was that way on the farm as well. He only did enough work to subsist. Peter didn't deem Matt lazy, but he lacked ambition and vision. Sadly, contentment to Matt meant just getting by.

Still, Peter's very few fond memories from his childhood involved his brother. At one time, he loved him. Or the closest thing to love Peter ever experienced.

Matt had been honorable enough to insist the money be a loan, not a gift. Pleasantly surprised by Matt's willingness to pay his own way, Peter gave him the money. At first, Peter kept up with Matt via phone calls, checking to see how his investment was coming along. Peter knew his brother would inevitably fail, but he let him fail. Valuable lessons are hard-earned. So Peter kept his mouth shut.

Eventually, Peter dropped contact. He assumed Matt wanted to sever all ties with his past, too. More power to him.

Twelve years later, Peter found himself in Kansas City on a business trip. He had some time to kill, so, on a whim, he called Matt.

An hour and a half later, Peter knocked on the door of his brother's house in a suburban Kansas neighborhood. He smiled derisively at the identical houses. *Still stuck in a rut,* thought Peter. An improvement over the hellish farm where they'd dwelled, but not by much.

A young girl with blonde hair and glasses too large for her face answered the door. She couldn't have been more than eleven or twelve years old. She said nothing, staring expressionlessly at Peter. He thought he had the wrong house.

"Ah, hello, I'm looking for Matt Strothers."

The girl continued to gawk. Finally, she stepped back and yelled, "Dad!" Peter couldn't believe it. He had no idea Matt had a child, let alone was married.

Matt came to the door bearing a warm smile. Unexpected nostalgia warmed Peter's chest. Just a pinch, though, before it skittered away.

"Peter! Come in, come in." The years hadn't been kind to Matt. Thinning hair, a bald spot threatening to overtake his scalp. A developing paunch suggested a lazy lifestyle, throwing in the towel. Contentment, Mattie style. "How are you?" Matt opened his arms, awaiting a hug. Peter stood still, arms anchored firmly at his side. Outside of handshakes, Peter liked to keep touching relegated to the bedroom.

"I'm quite well, Mattie. And you?" Peter extended his hand formally, dropping an ax on any forthcoming hugs. Matt accepted it and returned a limp shake. Same old, weak Matt. Peter fought to bottle a percolating sneer.

"Well, I'm okay. Oh, this is my daughter, Shannon."

Shannon watched the exchange with complete indifference, the way kids do once they reach a certain age. "You must be my Uncle Peter." She offered her hand, much more confidently than her father. Her entire persona transformed. A breathtaking smile flowered through her previously dour expression.

"I am, indeed." Peter took her hand and playfully kissed it. "And you must be the prettiest princess ever to reside in Kansas."

The girl blushed, gazing at her shuffling feet. Oddly enough, Peter found himself charmed. "Your father never told me he had such a beautiful daughter." The sudden warmth he felt toward the girl floored him. Finally, Matt accomplished something he could show off with pride.

"I'm not so…beautiful." Although her demeanor leaned toward shy, her smile spoke differently. "I have homework to do. Gotta bounce. Please say goodbye before you leave." She swiveled in her high-tops and ran up the stairs.

"Very lovely daughter, Mattie." Peter meant it, too. True compliments came hard by him; doling out shallow, hollow greetings was his usual comfort zone.

"Thanks. Let's go in here." Peter followed his brother through the hallway.

A woman wearing sweatpants sat on the sofa watching television. Peter thought she might have, at one time, been attractive in a sort of bland Midwestern way. But those years were long past. Her black hair looked straggly, somewhat wiry, like a scouring pad. Wrinkles stretched down along her mouth, a permanent scowl setting in. She glanced at the two men before returning her attention toward the television.

"Cheryl? Honey? This is my brother, Peter." Cheryl lifted an eyebrow, obviously bored—put out?—by Peter's arrival. A deep rush of shame for his brother's humiliation coursed through Peter.

"Hello," she muttered. She stood up and hurried out of the room.

Matt sighed and sat down. He motioned for his brother to follow suit. "Sorry about that, Peter."

"No need for apologies."

"It's just…well, we've been having some problems lately." Matt rubbed his eyes wearily. "Anyway. What about you? Are you married? Kids?"

"I'm married. No children yet." Peter feigned a smile. He wished to be anywhere but here. Marital drama made him uncomfortable.

"That's good, that's good. Look, Peter, I'm sorry I'm behind on my payments to you. Times have been rough."

"I don't really care about that, Matt. Money's no problem for me. Take your time paying me back. There's no rush."

"Well, I appreciate that." Matt cleared his throat, an uncomfortable foreshadowing of more trauma. "But I will pay you back. Definitely."

"It's fine, Mattie."

"Um, do you know about Mary?" Peter had no interest in exhuming the past. He'd talk to Matt about *Matt's* family—even his woes, if necessary—but the past was definitely off limits.

"No, I don't," said Peter. Nor did he want to, either.

"She showed up here a few years back. A total wreck." His hands fidgeted nervously in his lap. "She was pretty messed up." Matt paused as if expecting an acknowledgment. Peter remained silent.

"I had to put her in a home—a mental institution. She was raped and had a baby..." Matt trailed off.

As soon as Peter suspected the truth, he stood up to leave. "Matt, it's been nice seeing you, but I've got to go." He swept by his brother, making it to the hallway door before Matt called after him.

"Peter, she's your sister. Don't you care?"

He turned around to address his brother. "No, Matt, I don't care. Mary didn't care about me, nor did our mother, and especially not our evil son-of-a-bitch father. So now you're asking me if I care? No. I do not care."

"I think Dad did it." Matt sobbed on the sofa, hanging his face in his hands. "He raped her. He did that to Mary!"

"Goodbye, Matt. I'll see myself out." The thought of Edwin raping Mary filled Peter's mind with leaden numbness. Yet, it didn't come as a surprise. He knew the old man had it in him. Always did. Too bad about Mary. But honestly, she had never shown any kindness or affection toward him. Ever. Only disdain. And that was when she acknowledged him. Just like his mother and so-called father.

He had made a huge mistake visiting his brother because the worst possible result occurred. He felt vulnerably human again, and he loathed that feeling.

He yanked open the front door. The sounds of his crying brother filled the house with a pathetic morbidity.

Shannon, sitting on the stairwell, startled him with a sigh. She rested her chin on her knees, looking world-weary for her age. Her arms held her legs together tight, a compact ball of sadness.

"Goodbye, Uncle Peter," she said, her voice barely perceptible. If she had eavesdropped on their ugly encounter, it didn't seem to faze her too much. Probably she had grown used to her father's blubbering. "It was very nice to meet you."

Through it all, she still insisted on good manners. *Amazing.* Peter thought she could teach her father a few things about humility.

"Goodbye, Shannon. The pleasure was all mine." He offered her a charming smile. But with the grotesque sounds of his brother's sniveling growing louder, it seemed moot.

"Will we ever see you again, Uncle Peter?"

Obviously, emotional turmoil ran rampant through this household. Accepted as the norm. The girl sought comfort in the company of a stranger. Someone not dysfunctional. Peter remembered desperately hoping for visitors on the farm, anyone offering possible relief. He empathized deeply with her.

"I certainly hope so, Shannon," replied Peter. "I hope so." He pulled the door shut behind him, closing the door on his family forever. A pity, too. He wouldn't mind visiting his niece again over his weak-willed brother. But, due to her unfortunate heritage, he'd never see Shannon again.

That had been the last time Peter saw any of his family.

Until tonight. Until *now*.

He pulled onto the familiar driveway of the house where he had been beaten, tortured, starved, and humiliated.

His family home.

The hours crawled by.

Matt stared into the darkness, his headlights flitting across the highway. He felt alone, unprepared. But his father was an old man now. If it came to it, Matt wondered if he could take the old man in a fight. Matt cringed at the thought. His father still haunted his nightmares.

Trying to temper his dread and mounting fear, Matt reached into the past for comfort…

Matt had left home a few months after Peter. His brother's last words—

about how Matt should leave before things grew worse—had proved prophetic. Hard to believe, but their father had turned even meaner. And crazier. The beatings increased. And Matt's chores doubled. At times, Matt thought Peter's leaving hurt his father. In an odd way, Matt suspected Peter was his father's favorite child. Not that Edwin would ever admit it. He thought expressing feelings was "unmanly." Yet he took Peter hunting and spent more time with him than his other two children.

When Matt made up his mind to leave, he had no idea where the road would lead him. But Peter had inspired him. Matt packed his bag when his father was gone. The easiest way.

"You too?" his mother had asked. Her eyes were glassy, her pupils dilated. Peter always said she kept something secret stored away to endure the long hours spent with her husband. One look into her eyes and Matt finally believed it.

Mary stopped drying dishes. The pain etched on her face clearly broadcasted her thoughts. She was losing her only ally.

"Yes, Mom." Matt wanted to run back to his room and unpack. Maybe put it off for a few more days. Sleep on it. *No.* That was the old way of thinking. "I need to leave."

"Where will you go?" His mother's voice sounded hollow, void of life. Her spirit had long departed this mortal coil.

"I don't really know. But away from *him*. I'll call and write."

"No. Don't call. That will make your father very angry, but please, do write." His father never picked up the mail. Sometimes Matt wondered if he could even read.

"I promise."

The long silence draped over the kitchen like a death shroud. Matt waited for an emotional breakthrough, for *anything*. His family had never been demonstrative. His father wouldn't allow it. Or didn't know how, more than likely. But Matt couldn't leave without telling his suffering family how much he loved them.

He reached his arms around his mother. She flinched, pulling back slightly. Afraid of his touch. He felt her shoulders slowly relax in his hold as if thawing out from the cold. She patted Matt's back lightly, maintaining a good six inches between them.

"I love you, Mom." Matt hadn't said those words to her since he was a child. The sentiment hadn't been returned since then either. His mother sputtered, but words didn't follow. She released her son. "Goodbye, Mom. You protect Mary, okay? *Protect* her." She averted her gaze to the sink as if she didn't intend to honor Matt's request. Almost like she knew she'd already failed at the task.

Matt turned to his sister and hugged her. She clung to him. "I'm really going to miss you, Mary." Her tears wet his neck, tiny eyelashes fluttering against his skin.

"Please don't go."

"I have to, Mary. Come with me." The idea startled him. He hadn't planned on it. But it was the only option that made sense. The only way for her to do something with her life. He glanced at his mother to see if she'd protest, but her gaze darted around the kitchen as if wondering what chore to tackle next.

"No, I can't. My place is here."

"I love you, Mary." Matt released her. It felt permanent, too. No arguing with her. Not with the mindset Edwin had inculcated into her.

Matt scurried out the door before he changed his mind. His knees felt weak, his mind foggy. Walking down the driveway, he heard choking sobs behind him. He turned to see Mary, standing in the drive. "I love you, too, Matt!" She fell to her knees in the gravel. Her hands clasped to her chest as if praying for release.

As Matt drove on into the night, he cursed himself. He had abandoned his sister to his evil father, not once, but twice. When their mother died, God—or *something*—had sent Matt back to the farm to save Mary. He had failed then. Maybe God did, too.

But he wouldn't fail again. He wouldn't fail his daughter. After all these years, he had a third chance at saving a loved one. Whether delivered by God, fate, whatever, he didn't know. Didn't care.

I'm coming, Shannon. Hold on.

Chapter Nine

Fit to be tied and itchier than an alley cat.

That's how the little brown-haired temptress in the cellar made Edwin feel. A state of bound-up agitation, a scratch he couldn't quite reach. He had to admit, these stirrings felt good after lying dormant for so many years. What he at one time felt for Gretchen had long fled, years before her death. It became a chore fulfilling his manly duties with her. By *God,* if he didn't feel like a man again.

Some naysayers might consider these sort of lustful feelings as sinful. Well, hell, let the tongues wag. From God's words to Edwin's ears, the Good Book laid down the law. The natural order of things. God made woman to be subservient to man's needs.

His mind made up and fully justified, Edwin entered the bathroom. Smiling at his visage in the mirror, he liked what he saw. He washed his hands, wiping them on his overalls. In the Quail farmstead, towels became obsolete once Gretchen had passed.

"Boy, let's go visit our guests." Joshua came running, barely keeping up with Edwin's vigorous pace.

The girls hadn't budged an inch. Their obvious fear renewed Edwin's vitality. Staring at these two shivering little girls gave him a sense of power. Of potency.

"You," shouted Edwin. "Little Miss Lindsay Bellowes." He spat onto the dirt floor, cleansing his palate for the upcoming meal. "Stand up. You're comin' with me."

"No! No, Shannon!" Lindsay thrust her arms around the other girl, holding on tight. "Come with me, come with me…please come with me, Shannon."

"Nope, not just yet for you." Edwin stabbed a finger at the blonde girl.

"Can't I please go with her?"

"I said, no, dammit! Joshua, pick up the brown-haired sow."

Joshua tugged at Lindsay, but the girls stayed locked together, inseparable. With a grunt, Joshua yanked harder. Lindsay's fingers peeled away, reaching out for her friend. Joshua tossed her over his shoulder as easy as pie.

"*Please,* mister," pleaded the wispy girl.

"I'll be back for you later," said Edwin. "Let's go, boy." They backed toward the door. Lindsay kicked her feet against Joshua. Joshua grinned, taking it all in good fun.

In the living room, Edwin turned to his son and said, "Boy. You go on upstairs to your room for a while. And stay there." Confused, Joshua gaped at Edwin. Just like a kid on Christmas Eve, he didn't want to miss out on anything. Right now, though, Edwin didn't have the patience for any buffoonery.

"You heard me, boy. Drop the girl on the sofa and git."

Joshua lowered Lindsay onto the sofa. He sulked out of the room, head lowered. Edwin listened for his plodding footsteps on the stairs. Then he turned his attention back toward the girl. "Now, Miss Lindsay Bellowes, we're going to have us some fun." He ran his hand over his stubbled chin, anticipating the glorious wonders awaiting him.

The girl's eyes widened as realization set in. She cast her eyes about the room, searching for an escape route, Edwin presumed. "Please…can I use the bathroom first?"

Edwin hesitated. It was about *his* needs, after all, not hers. Then again, if he invited her into his matrimonial bed, he would want her clean.

"All right then, girl. Just remember to behave yourself. I'll be waiting right outside the door." He grabbed her hand, wrenching her off the sofa. "Come with me."

Holding her wrist tightly behind her back, he steered her toward the bathroom. Leading a cow to slaughter. The nape of her neck beckoned him. He bent, his nose grazing her neck. Sniffing, he drew in a deep breath. A nice scent, not unlike rain. Edwin noticed the girl's neck muscles tense.

He shoved her down the narrow hall, the floorboards creaking beneath their feet. They stopped in front of an aged painting of Jesus, smiling serenely down upon them. Edwin reached around the girl, pushing the bathroom door open.

"Get in." He slapped her back. "I'll allow you to shut the door 'cause I'm a gentleman, but don't even try the window. It's been nailed shut for years."

Lindsay closed the door behind her. She looked around the small room for a potential weapon. *Nothing.* Maybe if she came out swinging, she could overpower the old man. Yet the old man possessed surprising strength. Not the best plan.

She snatched the phone out of her pocket and then twisted the knob in the sink. A rusty-colored liquid slopped out of the faucet, eventually running clear. With unsteady hands, she turned on the phone. She punched the mute button before the musical greeting notes chimed. Carefully, she set it on the sink ledge. Her heart sank. No signal.

She peered into the toilet, gagging at the filth lying within. Amongst the excrement ringing the bowl, a green mold thrived, spreading onto the seat. A medicine cabinet hung on the wall above the sink. Suspecting the cabinet door might creak when she searched its contents, she flushed the toilet. Her hand fumbled, brushing up against the phone. The phone plunged into the toilet. Clamping one hand over her mouth, she thrust her other hand into the bowl. Her fingers latched onto the phone. Sludge oozed between her fingers. She shook the phone several times and patted it against a ragged curtain, praying for no water damage.

When she slipped the phone back inside her pocket, her fingers felt something sharp. The glass shard. Pinching it between two fingers, she edged it out. She wrapped toilet paper around one end, creating a workable handle. She placed it into her back pocket, the paper handle extended above the pocket-line.

"We ain't got all day, girl!"

The door flew open, loud as a thunder crack. Lindsay turned, her hands quivering in the air. The old man came at her, nostrils flaring, eyes burning. "Time's up."

Before Lindsay could reach for the glass knife, he yanked her toward him. His fetid breath expelled, sparking her gag reflex. She shut her eyes, unable to look at him. Using one hand, he cinched her wrists together. Holding them firmly in place, he dragged her into the hallway.

"You don't even remember me, do you, Miss Lindsay Bellowes?" He swayed back and forth, dancing with his unwilling partner.

"No. No…" She opened her eyes. "Have…we met?" Making conversation with this bastard might forestall the alternative. The *unspeakable* alternative.

"Do you know how insultin' that is?" Spittle landed on Lindsay's cheek. "From the American Royal last year. I demand your respect."

Suddenly, she remembered the old pervert hitting on her at the Royal. Something she'd laughed off and filed away. But she didn't recognize this man. Didn't want to try. *But if it is him…it's the only thing that makes sense. It must be him.*

"Wait! I do remember you. I do." Terrified, Lindsay weighed her words carefully. "You wanted me to go back with you to your farm, right? Is that what this is all about?" Lindsay chortled once, even though her survival instincts warned against it. But the sheer insane notion that this old fool kidnapped her because she rejected his awful advances notched up her hysteria to unmanageable levels.

"Don't you laugh at me, slut. We'll see who's laughin' soon. You're about to make me happy in more ways than one." He thrust his free hand onto Lindsay's breast and gave it a harsh squeeze. Lindsay grimaced. "Nice," he drawled. His hand fell to her side, following the contours of her body. Traveling dangerously close to the phone and knife.

"Can't we go somewhere else?" She had to redirect, change course. It surprised her how cool logic intervened, calming her. "Not the bathroom?" She attempted an alluring purr, came up with a stuttering child's voice.

"I'm not finished yet." Shoulders hunched, he pressed his face against her breast. His hand moved along her hip. Lindsay gulped, waiting for the inevitable. His thumb sidled over her phone. "What the hell's this?"

"It…it's my phone. I swear to God, mister, I didn't even remember I had it."

He released her wrists. Poking his fingers inside her pocket, he dug for the phone. She reached behind her back; then brought the make-shift blade around with an upward motion, slicing it across his cheek. Red tears crawled down from the thin incision.

"God damn bitch!" Stumbling back, his hand flew to his wound. "I'm a-gonna kill you!"

Lindsay jabbed the knife at him again, forcing him down the hallway. He raised a hand, attempting to ward off her attack. Lindsay contacted with his palm, feeling the shard hook deep, feeling satisfaction. She wrenched up sharply. The glass came free, a flap of skin flopping back into place. His palm gushed blood. He bellowed. Falling against the wall, he knocked Jesus's portrait to the floor. He dropped to his knees as if praying.

Screaming, Lindsay bounded over him. She raced down the hall, her foot catching on the edge of a rug. She hopped on one leg, quickly righted herself.

She turned a corner, found herself in a kitchen. Her hip jabbed into a chair, bringing it down with a blood-freezing *bang*.

A narrow white door. Ghostly light peeping in. *Outdoors!*

She wrenched the door open. The chain-lock snapped tight.

"Boy!" The old man's voice roared down the hallway into the kitchen. "Get her! She's making a run for it!"

Lindsay slammed the door shut and slid the lock free. A great thundering sound boomed overhead.

Oh, God, don't look back!

The door opened onto freedom. Taking a running leap into the darkness, she tumbled down four tall steps and landed on a grassy patch. She picked herself up, ignoring the pain. A low, drawn-out moan from inside gradually grew louder. She ran toward the gravel driveway, the moon lighting her way.

Please, God, let me get away. I'll come back for Shannon with the police. Oh, God, please…

Her legs carried her, pumping like pistons. Gravel kicked up behind her. Terrible thuds. Hoarse breathing, an asthmatic machine. An arm encircled her waist, solid steel. He picked her up and raised her toward the moon like an offering. Haphazardly, she waved the knife about. He shook her violently until she dropped the glass to the gravel with an impotent *clink*.

Twirling her around, his dead eyes looked into hers. He emitted a high-pitched shriek, an inhuman sound.

Lindsay's scream reached an even higher pitch and traveled across the desolate farmlands of Godland, Kansas.

Shannon heard her friend scream. Unmistakably her. Her blood ran cold.

"No, Lindsay! No!" She crumbled against the wall, sliding down its rough surface to the ground. Her teeth bit into her knuckles to stave off the image of her friend's death. Her vision blurred, her mind emptied. To keep from passing out, she dug her fingernails into her palms, inducing physical pain. She welcomed it more than mental anguish.

Temptation called. A serene place of retreat. A hideaway. *Gavin.*

Resolve pounded on the door of her happy place, an unwelcome intruder. But unavoidable.

She gathered her strength. Placing her ear against the door, she listened for sounds of life. Cicadas singing their repetitive song. Nothing else. Even the animals had quieted.

Despair washed over her. Now utterly alone with no way out.

She heard the outer cellar doors pull back. She scurried back to her corner, awaiting her turn to die.

The door opened. Joshua stepped inside, ducking so as not to hit his head on the frame. He held a length of rope and more rags. She shook with fear as he shambled toward her. When he opened his mouth, saliva fell in long strands.

"Joshua?" she managed. "Your name is Joshua, right?" Her bottom lip shuddered uncontrollably. She despised her inability to hide emotion. Particularly fear.

But he appeared pleased at her acknowledgment, a small hint of kindness in his upraised brow.

Good. Use his name often. Try to reach his humanity. "What happened to my friend, Joshua? Is she okay?"

He nodded tentatively, uncertain of his own answer.

"She's alive?"

He patted his hands together. If she read him right, Lindsay was still alive. Momentary relief washed over her.

Joshua dangled the ropes in front of her face as if presenting a gift. She remembered her earlier words to Lindsay. She needed to gain Joshua's trust. No matter how repulsive the idea. "Okay." Shannon held her arms up toward Joshua, wrists together. "You won't hurt me, will you, Joshua?"

Joshua shook his hairy head back and forth. He fell to his knees, wisps of dust rising from the impact. He delicately wrapped the rope around her wrists as if tending to a wounded baby bird.

"I'd like to be your friend, Joshua. Would you like that?"

Joshua craned his head, favoring Shannon with his good eye. His nearly toothless grin made him appear like a bearded jack-o-lantern.

"Do you have many friends, Joshua?"

The smile vanished. Miniscule whimpers, fragile almost.

"I'm…I'm sorry about that. Everyone should have friends."

Joshua stopped binding her hands. He sat down in front of Shannon, rocking back and forth on his haunches. The whining increased. Long, greasy hair whipped at his face, a self-flagellation.

Shannon took a clue and backed off. "It's okay, Joshua. I'll be your friend. Just remember…friends don't hurt each other, right?"

A sudden hush fell over him.

"It's okay, Joshua." Shannon couldn't help but feel a little pity for the man. She wondered if the old man—Joshua's father?—abused him. Judging by what she'd witnessed of the old man's behavior, she'd bet on it. "It's okay," she repeated calmly.

Suddenly, Joshua lashed out. He hooked a thick finger into Shannon's jean pocket and gave it a jerk, tearing the denim. The glass shard fell to the ground. The dim light from the overhead bulb played on the weapon's edges. Once again, the gentle beast transformed into a monster. Shannon's momentary pang of empathy vanished. He grabbed the shard, wagging it in front of her face. His deep-throated growl reverberated in her chest.

She couldn't help her involuntary shriek. Joshua jumped to his feet, hovering over her. His face contained little humanity, only animal rage. Shannon shut her eyes, folded her arms over her head, and dug in. She didn't want to see it coming.

After an endless moment of silence, she dared to open her eyes. Joshua studied her, his head at an awkward tilt. He attempted another smile. Shannon didn't know what unsettled her more—his smiles or the sudden, unpredictable temper tantrums.

Joshua wrapped another rag over her mouth. He pulled it tight, nimbly fastening a knot with his large fingers.

Shannon focused on the wall in front of her, looking past Joshua. She didn't want to emanate fear. She felt he could smell it on her. But every time she looked at him, terror filled her.

Joshua walked away, bumping his head into the light bulb. He swatted at it like an annoying housefly. Before he locked the door behind him, he looked at her once more. Shannon registered curiosity, maybe something else, something *decent.*

Okay, now I have something to work with.

Remain cool and calm. No more lapses into hysteria. Her overwhelming urge to survive trumped all.

Peter shut off his headlights as he coasted down the driveway. No sense in having his car noticed. His Town Car didn't fit in with the rest of the country bumpkins' choice of transport, mostly pick-up trucks.

As if to prove his point, Edwin's old truck sat at the head of the driveway. Peter couldn't believe he still drove that piece of shit. No, scratch that. The cheap son-of-a-bitch would drive it until it dropped. Just as he did his wife and would have done to Peter had he stayed on the farm.

No one would have ever called the house *nice*. Serviceable, maybe, but never nice. Now, though, it was a rotting pile of debris. Every inch, nook, and falling shingle aptly represented the rotting life inside the farmhouse.

Light trickled out from the living room's closed blinds.

Oh, good, Daddy dearest is home.

He walked up the steps to the kitchen door, the only door anyone ever used. The front door of the house had remained boarded up for as long as Peter could remember.

His hand trembled when he knocked. He willed it to stop. It did.

He hefted his heavy bag in front of himself to ward off any contact. And perhaps for protection as well.

When the door opened, Peter's heart knocked. His father stood in the kitchen, shorter than Peter remembered. Older, more weathered, but still the same bastard as always. Except for the new fashion accessories—a bloodied Band-Aid matted to his cheek and a cloth wound around his hand.

"Well, if it isn't the high and mighty Peter Brookes." Edwin's lip curled into a snarl, an expression Peter remembered too well.

"I thought we understood we aren't going to use names." Peter swept past his father and entered the kitchen. Everything remained as it had been twenty years before, except much filthier.

"It won't matter none anyhow. You got my money?" The old man framed his mouth into a skeletal grin, hungry like a wolf.

"Yes, I have your money." Peter dropped the bag on the kitchen table, unzipped it, and pulled out a smaller bag. "It's all there." Intentionally, he tossed the bag out of Edwin's reach. It plopped to the floor. His father snatched it up, greedily prospecting inside. His eyes lit up, displaying more life than Peter had ever seen from him.

"It's all the same to you, I'm a-gonna count it." Edwin sat at the table, humming, as he separated the bills into piles.

Peter noticed the computer. "You can afford to buy a computer, but you couldn't buy clothes for us?" He kept his tone even, but he wanted to kick the chair out from underneath Edwin.

"Hee!" With his gaze firmly locked onto the money, he said, "Didn't buy no damn computer, boy. That school in Karlin done gave it to me…a consolation prize…when things didn't work out in their fancy remedial schooling."

"What are you talking about?"

"You'll find out, boy. All in good time."

Not wanting to engage in mind games, Peter changed the subject. *Business, the only reason I'm here.* "You mentioned a surprise?"

"I've got you two gals. But it's gonna cost you double."

"I see." Peter kept his poker face in check. Barely. "So, you're asking for another five-hundred thousand dollars?"

"That's right." He pointed his finger at Peter, ever judgmental and always unnecessary. "And I want it soon."

"You'll get what's coming to you. You can count on *that.*" Of course, Peter didn't intend on giving him any more money. In fact, he looked forward to tying up this particular loose end. *His* way.

"You better get it to me. Otherwise, I might have to tell someone about our little arrangement."

"I said you'll get it, Edwin."

"Boy, in this house, you call me 'Father' or 'Sir'."

"Whatever you say, *Edwin.*" His father scowled at him. "Now. Where's my end of the bargain?"

"On my bed."

The smell of rot followed Peter down the hallway. Wallpaper rippled off the walls in waves. The ever-present painting of Jesus sat on the floor. A dust-free rectangle on the wall represented its old home. Shaking his head in revulsion, he pushed the bedroom door open. A girl lay on the bed, her hands tied to her feet. A gag pulled tightly into her mouth. Gift wrapped especially for him.

Peter sat next to her, drew a finger across her cheek. Her eyes widened, her fear nearly palpable.

"Hello, sweetheart," said Peter. "Before we begin our activities, I want to thank you for your participation. Your valiant sacrifice. It means a lot to me. And I want you to understand that it's nothing personal."

The girl flailed about on the bed, attempting to escape Peter's touch.

"We'll begin soon." Peter turned. A monstrous, deformed man blocked his path. "Jesus Christ!" The thing bobbed its head, its tongue lolling. Long, dirty hair dropped into his face, and food crumbs speckled his beard. Snarling, his one working eye focused on Peter.

Behind the behemoth, Edwin laughed. "Peter, say hello to your little brother."

The creature approached him.

This must be Mary's son. Good Christ.

"Get him away from me. I want nothing to do with him." Peter backed into the bedroom until his legs butted up against the bed. Nowhere to go.

Edwin balled his hands up to his eyes, feigning a crying gesture. "Joshua, looks like you're scaring your big brother. Poor baby. Go on upstairs now. Go on, boy. Git!"

The thing whimpered as it left the room.

Peter felt his adrenaline rush away, flipping the switch to his analytical side. This creature posed another problem he would have to deal with. He might have to get rid of it. No witnesses. Probably do it a favor by putting it out of its misery anyway.

Seething, Peter knocked into his father as he passed him. He sat at the kitchen table and opened his bag, checking the rifle thoroughly. "Cut the girl loose and bring her to me," he ordered.

Time to get 'er done, as they say in Hicksville.

Jason answered on the first ring.

"Hi, Jay. Just checking in as I said I would. I'm almost there."

"I'll be glad when you're done with…with this…*whatever*."

Matt sighed. "Me, too. Shouldn't take long." He hoped. The closer Matt drove to his childhood home, the more apprehensive he grew.

"What are you going to do, Matt? I mean, if your father has your daughter?"

After a long pause, he said, "I'm going to bring her back with me."

"If he has her, you really need to call the police. Don't try and do it on your own."

"Okay." Godwin had no police officers, though. A town with a low crime rate, Godwin residents found the idea of law enforcement to be a waste of tax money. On the rare occasion of a crime, a cop drove in from Karlin, nearly forty-five minutes away. But what Jason didn't know wouldn't kill him.

"I mean it. Don't do anything stupid."

"I won't. I've got to go, Jay."

"I love you, Matt."

Before Matt could respond, his phone beeped and died. He turned on the dome light. No signal bars. The now-worthless cell phone sailed up onto the dashboard. He hoped he would get a chance to tell Jason he loved him, too.

Chapter Ten

With the girl fighting him, Edwin had a devil of a time cutting the ropes.

"Damn it, girl, hold still. And don't you dare try and cut me again, you little bitch!" Disappointment saddled in when he realized he wouldn't have his way with the girl. No matter. With his newfound fortune, he could buy (and damn near *own*) a couple of sluts the likes of Miss Lindsay Bellowes. God watched over him.

Finally, he succeeded in cutting the ropes. He tore the rag from her mouth.

"What are you going to do to me?" Lindsay said.

"Why, I ain't gonna do anything to you. My son, on the other hand…" He broke into a chuckle. "Get on your feet." He yanked her off the bed and prodded her into the kitchen.

Peter looked up from his gun inspection. "Sit down, please."

The girl sat across from Peter. Edwin stood behind her in case she decided to make another run for it.

"Now, I'm a fair man," said Peter. "And I'm a sporting man. That's why I'm going to give you a head start." He looked directly into the girl's terrified eyes.

"What…what do you mean?"

"I'm going to let you walk right out that door." Peter extended his forefinger, his thumb cocked in the air, and pointed toward the kitchen entrance. "And I'm going to give you a ten-minute head start. I believe that to be more than fair. And a bigger challenge for me." He closed one eye and dropped the thumb on his fist as if shooting a gun.

"Don't be stupid, boy!" said Edwin. "She can get away."

"Please…shut…your…mouth, Edwin."

"Oh my God!" Lindsay's voice crawled to a dry whisper. She whimpered, inhaling deep, shuddering breaths. "What are you going to do?"

"I'm going to hunt you," said Peter. "Now, stop crying. You're going to need your wits about you."

Edwin's nerves were frazzled. The girl kept on blubbering like Mary used to do. It took all the control he could muster to not slap her into silence.

"Please be aware the closest neighbor is at least ten miles away. If you think you can make it there, then, by all means, have at it," continued Peter. "But it's going to be a long haul. You also might try following the gravel roads out to the highway. But that's also a good fifteen-mile stretch. It's your decision." He placed his hand gently on the girl's arm. "Do you understand?"

"Why are you doing this?"

"Because I *can*," replied Peter quietly.

Edwin smiled; his heart warmed. *There may be hope for Peter yet.*

"Your ten minutes begin now." Peter checked his watch. "If I were you, I'd get going." She sat frozen, barely moving. With a couple of chin juts, Peter urged her on. Slowly, she pulled herself up and out of disbelief. She dropped one last doe-eyed glance at Peter, her fingers running over the back of the chair. Then she walked toward the kitchen door, picking up her pace as she went. With one last sniffle and a sleeve pulled across her running nose, she ran out into the night.

Edwin watched Peter polish his gun, chuckling at his lustful touch. How a man might treat a whore.

"You gonna kiss that gun next, boy?"

Peter stopped long enough to glower at Edwin. "Maybe I should make you kiss it, you bastard."

"Big, hollow threats from a little man. You ain't got the guts." It was never wise to goad a man with a loaded gun, but Edwin knew Peter didn't have the balls to follow through.

"You might be surprised."

"What'd you say, boy?" Edwin thought he'd heard Peter right but couldn't be sure. He'd tolerate no insolence from his kin.

"Never mind." Peter reached into his bag, pulled out a knife and something resembling binoculars. He strapped the device around his head.

"What in the hell?" Edwin howled at the sight of his boy. Made him look like a damn giant bug.

"I realize you're not intelligent enough to grasp the concept, but these are night-vision goggles."

"Some hunter you are. Christ Almighty. I never had to use anything like that."

Peter stood, carefully securing the hunting knife in his belt. Everything he did appeared prissy to Edwin. He wondered if he might be one of them queers.

Next, Peter slung the rifle around his back and checked his watch. "It's time." At the kitchen door, he said, "I'll be back for round two."

Edwin felt good. Better than good; he felt *great*. He looked around the house, ruminating on his last night here. *Good riddance.* By this time tomorrow, he'd be on his way to Florida.

The later the night dragged on, the colder the cellar grew. With her arms bound, Shannon couldn't warm herself. She looked up at the jars, wishing she still had her glass shard. She wouldn't hesitate to use it either. No more Mr. Nice Guy.

Since Lindsay had screamed out earlier, she strained to listen for something—anything. She closed her eyes, even held her breath, hoping to hone her auditory senses. At one point, she thought she heard a car crunch over the gravel. *Maybe a police officer?* She never heard the car leave. It gave her a sliver of hope to hang onto.

Later, a sharp crack rang out in the distance. The reverberation across the flatlands made it sound like several explosions. Her heart pounded. Her temples throbbed.

A gunshot? But who got shot, and who was doing the shooting?

Shannon recognized the heavy footfalls of Joshua coming down the stairs. After fumbling with the lock, he came toward her with an immobile face. Determined. This time he didn't indulge his curiosity.

He carried her out and up the stairs to the farmhouse.

Remembering the steps this time, Lindsay leaped down them. She hit the gravel running, high school track paying off in spades.

Her heart raced faster than her legs.

She couldn't comprehend this unfathomable scenario. A horrific, surrealistic nightmare, the kind that repeats over and over. Except this was *real*.

Shannon's words looped through her mind. If she didn't pull it together, they'd never make it out alive.

Running past the cellar, she paused. But just for a second. She couldn't open the padlock. If she could make it to a neighbor's house, she'd come back for Shannon. With lots of armed cops. Make the sons-of-bitches pay.

Like it or not, she was their best chance at survival now.

Time to drop the cry-baby diapers and put on my big-girl panties. Be cool.

She studied the farm and the land surrounding it. Pigs squealed out from a fenced area next to a battered barn. If she hid in the barn, the clamoring pigs would surely give away her position. A sitting target.

A wooded area lay beyond the cornfields. Within reach. But she might end up lost. A better option than being murdered by savages.

She guessed two minutes had passed since she left the house. The new man said she would have a ten-minute head start before he came after her. Ten minutes to live. A lot could happen in ten minutes.

Wiping the last of her tears away, she took a deep, calming breath—the way her coach had taught her—then sprinted toward the cornfield.

The dry stalks snapped briskly as she trampled through them. She plunged into a narrow, empty row. Unimpeded by the stalks, she ran down it, quieter, faster. The woods were in sight, as was hope.

Her legs grew heavy as if she'd been running for hours. Mentally, she had been. She needed to rest. *Out of the question.* She had to put as much distance as possible between her and the madmen at the farm.

Across the field, she heard the kitchen door crack open, echoing sharply across the grounds. Her newfound bravery abandoned her. Paralyzed with fear, Lindsay dropped, shaking in the field.

Peter stepped off the stairs and adjusted his goggles. Much better. He scanned the area, everything tinted green via his night vision.

If I were a girl, terrified for my life, where would I go? Peter smiled. People were so easy to read. *I'd head for the gravel roads, looking for traffic.*

Little does she realize, though, traffic is rare in this hellhole, particularly at night.

Peter cocked his rifle. *Ki-chak.* A good hunter is always prepared.

He jogged down the driveway to meet the gravel road, eyes and ears alert, checking both directions. The road appeared empty. By his estimation, the girl could've possibly run three-quarters of a mile in ten minutes. Particularly in as good a shape as she appeared. The road lay flat enough for him to see that distance.

She's hiding, still on the farmland.

At first, he thought the girl weak. Easy prey. Maybe he underestimated her, as unlikely as that seemed. But she could be more formidable than he gave her credit for. The thrill of the chase kicked in, and Peter's senses heightened, rising to the challenge.

He ran back up the driveway, searching the area. His gaze locked onto the cornfield. Should have been his first destination. Most likely was hers. Squinting, he spotted several unnaturally broken stalks bent toward the ground like surrendering soldiers. He slung the gun around his shoulder and hurtled toward the field.

Peter crouched down before entering as his pulse picked up. He realized he'd been grinning like a lunatic. Couldn't be helped. He wished the pursuit to go on, sad at an abrupt conclusion. The impending conclusion thrilled him more than any sexual conquest could.

He picked up the girl's trail much more easily than a deer's. More broken stalks led off to the right. He followed the path. Then the trail went cold. Just stopped like she'd been whisked away. Backtracking, he found light footprints in the dirt and tracked her steps. Again, they ended abruptly. He stood. Focused. Listening for his quarry.

Close. So very close, he could feel it in his bones. The clatter of crickets stopped. Weeding out the distant calls of animals, he heard something. The faintest of sounds, something unnatural to a farm's habitat. Muffled breathing, quiet as an infant's whisper. About thirty feet from where he stood. Cradling the gun in the crook of his arm, he stealthily stepped between two stalks. The breathing grew louder, possibly one row over. He sidled between two more stalks, cautiously avoiding brushing against the dried plants. In front of him, a tall stalk shivered. A dark figure huddled behind it. Hoisting up the gun, Peter captured her in his sights.

"Got you," he whispered.

The girl shot to her feet and whirled right, ran toward the road. Peter pulled the trigger. The rifle cracked, blowing back sharply into his shoulder. Blood and splintered bone exploded from the girl's arm. She crashed down into the dirt.

Unexpected dizziness overtook Peter. He dropped to his knees. The impact knocked his teeth together. He pitched forward, chin in the dirt. The contents of his stomach emptied. A bitter taste filled his mouth; an even sharper feeling flooded his soul.

Not the experience he'd hoped for.

His repulsion stunned him. The sight of the girl's arm torn apart by his bullet should have been invigorating, sexual in its power. But it wasn't at all like killing an animal. Animals never looked back. Before the girl fell, she looked his way. Caught his gaze for one unforgettable second. Shock, sadness…life fleeting away.

He wanted no part of this. Not cold-blooded murder.

Yet… Yet, the girl was still alive. Hard to die from an arm wound.

He could leave. Pack up his gear and get the hell out of here. He didn't think she'd heard his name. But could she identify him?

Somehow, the girl pulled herself to her feet. Cradling her shattered limb with her intact arm, she stumbled through the field, wobbly, uneven. Dazed.

She'd almost made it to the road when Peter spotted the car. She screamed, unable to wave, trying to catch the driver's attention.

Peter winced. He pulled the gun up and captured her in the rifle's sights. She left him no choice. A killing blow to put her—and his own fears—out of their respective misery.

Sorry, honey. Survival of the fittest, the law of the land.

The girl dove in front of the car. Gravel scraped and shot up like buckshot as the driver braked. The vehicle barreled into her. A meaty *thud.* Her body twisted into the air and landed on the hood.

Peter collapsed again. Dry heaving racked his body. Someone inadvertently delivered the killing blow to his prey. Much as he had done for his brother's deer so many years ago.

Sickness gave way to a comforting sense of relief. All was well once again in his world, his hands still clean from human blood.

Now he needed to tell Edwin the deal was off. And get the hell out of Godwin, hopefully without leaving a trail.

"Shit!" Matt screamed as the girl ran out from nowhere. He swerved, slamming on the brakes. Not soon enough. The car slammed into her head on. Her body flew up—a suspended moment of nightmarish ballet—then crashed down onto the hood. The car slid into the ditch, tossing the girl to the ground. His chest crunched against the steering wheel when it stopped.

He instinctively reached for his phone. Still no signal. He jumped out, barely keeping hysteria at bay.

Unbelievably—miraculously—he saw her chest rise and fall. Her eyes were glassy with shock. An arm clung to her body by filaments of flesh. Shattered beyond repair, bone and blood jutted out of her damaged limb.

"Jesus, God, I'm *sorry!*"

Gulping for air like a land-locked fish, she struggled to form words.

A thought struck Matt. He remembered the name of his daughter's friend. A long shot, but one worth taking. "Are…are you Lindsay?"

Her eyes wandered, not necessarily moving in the same direction. Matt repeated the question. She nodded her head.

"What happened to you? Where's Shannon?" Hellish urgency pushed him to grill the girl more than he should have. She was barely coherent. Barely alive.

"They…have…her…" Every word a chore.

Matt understood. And he hated himself for what he had to do. "Lindsay. I'm sorry…but I have to go save Shannon. I'll come back for you later."

Matt couldn't bear her anguished look, the dislocated jaw he caused. He turned, setting out for the farmhouse. Behind him, he listened to Lindsay's bubbling pleas for help, not even words now. But he had to leave Lindsay. He just *had* to. His crazy father had his daughter. *Look at what Edwin did to this poor girl.*

"God damn it!" No matter how badly he wanted to find Shannon, he couldn't leave this girl dying on a country road. Matt ran back toward Lindsay.

The girl was staring at the moon, her cheeks glistening from her tears. She squeezed her eyes shut when she saw Matt. He carefully picked her up and laid her down on his back seat

"I'm going to get you some help, Lindsay. Just hang in there!" He gunned the car into reverse, squeezing the pedal down. The tires spun before grabbing traction. Miraculously, the car jettisoned out of the ditch and onto the road.

Matt stopped and looked down the road. Lights lit up the farmhouse.

"Hold on, Shannon," he said quietly. "I'll be back for you as soon as I can." He pulled a U-turn and shot down the road.

"I'm going to take you to the nearest neighbor, Lindsay. They'll be able to call for an ambulance." She sobbed softly, encouraging signs of life.

"What did that bastard do to you?" Matt tried to keep her conscious with non-stop questions. "Is Shannon okay?" Saying the words aloud re-awakened his fear of losing his daughter. This time forever.

"Hunting…us. Shannon's…in cellar…" she trailed off.

My God. He knew his father wasn't a good man, insane, even. But hunting teenage girls? His own granddaughter? Evil, *sickening.*

Matt barreled down the road at nearly ninety miles per hour toward the Sowers' home. His hands shook violently over the steering wheel. Sweat—or tears—stung his eyes. He pulled into the driveway of his neighbor from twenty years ago, relieved to see a light on inside.

"I'll be right back, Lindsay," he shouted, already halfway to the front door. He pounded on the door until the outside light popped on. Matt squinted from the sudden brightness.

"Who is it?" An old woman peered from behind the door's curtain.

"It's Matt…Quail. I used to be your neighbor, Missus Sowers." He hated using his birth name, but it would gain him easier entry. "I need your help!"

Hesitantly, she opened the door. "Oh, I think I remember you…" She sized him up and down.

"Missus Sowers, there's been a terrible accident. I hit a girl with my car, and she needs help!"

Mrs. Sowers called for her husband. Mr. Sowers appeared, looking about the same as he had twenty years ago. "It's Gretchen Quail's boy, Earl. He hit a girl with his car!"

Without saying a word, the old man sprinted out toward Matt's car, long legs outrunning Matt. Mr. Sowers yanked open the door, bent, and studied Lindsay. He straightened and narrowed his eyes. "The girl's been shot!"

"I…didn't know that." Matt's heart fluttered, urgency frustrating him. "Look, I'll come back later and explain everything, but right now…someone else needs my help. If you could call an ambulance and maybe help stop the bleeding?"

"Yup. I'll do what I can." He rubbed his jaw, staring at Matt. "Maybe I'd better call the police while I'm at it?"

"No…not just yet. I…need to find out what's going on first."

Mr. Sowers took in a whistling breath between clenched teeth. Suspicion clouded his eyes, then lifted. Thankfully, Lindsay's immediate needs came first. "Let me get this poor girl indoors." He scooped up Lindsay and hurried back inside.

Matt jumped into the car, flooring it out of the driveway. Speeding toward the farmhouse, he hoped he wasn't too late.

Chapter Eleven

Learning from his past mistake, Edwin kept this girl's hands tied. Joshua dropped her onto the sofa and sat beside her, stroking her hair. Playing with dollies, for God's sake.

On the other hand, Edwin lorded it over his captive as she wept. At least she kept the waterworks to a dull roar this time. "Now, you just hush. It ain't doing you no good. It'll all be over soon."

Peter entered the house, whiter than a picket fence. "Game over," he said.

"What're you talking about, boy?" Edwin strutted into the kitchen. He had a bad feeling about this. Practically could see his money going up in smoke.

"I said, 'It's over!' I'm done with all of this." Peter sat at the kitchen table, packing up his hunting supplies.

"Now, wait a damned minute, boy. We had a deal."

"I don't care, Edwin. I'm finished, and I'm leaving. Now."

"You haven't finished your huntin'! You're only half done."

"I am not hunting the other girl. Take her back—or let her go. Do what you want with her. I don't care. But I don't want anything to do with it."

"What's the matter? Lost your guts for it?"

Edwin watched his son nearly rise to the occasion, halfway out of his chair. Then he backed down. "It wasn't what I expected."

"What the hell happened out there?" That bad feeling sank lower. He had counted on Peter doing the dirty work, but the boy had let him down. Again.

"I wounded the girl. Then some car finished her off."

"*What?* How do you even know she's dead?"

"I'd count on it." Peter's voice lowered, his eyes haunted.

"Goddamn it! What if she ain't dead? What then, boy? What if they connect her back to us?"

"That's *your* problem. I'm certain the girl can't be traced back to me. You'd better cover your own tracks. And so help me, Edwin, if you breathe a word of my involvement to anyone, I'll come back for you."

"You think you can't be identified, you dumb son-of-a-bitch? Well, we'll just see about that. Joshua, bring the other girl in here…*now!*"

Joshua carried her into the kitchen, taking his sweet time positioning her into a chair. Still playing with dollies. *Jesus Christ a'mighty.*

"No!" Peter zipped up his bag and rushed toward the kitchen door.

Edwin yanked the rag from the girl's mouth, tore the blind from her eyes.

"Peter? Uncle Peter?"

With a hand on the doorknob, Peter froze. His shoulders collapsed. He turned slowly, avoiding looking outright at the girl. Peter sat back down and unzipped his bag. If Edwin didn't know better, he thought the boy looked downright remorseful.

"What the hell's going on here?" asked Edwin. "Do you know this little girl, Peter?"

"Hello, again, Shannon," said Peter. He sighed as he rolled his rifle onto the table. "Looks like the hunt's back on."

Shannon screamed.

Peter turned toward his father. "You stupid, old fool. You've grabbed your own granddaughter."

Edwin dropped into a kitchen chair. He poked the bill of his cap up, considering things.

"It's Matt's daughter." Peter shot the girl a look, loaded with guilt. "You ignorant asshole," he hissed.

"Well, I'll be goddamned!" Edwin coughed out a dusty laugh, dry as the desert.

Like a bound-up toddler, the girl rattled her fists. Building to a tantrum. Then she ripped out a teeth-jarring shriek, a fine how-do-you-do to her grandfather.

Matt parked his car a mile from the farmhouse and ran the rest of the way. The jog winded him, but he couldn't risk driving up to the house. If his father was sick enough to hunt humans for sport, then stealth was the best option.

For the first time in many years, he prayed. He'd long ago felt abandoned by God. But desperate times called for desperate measures.

With the house in sight, Matt paused to catch his breath. Dropping to a crouch, he made his way toward the driveway. A new Lincoln Town Car sat in the driveway, a vehicle he didn't recognize. Couldn't be his father's. He'd never buy such an extravagant car.

Light dribbled through the kitchen and living room's drawn blinds. A sure sign *something* was happening. In the past, his father made damn sure the lights stayed out if a room remained unoccupied.

Matt peered through the living room window. Three figures crowded around the kitchen table. His father flailed his arms about, shouting. Next to him sat Shannon. It *had* to be her. Even though she'd grown and matured, her features remained the same. Pale and obviously terrified, her simple and natural beauty still took Matt's breath away. At that moment, he wanted to hold her, protect her, and take her away from his father's madness. But he couldn't. Not just yet.

Across from Shannon sat the third figure, an unwelcome surprise. His brother, Peter. Matt couldn't believe it. Never in a million years would Peter return to the farm. *Never.* Matt took a closer look. Peter sat calmly, nonchalantly cleaning a rifle. Bile rose in Matt's throat. His head pounded, his pulse lively in his ears.

Peter…not Peter… My God, he's a part of this…

A low rumbling growl came from behind Matt. He swiveled, nearly stumbled, and steadied himself against the house. The hound dog's eyes appeared dangerously uncertain, its body language threatening. Hackles rose across its neck. Then it bared its teeth. Rear legs tensed as it prepared to attack.

Holding out his hand, Matt stooped down. "Easy, boy…good dog," he whispered. "It's okay…good boy."

The succession of barks blasted off like a string of firecrackers. Matt shot to his feet and made for the cover of the Town Car. The dog raced toward the kitchen door, panting between barks. Kneeling behind the car, Matt risked a glance through the back window.

The porch light flared. The front door banged open. Edwin stood on the top step holding a flashlight. He swept the beam across the yard.

"Shut *up*, Jeremiah," he shouted before delivering a kick to the dog. Tail between its legs, the dog ran for the safety of the barn.

Footsteps crunched across the gravel. The stream of light played over the car's roof before falling into the car, barely clearing Matt's head. Matt, his knees burning from squatting, held his breath. The beam snapped off, and Edwin returned to the house, humming a gospel song. Matt heard the kitchen door open and close. He waited a few seconds before lowering himself to the ground. Finally, he expelled his breath.

He sat for five minutes before he dared to move again. Seeing his father again scared him. Bigger than life and twice as bad as death.

A shiver overtook Matt. He looked over the familiar grounds. From the vantage of the cornfield, he would be able to keep an eye on the house.

Matt sprinted for the field and settled in behind the first row of corn. Again, squatting proved hellish to his knees, so he sat on the damp ground. The cold seeped through his clothes, his flesh, his bones.

If his family intended to hunt Shannon, they'd let her go first. His brother always liked the challenge of the hunt. At least he *hoped* he'd give her a chance. Once they released her, Matt would grab her and get the hell out of Godwin.

Shannon stared at her uncle with disbelief. She had only met him once, and briefly at that, but she had felt an instant kindred to him. She'd felt he *understood* her. Something she didn't get from her squabbling parents at the time.

Now he could barely look at her. All his attention stayed firmly planted on his gun as he polished it with relish. It seemed unfathomable this man— her uncle—would do this to her.

"Why?" She heard the quiver in her voice but was determined to stay strong.

The long moment of silence before he looked up seemed interminable. "Excuse me?" He spoke softly, but his eyes remained as cold as the steel in his hands.

"Why? Why do you want to hunt me? Tell me why."

"Shannon, I don't *want* to hunt you. It's just how it played out…through no fault of my own, I might add."

"Then why do it, Uncle Peter?" She emphasized "Uncle" every chance she got.

His eyes flitted about the kitchen, unable to meet her gaze as if suffering guilt. "I don't want to hurt you, Shannon. Believe it or not, I'm truly sorry it has to be this way. It's nothing personal, I assure you."

He reached across the table, placing his hand over her two bound ones. Shannon snatched her hands away at his foul touch.

"I honestly believe had things been different, I could've grown to like you, Shannon."

"Why does it have to be this way?" Tears welled up in her eyes, the dam breaking again.

"Because now it's a matter of my survival. Had your sick bastard of a grandfather not dragged you in here and had you not identified me…" He shrugged. "Well, it was my every intention to see you released."

"I won't tell anyone, Uncle Peter. I swear!"

"I'm sorry. I don't believe you."

"What did you do to my friend?" Shannon dreaded the answer, but she had to know.

"I shot her in the arm. Then a car ran into her, killing her." Lines wrinkled his forehead as he grimaced. "She didn't suffer long."

Shannon couldn't stop crying. Just couldn't do it. And she absolutely hated herself for showing weakness. She hated reacting like a simpering, helpless little girl. But mostly, she hated these men. Her so-called "family."

"Is…is he really…my grandfather?"

"I'm afraid he is." His upper lip curled up like a dried leaf; obviously, there was no love lost between father and son.

"And who is Joshua?"

"I'm not even certain *what* he is."

The kitchen door opened. "Well," crowed Edwin, "as I told you, nothing to worry about 'cept for an ol' 'coon, probably."

"Are you sure about that? You've managed to screw everything else up."

"You'd better show me some respect in my house, boy. I'm not the only one who messed things up tonight." He leered at Shannon. "So, how's my precious little granddaughter doing? I can't believe something so pretty came from my useless son." He caressed her hair. Then his fingers ran down her neck and dropped to her shoulder. Shannon shuddered from his cold, leathery fingers. When she tried to pull away, he grabbed her shoulders, pulling her back into the chair. From the living room, Joshua grumbled, low and menacing.

"Leave her alone!" Peter bolted upright, sending the chair sliding behind him.

"I'm just showing my granddaughter some love. Ain't no harm in that."

"Yeah, like you showed your children 'fatherly love'…especially, Mary."

The old man dropped his grin. He stormed toward Peter, prodding a finger into his face. "You watch what you say to me, boy."

Tension, thick as smog, filled the room. Finally, Peter broke the silence and said, "Let's get this over with." With a knife, he cut through the ropes binding Shannon's hands. Peter leaned over and whispered, "Shannon, you'll have a chance, I promise you that. I'll give you a ten-minute head start. Your best bet is the woods. It's about ten miles from there to the nearest farm."

Shannon stared at her uncle, confused.

A head game? Or is he actually trying to help me?

"Now, go."

Without hesitation, Shannon pushed through the door and ran for her life.

Peter couldn't believe what he had done. Peter Brookes, king of sexual conquests and destroyer of financial empires, never cut anyone a break. Yet, a teenage girl singlehandedly reduced him to a man of lesser worth. Peter put the welfare of his niece before his. Gave her a chance at survival. A *first*.

Maybe he helped her because of his brother, Mattie. After all, Matt was the only member of his family he had any feelings for, small as those were.

Yet, he knew something else—something inexplicable—had compelled him.

Single-minded earnestness burned in the girl's face. Intelligence brushed past the tears in her eyes. Faced with impending death, the girl had sought answers. A true warrior.

He saw great potential in her. A shame, really, to blow it away. She might be the first person related to this God-forsaken family who could possibly rise above the horrors of the past and move on to a normal life.

He wondered if he'd truly given her a fighting chance, though. Or had he cheated, as he had all his life? He knew she'd take the route he suggested. Maybe he had not played fair. Or maybe he told her the best survival strategy merely to assuage his guilt? *Guilt.* A strange feeling—one he couldn't wrap his head around.

Peter cocked his rifle and prepared to bury his guilt along with his niece. Edwin grinned. The inbred boy moaned from the shadows of the kitchen corner. Peter purposefully avoided looking at Joshua as he made for the door.

Once outside, he strapped on his night-vision gear again and secured the knife in his belt.

Then, as he raced down the driveway, the comfortably familiar feeling of anticipation flooded him like a shot of adrenaline.

About a mile down the road, he spotted a parked car. The car appeared similar to the automobile that had run over the other girl. Earlier, he had watched the car flee the scene. Why would it have turned back? A chill ran up and down his spine.

Peter scrambled for his car keys. He gunned his car into reverse and roared down to the parked car.

Fifty feet from the car, Peter flashed on his bright lights. The smashed hood verified it as the same blue hybrid he saw earlier. He left his car, leaving the door open. The headlights illuminated his path. Hitching up his rifle, he approached the vehicle. Trash littered the floorboards. A cell phone lay on the passenger seat. At the back of the car, Peter knelt at the license plate. Kansas tags, but definitely not from this county. From what he recalled, the "JO" stood for Johnson County. A Kansas City suburb.

Peter pulled at the door. *Locked.* Why would someone abandon a car in the middle of nowhere? The only residence for miles was Edwin's shithole. Someone—somewhere—was out there.

This changes everything.

A nearly sexual intensity filled Peter with the prospect of a new player in the game. His niece had an ally. Perhaps the earlier driver wanted to atone for running over the girl.

Peter's fleeting compassion drifted away like a forgotten memory. Humming a Sondheim tune, he plunged his knife into the hybrid's front tire. The tire hissed and deflated to the gravel. Smiling, he flattened the rest of the tires.

Peter pulled his car partially into the ditch. He grabbed his gear and locked the doors. Plunging into the cornfields, he pursued his prey with a newfound zest for life. And death.

Matt crouched in the cornfield and realized he had no idea how to approach Shannon. Eight years was a long time. The last time he saw her, when he'd said his goodbyes, she had just been a little girl. She might not even recognize him. More to the point, would she even *want* to see him again? There certainly wouldn't be time for apologies or explanations, as much as he desired to offer them.

The door cracked back and hung open. Shannon sprang from the house. He climbed to his feet, a cold lack of sensation in his knees. She rushed toward the field, not far from his hiding place, and leaped inside. He followed her, crashing through the stalks. Much faster than him, she pulled away with a frenzied speed.

"Shannon! Stop!" She didn't hear his whispers at first. He raised his voice. Down the row, she stopped, uncertain. But just for a second. Matt pushed on, every footfall resounding in his head. Nearing her, he jumped, snagging her by the ankle. They tumbled to the dirt. Stalks snapped beneath them like cracked knuckles.

The ground met Matt's chin with a sharp blow, but he held firmly onto her foot. Shannon lashed out at him, feet kicking into his face. His hand slipped down to her tennis shoe. "Shannon, stop! It's me! It's Dad! It's okay. I'm gonna get you out of here."

Shannon looked back, hesitated. Then her foot landed squarely in Matt's face. He fell back, stunned, dizzy. She leaped to her feet, squatting, fists balled up. Climbing to his knees, Matt launched himself at her, tackling her to the dirt. He held a palm over her mouth as he pinned her to the ground. "Shannon, I'm trying to *save* you! Stop screaming!"

A car barreled down the road next to the field. They froze. Heading in the opposite direction of the farmhouse, it had to be Peter or Edwin. Lying still, they waited for the car to pass.

Shannon stopped resisting. Tears rolled down her cheeks. When Matt slowly removed his hand from her mouth, she immediately clamped her hands there. Stilling sobs. Her body shook with a feverish intensity. "Shannon, it's me, your father. We've got to get out of here. *Now.*" Sitting up, he extended a hand toward his daughter.

"Dad?" Doubt, close to hysteria, colored her voice. "Dad? Oh, my God. Are you part of this, too?"

"What? No. God, no! I want to get you out of here."

"No...no, no, *no*... I don't *believe* you."

Matt placed a finger over her lips. "Listen, Shannon. You've got to trust me. I'm going to get us out of here. I know you don't have any reason to believe me. I know I haven't given you any reason to. But we've got to get out of here now!" Matt pulled her to her knees. "Are you ready?"

Shannon gave a lifeless nod.

"I have a car close by. But we need to go." They stood, Shannon warily eyeing him. When Matt reached for her hand, she recoiled. Then she offered it back to him, a small sign of hope. Matt grabbed it, held on tight. Gave it an extra squeeze like eight years hadn't passed. He pulled her onto a path unencumbered by stalks. Scurrying down the aisle, they headed toward the road.

Matt stopped. Ahead, stalks rustled. He turned to Shannon, finger to his lips. Her eyes widened, practically glowing beneath the moonlight. A delicate sound, so minimal it might be an animal. Or someone not wanting to be heard.

Matt whispered, "We've got to get out of the field."

Pulling aside several stalks, Matt searched for a clear exit. Plowing through the stalks would raise too much noise. A risky decision—but their only option—they had to go back. Turning, Matt pulled Shannon along behind him. They ran quietly, traveling down the dirt path.

Lights blazed in the distant farmhouse. Matt stopped, listening for the intruder behind them. *Silence.* He gestured toward the gravel road. Shannon nodded. Squatting, they made their way to the road, staying within the tree's shadows.

Matt stepped onto the gravel road, glancing back at the house. With his distance eyesight failing, he saw no activity, blurry or otherwise. Then he noticed Shannon's eyeglasses were missing. Both of them were now effectively blind.

Matt tiptoed across the gravel. Shannon released his hand—the impatience of youth—and sprinted across the road. She stood on the other side, arms folded, waiting. Matt abandoned stealth and ran to join her, and they crouched in the roadside ditch.

Barbed wire marked the territorial line of an abandoned field overgrown with tall grass and weeds. Perfect cover. Matt carefully held up the lowest strand of wire, motioning for Shannon to crawl through it. She maneuvered underneath and then pulled it up for Matt. The wire caught him, a slight jab pricking his belly. It didn't matter. Nothing mattered but his daughter's safety. They were almost home free. Soon the nightmare would be over.

"We're almost there," he whispered.

Shannon remained emotionless, and it stung Matt deeply. Their first father–daughter outing in eight years, a life-or-death situation. Not the way he had envisioned it.

Matt led the way through the cutting grass, blazing a trail as best he could for his daughter.

A glint of moonlight bounced off the hybrid's roof, a life-saving buoy. "There's the car." Tension visibly slipped away from Shannon's face. Her hand loosened in his. Even though exhausted, they ran the last leg at full speed. Overtaking Matt, Shannon crawled underneath the wire before Matt reached the fence.

By the time Matt climbed up the ditch to the road, he saw Shannon facing the car, immobile. Her shoulders slumped, folding within her tiny frame.

"Shannon?"

She turned, mouth open, eyes dulled. Matt peered around her.

All four tires were flat.

"What now? What now, Dad?"

Standing helpless on a desolate Kansas back road, Matt felt like roadkill waiting to happen.

Chapter Twelve

Edwin didn't believe in coincidence, had no use for it. God planned everything. Now God was testing his loyalty as surely as God had commanded Abraham to kill his son, Isaac, as a test of faith. Plain as the nose on his face, it was obvious Edwin's granddaughter should be punished for her sins. Who better to do the job than her own kin?

Edwin pulled his hunting rifle off the wall and loaded the chambers.

Time to join the hunt. God's plan. Nothing was going to stand in the way of his receiving his just reward. After all, the Good Book says *the meek shall inherit the earth.*

"Joshua," he called. "I need you, boy!" Joshua pounded down the stairs at a speed that always took Edwin aback. Surprisingly, he never tumbled down the steps. But the boy had a Godly grace in his huge body. "We need to go and take care of the girl. That girl means to hurt your daddy, Joshua. You don't want that, do you?" Edwin spoke slowly, but his son would try even the patience of Job. "So, we need to hurt her before she can hurt me. You understand, boy?"

Joshua muttered an agreement. For what the boy lacked in intelligence, he certainly made up for in loyalty. More than Edwin could say for his other offspring.

"Well, then, let's go get her." Edwin strolled toward the door, rifle in hand. "I heard Peter tell the girl to run into the woods. I need you to look there. You understand?"

Joshua nodded.

"Good boy."

When Edwin stepped outside, he took in a deep breath. Remembering the smell of the land for the last time. Edwin pointed out toward the woods with one simple gesture. Joshua flew through the cornfields toward the woods, faster than any horse Edwin had ever seen.

As Edwin climbed into his truck, he cleared his throat and spat.

"Amazing grace, how sweeeeeeet the sound, that saaaaaaaaved a wretch like meeeeeeeeeee! I once was losssssst, but nooooooooow am found, was blind, but nooooooow, I seeeeeeeee…"

In the field, Peter heard whispers followed by retreating footsteps. Changing direction, but undoubtedly winding their way to the car. Fine, let them reach it. They'll be in for quite a surprise.

Peter remained hiding, the car within his sights. Voices sounded from the road. He pulled back a stalk to scope out his targets, the rifle wedged squarely against his shoulder.

His brother, Matt, stood next to the car. Stymied, Peter lowered the rifle. He peered through his goggles to make sure.

Although he hadn't seen Matt in years, it was unmistakably him. Heavier, with less hair, maybe. But Matt carried the same sense of self-defeat in the way he moved and walked.

He didn't want to kill his brother, would prefer not to, actually. But Peter saw no other way out. His freedom was at stake.

Dammit.

He dropped the gun again. He couldn't bring himself to shoot his brother in cold blood. Could he? Mattie had suffered alongside him in those painful, early years. He spent his childhood trying to protect Matt from their father. An unexpected surge of emotion punched him in the gut as he remembered one of their last days together on the farm…

While their father plowed the fields, Peter and his brother pitched hay. A tedious, backbreaking job that Peter never fully understood. Sometimes he thought their father made them do it just to torture them.

"Mattie? What're you going to do when you leave here?" Peter wiped sweat from his forehead. He jabbed the pitchfork into the hay.

Matt sat down on a hay bale, considering Peter's question. "I dunno. But I've been thinking about it. You know, before, I just accepted *this* was everything. Farming. But you're right, Peter. This is no life. I think I'd like to go to college."

"Really? What would you study?"

Matt shrugged. "Beats me. Took me a while just to decide on college."

Typical Matt. He never could make a decision about anything, especially his own life. But Peter admired him for trying to better himself. "Well, I think you can do it, Mattie. I think you *should* do it."

"Thanks." The boys leaned back in the hay, enjoying a brief respite from their chores. The sun toasted their faces with comforting warmth. Then it all came crashing down.

"Well, I'll be dipped in shit!" The boys jumped to their feet as Edwin swaggered in front of them. He picked up the pitchfork, prodding it at them like a lion-tamer. "I can't believe what my ears are hearing."

Trembling, Matt stooped to scoop up hay with his hands. Peter boldly held his ground.

"Tell me again, boy. What you gonna do with your life?"

"I want...to go to college..." Matt's voice crawled to a tiny whisper.

"College? Why, you're too dumb to go to college!" The old man slapped his overalls, enjoying his son's discomfort. Matt's eyes filled with tears, his cheeks burning a deep red. Peter wanted to defend Matt but knew when to keep his mouth shut. Even then, his survival instincts were firmly in place.

"That's what I'm going to do," Matt said it under his breath, but his attitude surprised Peter.

Edwin's jaw dropped. No backing out now; Matt had unleashed the beast.

"Well, now. I'm going to give you your first lesson in higher education, boy." Edwin narrowed his eyes. "Take off your clothes."

"What?"

"I said take off your damn clothes." Before Matt could respond, Edwin raised the pitchfork and brought the wooden handle down upon Matt's shoulder. Matt cried out as he dropped into the hay. Peter clenched his fists, moving toward his father with violence in mind. Just as suddenly, he stopped. It'd suit no purpose for them both to be beaten.

"Get those clothes off. *Now!*"

Matt crawled to his feet. His overalls slipped to the ground. Other than his sunburnt face, neck, and arms, he stood pale, white as snow in his underwear. Covering his chest with his arms, Matt stared into the dirt. Peter shot a hate-filled glare toward their father. How he had wanted to wipe that sadistic leer from his father's face. Beat it off him with his fists.

"Kick them boots off."

Matt hesitantly complied. The old man pinched his arm and dragged him toward the farmhouse, with Peter following a safe distance behind.

"Now, stay right there. Don't you dare move. Idiot!" Edwin planted Matt several feet in front of the kitchen window before going around the side of the house. Peter caught Matt's eyes and shook his head. He felt impotent, powerless.

Edwin returned, holding the water hose, cranked on at full force. He cackled as he unleashed the torrent onto Matt.

"Here's your goddamned education, you moron. You worthless piece of crap. Get this through your head. You're too stupid to go to college. You'll never amount to nothin'!" Their father hosed Matt for thirty minutes. He danced around, seeking out different angles, braying like a hyena. Matt, with eyes clamped shut, shook under the onslaught.

Peter wanted to kill his father, plain and simple. What a nice feeling.

"Now, I don't want to hear no more talk about college. You're gonna stay out here tonight, no food, no clothes, no nothin', 'til you learn your lesson." He tossed the hose to the ground, storming away to turn off the water. Peter ran to his brother.

Edwin popped his head around the side of the house like a demented jack-in-the-box. "You want the same treatment, boy?"

Peter shook his head.

"Then go back and do your damned chores."

Peter raced back and snatched up the pitchfork. Every time he jabbed it into the hay, he envisioned Edwin's throat as the mark.

The rest of the day, Peter stole glances at his brother. Matt shivered and sobbed continuously. After the sun went down, Peter threw caution to the wind and went to his brother. The old man was still out in the field.

"Are you okay, Matt?" he whispered.

"I…guess so. Go…go in the house, Peter…before you get in trouble, too." Their cruel father had drained away Matt's earlier optimism. Siphoned it out of him like a leaky bucket. Hours ago, Matt seemed excited about the prospect of a college education. Now he resigned himself to a future full of nothing but tedium, hard work, and abuse.

Throughout the night, Peter looked outside. In the dark, Matt wriggled like a nightcrawler in the mud, ready to collapse from weakness. After his parents went to sleep, Peter grabbed the blanket off his brother's bed. From the refrigerator, he stole what food he thought wouldn't be missed…

Peter snapped out of his reverie. He didn't want to think about what happened next. Too painful. Too damned humiliating what he had said to Matt.

Particularly given the current circumstances.

Ironic that Peter spent all those years trying to protect his brother. And now he was faced with a situation where he had to kill Mattie. Cruel, unjust irony. But that was the nature of fate. Fairness didn't enter into the equation. Fickle bitch, that fate.

But Peter's own life and freedom were in jeopardy. That trumped any misguided feelings he had for his brother.

Peter sighed as he walked out of the field. Matt stood at the back of the car, his head lowered into the open trunk. Shannon was nowhere to be seen. Matt must have sent her running down the road to perceived safety.

Peter swung the gun up and leveled it at his brother. Family reunion time. "Hello, Mattie."

Matt looked over the trunk lid at his brother. "Peter," he replied evenly.

Peter crossed the road, his rifle leading the way like a divining rod. "How've you been, Mattie?"

Matt lowered the trunk slowly. "Are you really asking me that with a gun pointed at my head? *Why* are you doing this, Peter?"

"I never set out to harm you or Shannon, Matt. But through some great cosmic fuck-up, here we are." He stepped closer, good-natured charm on his face. The way he looked after he'd left the farm. "I'm sorry. It's just the way it has to be. Goodbye, Mattie."

Peter squeezed the trigger. Matt flung the trunk up and dropped to his knees. The bullet passed over Matt's head, boring a hole through the trunk lid. Kneeling, Matt waited for the next shot. The rifle *clacked*, a bullet sliding into the chamber. Peter's feet scrabbled across the road. Then a moan.

Matt peered from around the rear of the car. Peter lay face down in the gravel, unmoving. Shannon stood behind him. With the crowbar raised above her head, she appeared more than ready to deliver another blow. She kicked Peter, did it again. The crowbar fell to the pavement with an alarming *clang*. Her chest heaved in and out. She looked at Matt with shock in her eyes, as if she couldn't believe she wielded such power.

Matt inched the rifle from Peter's grip. Searching through his brother's pockets, Matt found the car keys.

"Get in the car, Shannon!" She literally shook herself alert and, following her father, she slid into the passenger side. Matt jabbed the key into the ignition. The key didn't turn, frozen in place like Matt's anesthetized emotions.

"Damn it!" Matt spotted a small compartment to the left of the steering wheel. He popped it open and saw a fitting for a finger. State-of-the-art fingerprint auto security. Something only Peter could afford. Matt jumped out of the car and sprinted toward Peter. Lifting him by the arms, he dragged Peter across the gravel. He almost broke out a smile when he heard Peter's expensive outdoor clothing tearing.

About a mile down the road, two pinpricks of light bore down on Matt. One of the lights shot off to the side like a lazy eye. His father's truck. The engine's sputter grew louder. Matt dropped his brother. No time.

"Shannon, let's go. *Now!*" Shannon scrambled out onto the road. "Back to the cornfield."

Holding onto Peter's rifle, Matt pulled his daughter into the field. Seconds later, the truck slowed where Peter lay. Matt nudged Shannon ahead and followed. The truck continued down the road at a hellish pace.

Where is he going?

They tore through the field, this time not taking care to be quiet. The cornstalks popped, scratching their arms and faces with dried-up, leafy tendrils.

If they reached the safety of the woods, they might make it to the Sowers farm. Their only chance.

Behind them, something powered through the field. At first, Matt thought it sounded like machinery, the pumping of pistons grinding closer. But then Matt recognized the sound as footfalls, inhumanly fast, snapping over the stalks like machine-gun fire. Repetitive, evenly measured, and frighteningly urgent.

"It's Joshua," said Shannon.

Joshua. He must be Mary's son. Matt had forgotten about him, thinking him dead. But the dead don't run that fast.

Matt slung the rifle over his shoulder. Only one bullet left. He had to make it count.

Joshua closed the gap, footfalls drawing nearer. Matt increased his stride, Shannon easily keeping step.

The end of the cornfield lay ahead. Then another few hundred yards to the woods. They broke through the last of the stalks like runners crossing a finish line. The ground sloped toward the woods, their momentum increasing as they descended. Matt looked back, never breaking his gait. Joshua hadn't emerged from the cornfield yet. No sound. No movement amongst the stalks. *Nothing.*

Why? He could've easily caught up to them. Was he watching them?

Toying with them?

They reached the woods, trampling on dead leaves. Tree branches entwined above, creating a tunnel of darkness. Moonlight struggled to slip through the barrier, its light vanishing with the wind's whim. Matt stuck his hand into the blackness, using it to guide them deeper into the forest.

Thirty minutes in, two beams of light pierced the woods. Parked in the middle of the opposite field sat his father's truck. Cradling a gun in his arms, Edwin sat on the hood. Talking to himself, laughing.

If they tried sidling through the woods, his father could easily catch up to them in the truck. Joshua had them trapped from behind. Boxed in on both sides, no way out.

Matt turned to Shannon, her features barely visible in the dark. "Shannon, this Joshua…is he a part of this, too? Is he dangerous?"

Shannon nodded. "Yeah...there's something wrong with him."

"Do you know if he has a gun?"

"I…I don't think so…I've never seen him with one, at least."

"How good are you at climbing trees?"

"I can do it." She said it without hesitation, a sturdy willfulness returning to her voice.

From the truck's meager headlights, Matt made out an old oak tree with low-hanging limbs. He pulled Shannon toward it. "Quietly." Matt pointed up. "And take the gun."

Shannon reluctantly took the rifle and slung the strap over her shoulder. Matt watched her scrabble up the tree with an athlete's prowess. After she put enough distance between herself and the ground, Matt dropped his bombshell. "I've got to go back to the farm."

"What…what're you talking about?" Even through her whisper, Matt felt her panic.

"I have to go. I need to call for help or maybe get another gun. *Something.* Maybe I can even get the car on the road started. But right now, we're just sitting ducks in the woods. They've got us covered on either side."

She said nothing, but her quiet sobs, muffled as though she were covering her mouth, said more than enough.

"I'll get you out of this. I promise, Shannon."

"Don't leave me again."

Matt felt a blow to his chest. The words hurt more than bullets ripping his body apart.

"I won't, I swear." The lump in his throat threatened to explode. He bit back his tears and words. So much he wanted to say to her. But not now. *Later.* He needed his mind clear, his emotions held in check. "I'll be back."

Matt blindly groped his way through the woods. He hoped his last words to his daughter wouldn't prove to be another hollow promise.

Peter sat up in the road, shaking his head. He winced upon feeling the knot on the back of his head.

He couldn't believe Shannon had gotten the drop on him like that. Admirable. A much more worthy adversary than the first girl or his brother. Peter no longer suffered any pangs of guilt about killing her. Obviously, she was fully prepared to fight back, and he welcomed her challenge.

Clapping his hands together, he knocked away the gravel dust. *Time to get back to work.*

Entering the woods without a gun seemed like a particularly bad idea, especially since they had stolen his rifle. He patted down his pockets. All his bullets were there, but the car keys were missing. Peter pulled himself up and stumbled to his car. They left the keys in the ignition. Dumb move on their part. He slipped his finger into the security module and started the car.

The trail had gone cold. He'd have to start over again.

Good.

Matt stood at the edge of the woods, listening. Then he flew across the clearing to the cornfield.

Somewhere along their survival run, Matt had dropped the crowbar. And Shannon had the gun. Even though he had no weapon now, he didn't regret his decision. It gave Shannon a fighting chance. She had her entire life ahead of her, after all.

He hadn't realized how strange it would be seeing his daughter again. Even disregarding their current dire circumstances. He had missed her more than he thought possible. Those feelings didn't fully emerge until he saw her, though. Bright and resourceful, she had fared well without his fatherly guidance. It hurt, but at least Matt knew she could handle anything. He felt extreme pride, even if he hadn't earned it.

The driveway sat empty. A single light shone from the kitchen, but he doubted anyone was in the house. He left the cornfield and ran for the farm.

As Matt entered the yard, an automobile approached. The car slowed, crunching into the driveway.

The barn stood in front of him, his best chance for shelter. He could hide in the barn until the person left. If it was a police officer, he'd come out, arms waving, white flag held high.

Before the car's headlights washed over him, Matt broke for the barn. He plunged past the splintered door, his feet landing on a thick blanket of hay. Pigs squealed at his intrusion, their cries bouncing off the walls.

A huge mistake.

He ran to the broken window and looked out.

Now where in the hell is Edwin?

The bastard might be planning to steal Peter's killing blows. Peter wouldn't stand for it. He had worked hard for that singular pleasure, and he fully intended to collect on it.

Peter gave the grounds a quick once-over. Nothing looked out of the ordinary—same old run-down house and land. He climbed the steps to the kitchen door and then stopped. Something sounded off.

He heard the usual clatter of farm life. Buzzing crickets. Something howling in the woods. Pigs shrieking in the barn. More raucously than usual, from what he recalled. Pigs only wail like that for two reasons—feeding time or slaughtering time. And there's always a human present for both events.

Someone's in the barn.

He plucked the knife out from his belt. Setting his goggles back into place, he stalked into the night, making his way toward the barn.

Matt watched Peter exit his car, his gait unsteady. His brother stiffened on the top kitchen step and turned around.

Matt's attempts to silence the pigs with manic hand gestures failed. He really should've known better, too, having grown up on a farm. The animals bounced off one another, raising holy hell and clattering into the wooden gates. He kicked the fence several times, hoping to chase them outside. Several pigs scurried out of a sawn-out hole in the barn's wall. Too late. The noise would surely draw Peter's attention.

Matt raced back to the window. Peter had vanished, but he knew his brother was coming for him.

Chapter Thirteen

Exhausted, unbelievably so, Shannon felt like she'd been on the run for days. Perched in a tree, however, seemed like the wrong venue for a nap. She let out a chuckle, short and forced. The best way to remain sane.

Underdressed in her t-shirt and jeans, she shivered in the breeze. The bough she sat on bobbed and swayed, bouncing her up and down. Goosebumps broke out on her arms.

Shannon freed one hand long enough to rub her arm. The tree limb sagged. Quickly, she wrapped both hands around it again.

For the first time since she left the cellar, Shannon had time to think. Especially about her father. *What is he doing here?* He said he was here to rescue her, but did she trust him? Truthfully? Some might call it paranoia, but honestly, she'd earned the right to feel this way. Practically earned a merit badge in paranoia after this night.

She shook her head, the tree limb jostling as if agreeing with her. No, her father's actions were definitely at odds with the others'. He'd left the gun with her, after all.

On the other hand, her father had abandoned her eight years ago. He had wanted nothing to do with her then. Mom told her he never wanted to see her again. Her father's new life didn't have a place for Shannon.

He was nothing but a total stranger to her. Suddenly, he shows up out of nowhere, trying to save her life. After eight years, was he trying to make amends? Did he just stupidly walk toward his death in an effort to save her life?

No. He's not getting off that easy.

He needed to explain *why* he'd been an absentee father. And he needed to know how she had retreated into herself during those long, miserable years. He had to understand the pain she felt, the guilt she carried. He was not going to die before he heard those words.

Shannon knew she had to return to the farmhouse.

She hated leaving behind the moonlight touching her through the tree-tops. In comparison, the heart of the woods looked pitch-black, overbearingly so. After losing her glasses, she couldn't see more than three feet in front of her. But in the woods, she saw only darkness.

Enough excuses. Get out of this damn tree.

She shifted the rifle strap over her head and tightened it across her chest. Extending one leg below her, she searched for a solid foothold. Her dangling foot left her feeling unsafe, inches from plummeting to the ground. She reached out and hugged both arms tightly around the trunk. With a deep breath, she hopped off the branch. Her legs swung against the trunk, and she immediately clasped them around it. Hugging the tree, she inched her way down, her toes her guide. She touched a stable branch. Dropping one foot upon it, she tested it by pushing down lightly. When it didn't break, she eased her other foot onto it. Shannon groped her way down the tree, applying the same search-and-conquer technique. The branches grew larger the farther down she traveled. The wind had all but died, and the limbs grew sturdier under her weight.

How had she managed to zip up the tree so fast? Pure adrenaline, she supposed, even though she didn't remember the climb up at all.

She slithered down the bottom part of the trunk, the limbs becoming more sparse, scraping her hands over the rough bark. Every inch or so, she stretched one leg out, hoping to find another limb. She must be nearing the bottom.

Shannon scrabbled down faster. Finally, she touched the ground. Planting her feet firmly, she stamped the leaf coverage, ensuring it wasn't a trick of the darkness. Solid ground. She leaned back against the trunk, relieved.

The darkness grew deeper, the air clammy and still. The airflow in front of her cut off. Almost stifling. She breathed in deeply. A familiar stench filled her nose. She felt an intense, almost palpable heat in front of her. Then she heard a gurgle.

Joshua loomed in front of her.

"Joshua? Joshua…remember me? Your friend?"

Joshua remained as still as the nightlife in the woods.

"That's right, Joshua. Your friend." Shannon edged away from the tree trunk. "I can help you, Joshua. I can get you away from your bad father. Get you some help—"

The blur of his arms rose swiftly above his head. He roared.

A rush of air brushed over Shannon as he reached for her. Grabbing her shoulders, he shook her like a sheet on laundry day. She knocked into the tree. His hands fell away. Stunned, she slipped off the trunk, rolling onto the ground. The rifle's strap caught around her arm. Joshua growled. The rifle pulled free. He hovered over her. She swung the rifle up, and jamming the barrel into his belly, she pulled the trigger. Joshua's shadow wavered above her like a drunken man. He let loose a moan before pitching to the ground with a *thump*. Shannon screamed.

Hurling the rifle behind her, she then jumped to her feet. She ran through the woods, hoping she was headed in the right direction. To find her father. And God help anyone who got in her way.

Tired of sitting, Edwin slid off the hood of his truck. He cupped his hand over his brow and squinted into the woods, a habit he picked up from those sunny days in the fields.

If his granddaughter was still out there, he hadn't heard nary a peep from her. She remained in hiding, a frightened rabbit. A miserable waiting game. Edwin hated waiting. He'd waited all his life, it seemed.

The gunshot blast startled Edwin. The gray hairs on his arms bristled. Bats fluttered into the sky, abandoning the woods. Joshua's bellow began low, grew, and climbed above the treetops. The girl's scream followed. Edwin had no idea how Joshua got hold of a gun—didn't know the boy even knew how to use one—but the hunt had ended. Confidence filled him that the boy had taken care of the girl, and he hoped the kid enjoyed his damn self doing it, too. He climbed into the truck and set his rifle next to him where Gretchen used to ride; the rifle was a much better companion.

Turning the truck around, Edwin swept his headlights through the woods one last time. He floored the gas, popping his truck over the ditch and onto the road. Even though his plan had hit a few snags along the way, the end was near.

Still, something nagged at him.

Earlier, he'd passed Peter lying in the road. Now, Peter and his car were both gone. The damn chicken-shit must've high-tailed it back to New York. But what was that other car doing there? He didn't have time to pay it no heed before. All four tires were flat. Peter's handiwork, no doubt. He just hoped the boy cleaned up all his messes before he left. Never leave a man's work to a boy.

But the car and its unaccounted-for driver still niggled, like a chicken scratching to get out of a henhouse.

Well, no matter. Once he got back to the farm, he'd just pack up and leave. For good.

From across the woods, Matt heard a single gunshot. Then, a beastly moan. Shannon's scream played out as the heart-freezing coda.

The gun report stopped him in his tracks. But he couldn't dwell on negative thoughts. Shannon had the rifle. She screamed after the gun went off, meaning she wasn't the gunshot victim. He had to have faith in this scenario. He had to.

Matt climbed over one of the slat fences. He wondered if that was how pigs felt—captive and awaiting their impending fate. He crawled through the hole in the wall. Better to be outside than trapped inside the barn.

Matt dropped to his knees and crawled across the enclosed pen. Trying to stay within the pig herd, he grabbed at them, but they raced off in other directions. Matt reached the outer fence. Looking at his mud-covered hands gave him an idea. He caked mud onto his face, his shirt, and his arms, camouflage for the night.

The pigs' squealing fury built up. As he pulled himself up using the fence for support, splinters pierced his hands.

"Hello, again, Mattie." Peter faced him on the opposite side of the fence. Brandishing a knife and wearing goggles, he looked like a giant insect with particularly nasty pincers.

Matt fell into the mud, scrabbling backward.

Peter climbed the fence. "You can run, but you can't hide, Matt. I know it's an old cliché, but honestly, it's true."

"Peter, why are you doing this?" Matt screamed, not caring who heard him anymore. "Why?"

Peter leaped agilely into the pen, always the athlete. "We really don't have time for a lengthy discussion now, Mattie."

"For God's sake, Peter! You're my brother. My protector. You—" Matt pulled himself out of the mud. He stared into Peter's eyes. "Peter, remember the last time we were here? In the barn?"

It took a minute for Peter to reply. "Yes."

"And do you remember what you told me?"

"I don't remember, no." But Matt knew he was lying…

After his father had soaked him with the hose, Matt dutifully stood where he'd been told to stay. Didn't have a choice in the matter. Of course, it was barbaric, absolutely so. But Edwin was his father. Love him or hate him, he felt duty-bound to show him respect.

Freezing, he rubbed his shoulders. The kitchen door quietly opened and closed. He cried with relief when he saw it was Peter, not Edwin returning to administer more punishment.

"P…Peter?"

"Here, Matt, take it." Peter draped a blanket around Matt's shoulders.

"Come on." He took Matt's hand, leading him to the barn.

"Stay the night in here. I'll get up before the ol' bastard and wake you so you can go back to where you're supposed to be." Peter handed him a chicken leg. "Eat it."

Matt wolfed down the chicken, then gnawed at the bone for the marrow. "Thanks."

"Matt, don't listen to him."

"What if he's right? What if I'm too stupid for college?"

"He's not right. You can do it."

"I don't know anymore. What if God means for me to stay here on the farm?"

"That's just what the bastard wants you to think, Matt. You need to do something for yourself. Make your life better. Go to college."

"You really think I can do it, Peter?" Matt's eyes lit up.

"Yes, I do." Peter squeezed his brother's hand. "I've made up my mind. I'm leaving soon."

"What will you do?"

"I don't know, but it sure as hell's gotta be better than this." Peter stood up, flicking hay from his jeans.

"Peter?"

"Yes?"

"I love you." Matt had never told Peter this before, but it was true. Peter appeared confused by the sentiment, various expressions passing over his face.

"I love you, too, Matt," Peter said to the ground. Then he fled the barn.

"'*I love you, too, Matt.*' That's what you said."

Peter shook his head and sighed. "Different planet, Mattie. What's in the past stays in the past. Things change. Now, it's just the present and *my* future that matters." He took a step toward Matt.

Matt turned and stumbled over a pig. His foot skated across the mud before he regained his balance. Peter laughed, his feet squelching in pursuit behind Matt.

Matt whirled. Reasoning didn't work. Nor did appealing to the brother he remembered from childhood. Time to fight for his life. Matt dropped into a squat, hands thrust out.

"Come on, Matt! You know you can't take me. Never could, never will. I mean, look at yourself."

"Maybe, maybe not. But I'm not going without a fight."

"Okay, then, let's do this, Mattie." Peter ripped off his goggles and tossed them to the ground, slashing the knife through the air. They circled one another, each waiting for the first move. Matt's feet were weighted down by the mud, sticking with each step.

Matt leaped. His weight took both of them tumbling down. Pigs scurried away from the fray. Matt grasped Peter's knife. His hand slipped along the blade, cutting deeply. Fighting through the pain, Matt clawed at Peter's hand again.

Peter landed a blow on Matt's chin. Stunned, he fell back. With his fingers wrapped around Matt's throat, Peter squeezed. Matt tore at Peter's face with his fingernails, drawing tears of blood across his cheeks. Peter straddled his brother then raised the knife. Matt blocked the knife's trajectory with his forearm. The tip of the knife bit into his flesh before sailing away. Peter flailed his hand about in the muck, searching for the knife. Then Matt punched him in the groin. Repeatedly.

Peter groaned. He rolled off, curling into a fetal position. Matt tried to stand but crashed back down. He crawled back into the barn; it was faster than trying to right himself. Behind him, Peter got to his feet and trudged through the mud, gaining speed.

Inside the dark barn, Matt sprang to his feet, slamming his face into the fence. His teeth cut into his lip. He clambered over it. Peter snagged his left foot, pulling him down. Matt kicked back with a satisfying connection. Peter yelped, releasing Matt's foot.

Matt groped blindly for the gate's latch. He managed to disengage it, then pulled the gate open. Standing behind it, Matt screamed, "Here, pig, pig, pig!" in the high-pitched manner his father had taught him. "Where, pig, pig, pig!" As the pigs thundered out of the barn, they rushed toward Peter. Peter collapsed beneath the rampage.

Matt fumbled his hand over the tool shelf. Moonlight from the window highlighted a handle in the corner. A rusty scythe, still very sharp. And deadly. Matt raised it and spun around to meet his brother.

Peter had found his knife. Pointing the mud-caked blade at Matt, he held out his other hand, fingers splayed.

"Don't make me do it, Peter!" cried Matt. "I will! Just let us go!"

"I'm sorry. I can't do that. It's too late." Peter lunged. Matt countered, lowering the scythe between them. Peter jumped again, pinning Matt against the window. With a whoosh, Matt brought the scythe down. He missed as Peter hopped back a step.

"Come on, Matt! Just drop the goddamn thing!"

Matt raised the scythe again. He pressed forward, forcing it down, hard. The metal sliced into flesh and bone. Three of Peter's fingers flew through the air. Blood sprayed over the hay-covered floor.

"Jesus Christ!" Pinpoints of light dotted Peter's peripheral vision. Numb, he stared at his hand. Nothing but a thumb and pinky finger remained. Nausea burned his stomach. Time stood still. Peter ridiculously thought of a chocolate fountain when he looked at his hand, the kind his wife loved. Three streams of dark chocolate gurgled down to the ground. Just not chocolate.

Awareness returned, sparked by fiery pain. Peter dropped to his knees. He moved fast, searching for his detached digits amongst the rampaging pigs. To his right, two pigs went at it snout to snout, fighting over one of his fingers.

"No! Jesus, God!" He plunged the knife again and again into one of the pigs. Its shrieks grew with each stab. The pig flopped over, the finger dropping from its maw. The other pig raced for the spoils of victory. Peter slit its throat. He moaned when he fished the masticated finger out of the pig's mouth. Nothing but a lump of bone and gristle. Peter ran his good hand across the ground. Unbelievably, the remaining fingers were intact.

Peter trembled, in shock. He ripped off his shirt and cut it in half. Cradling his two detached fingers in one-half of the shirt, he slid them into his pocket. With the other rag, he tied a makeshift tourniquet over his mauled hand. Blood seeped through the white cotton.

Matt crouched by the window, cradling his instrument of death.

"What have you done, Matt? What have you done?" Peter staggered out of the barn. His legs wobbled, threatening to give out. Behind him, he heard his brother heaving.

What if that fucking pig ate the finger that triggers my ignition? Peter fished his keys out of his pocket and opened the car door. He took his fingers out of his pocket and placed one in the auto-ignition device. *Nothing.* Peter cried. First time in many years. Sobbing loudly, he inserted the other detached finger into the compartment. The car turned over. Peter released a triumphant roar.

Okay, Peter, get yourself together. He laughed as he recognized the irony of the thought. Like Humpty-Dumpty, he needed to be put back together again.

He had to get to the hospital in Karlin as soon as possible. Maybe they could reattach his two fingers. Then he'd be on his way. Peter turned his car around. Blood ran down his arm and onto his leather interior.

Be careful. Think straight!

He had already concocted a scenario to tell the emergency room doctors. Farming accident, a no-brainer in these parts. And he'd need an alias. He'd burn his wallet on the way or toss it into the river. Knowing small towns, the doctors would work on his hand first before asking for insurance. Once patched up, he'd simply leave. Sneak out, if necessary, leaving nothing behind connecting him to the occurrences in Godwin, Kansas.

Life was over for "Peter Brookes." Time to "kill" his alter ego. Too many loose ends—his father, brother, niece. Just a matter of time before the authorities put it all together.

It was good to have a Plan B. Peter had several offshore accounts and enough assets to liquidate with a simple phone call. He could still live life as a very wealthy man. New identification would be easy enough to procure. He'd mastered it before. Leaving the country sounded like his best bet. The Caribbean might be nice this time of year.

Peter would never see his children or wife again. A blessing in disguise. *God's plan.*

He mustered a smile, ironically unaware of it.

His foot slipped off the gas pedal at the end of the driveway. The car ambled into the ditch, hit a telephone pole, and rattled to a stop. His head fell forward onto the steering wheel, the horn blaring into the night.

The Caribbean…

Chapter Fourteen

As soon as Edwin reached his driveway, he knew things had gone south. Peter's car sat in the ditch, the horn blasting to high hell. Edwin whipped the truck into the driveway and jumped out. Wrenching the car door open, he pulled his son's head off the horn. *Damned fool idiot!* Based on the amount of blood soaking the car's interior, Edwin reckoned him dead. Just another thing he'd have to tidy up. Even dead, Peter was a pain in his ass.

But if Joshua took care of his granddaughter, who had done this to Peter? Maybe Joshua? Edwin would be sure to fill Joshua's food bucket to the brim before he left tonight. A going-away gift for his son's fine work.

He gunned the truck toward the house. From the barn, the pigs raised a holy ruckus. And his damned dog wouldn't shut his yap.

By the dim light, Matt watched the pigs gnaw at their dead brethren.

He replayed the carnage repeatedly in his mind, a stomach-churning film loop. He'd never forget the look of shock on Peter's face—the *betrayal*—when he sliced off his fingers. Matt hadn't wanted to do it, but he had no other choice. Peter meant to kill him. And if Matt died, Shannon would die as well. Kill or be killed. Simple as that.

So why did he feel sick? He spent several minutes throwing up until he had nothing left to vomit.

Matt refocused. *Shannon.* The most important factor. He had to get her to safety. With the scythe clutched in one hand, he searched for Peter's knife. Nudging the pigs away with his elbow, his fingertips grazed over the knife's blade in the hay. He slid it into his pocket.

Then the car horn blasted, long and steady. Shannon trying to grab the attention of inexistent neighbors? He stumbled toward the barn entrance.

The car horn stopped. From the barn door, he watched Edwin's truck amble down the drive. The headlights flashed over the barn entrance, forcing Matt to jump back. Behind him, a growl, lower than the pig's squeals, emerged. *The hound dog.* The growl erupted into a rapid succession of barks.

Matt knelt. "Here, boy," he whispered. "Come here, boy." The barking continued. Matt jumped, forcing his weight on top of the dog, restraining it to the floor. "I'm sorry, boy. Just, shhh. Please…shhh." The dog nipped, hooking Matt's finger on a tooth. He managed to get a hand around the dog's jaw, holding it shut. The dog struggled, shaking its head. "Quiet, boy!" Matt scooted up, covering the dog's jaw with his chest. Although old, the dog bucked up against Matt before falling flat on its back. The dog shuddered. Matt pressed harder until the dog quit moving. He stayed in that position for a seeming eternity. He rolled off the dog. The dog's chest felt warm to the touch, unmoving. Matt's stomach heaved again as he blinked back tears. "I'm really sorry, boy." He stroked the dog's coat. "I'm sorry…"

Matt seethed with hatred. Peter's last words echoed in his mind. *What have you done to me, Matt?* Matt wanted to ask the same thing of his father. Before tonight, Matt respected all life. He used to move insects outside rather than swat them. But his father had reduced him to a killer. First, his brother, and now, an innocent animal.

I've come this far. It's time to finish it.

Covered in mud and blood, Matt stalked toward the farmhouse for the final showdown.

Finally, the dog stopped its yapping. Probably in a tizzy over Peter's car horn.

As he opened the kitchen door, Edwin froze in his tracks. In Godland, there'd never been any reason to lock up the house. But what about his money? What if the stranger from the abandoned car robbed him?

He heaved a sigh of relief when he saw the bag sitting on the kitchen floor. Stopping inside the doorway, he listened for sounds of an intruder. The linoleum squeaked beneath his feet as he took a few tentative steps. Other than that, he heard nothing but the usual settling of the house, small clicks and sighs and bad pipes in the walls.

But something filled him with tension. One of those feelings you can't quite put your finger on.

He raised his rifle and peered up the stairwell.

"Joshua? Joshua! You here, boy?" He waited. A heavy silence.

Where is that damned fool boy? He surely had time to make it back by now. Maybe he was indulging his manhood, having fun with his sister. Or what remained of her. Well, the boy sure had earned himself some recreation.

Originally, Edwin had planned to leave in the morning, before Joshua woke. Easier that way. Now that things had gone belly-up, he figured it best to err on the side of caution. Time to hasten his departure.

Edwin entered his bedroom. He pulled the solitary suitcase he and Gretchen owned from under the bed. Not like they'd ever used it before, either. It had been a wedding gift. The suitcase's lid cracked like a jag of lightning, cheap plastic material flaking off in his hands. But it would do just fine until Edwin reached Florida. Might even buy a new suitcase once there.

The kitchen door creaked open, then crept closed. Probably Joshua, but then again, since when did the dimwit *not* slam the door? He grabbed his rifle.

"What in the hell?" In the kitchen, covered in muck, the stranger's eyes nearly glowed white, crazed looking. Edwin cocked the gun and aimed. "Don't you move none, or I'll blow your fuckin' head off! Who are you? What do you want?" Scythe in hand, the intruder resembled the Grim Reaper. One last challenge sent from God.

The man placed the scythe by the stove, pulled out a chair, and sat quietly at the kitchen table. He craned his head, taking in the sights of the kitchen. "Hello, Father." His voice remained measured despite his hellish appearance.

Edwin lowered the rifle and cautiously approached the man. "What'd you say?"

"I said…Hello, Father."

Edwin thought he recognized the pathetic, weak voice but couldn't be certain. "Matthew?"

"That's right. It's Matt. I've returned to Godland."

"Well, I'll be tarred and feathered and dipped in shit." Doubled over laughing, he sat down at the opposite end of the table. "I'll be goddamned!"

"Yes, you will."

"What did you say, boy?"

Matt answered him with a blank stare.

Edwin swayed his hat through the air. "If this ain't a day for the books. This is one helluva family reunion." He slapped his knee, bringing up a wisp of dust. "What are you doing here? Where's Mary?" Bugging his eyes out, he playfully peeked underneath the kitchen table like a child.

Matt slammed his fists down on the table. "You ruined her!"

"You watch your mouth in my house, boy." An uneasy feeling crept over Edwin. A sense of menace. He swept the rifle up again. "Why're you here, Matthew?"

"I'm going to kill you, old man," Matt shot back. Grabbing the kitchen table, he upended it, sending dirty dishes clattering to the floor. Edwin's chair splintered as he crashed to the floor, a grotesque piñata. Matt landed on top of him, along with the table. Even with his arms restrained, Edwin managed to hold onto the rifle. But he couldn't edge it out to kill his son. *Yet.*

Matt pressed down on the table, attempting to crush the life out of his father. No regrets. He had walked into the house where he'd grown up intending to kill his father. Once you've walked through hell, murder didn't seem so bad.

"Wait…a…minute…boy," croaked Edwin. "Let…me…explain."

"Too late." Edwin put up a surprisingly solid fight. But he'd always been a strong bastard.

"I can…give…you *money!* Lots and lots…of money…"

Matt stopped. He eased up, keeping his hands firmly on the table. "What do you mean?" Against his better judgment, curiosity drew him in.

"Get this goddamn table off me and I'll tell you."

Matt slid the table roughly off Edwin's face, ensuring his arms remained pinned. "Talk."

"Look in the bag by the stove."

Matt glanced over at the stove. Nestled between the refrigerator and the stove sat a burlap bag. Green bills spilled from the top.

"I'll give you half that money—two-hundred-and-fifty-thousand dollars." His initial cough turned into a laugh.

Matt considered. It would be a way out of his financial problems. But how did Edwin come by this kind of cash? He had always been dirt poor.

"Where'd you get the money? Tell me." Matt suspected the answer, but he needed his father to say it.

"That ain't important, right now. *Son.*"

Matt's hatred for Edwin spiked. And clarity washed into his mind like a tidal wave. He suddenly understood Peter's motivations. Peter was merely fulfilling the blood lust his father had bred into him. Mentally unstable, but understandable. But his father—he'd done this for money. Shame washed over Matt for having even contemplated taking the blood money.

Behind Matt, the kitchen door crashed open. Shannon screamed, "Dad!" Matt whipped around. The table slid from underneath him. Edwin scrabbled away like a wrinkled, red crab.

Shannon ran to Matt's side. Momentarily distracted, Matt turned his attention back to his father. Edwin, now on the living room floor and aiming with one eye closed, pointed the rifle at Matt. Matt dove in the opposite direction, trying to draw fire away from Shannon. A blast ripped through the small room. Gunshot tore through Matt. Immense pain set his body on fire before he collapsed.

Shannon watched her father twist in the air and drop to the floor. "Dad! Oh, God!"

The old man appeared shaken for a moment. He swung his rifle toward her. Shannon froze. Her grandfather leered, his green teeth nearly incandescent.

Matt stirred. "No!" Clutching his side, he dragged himself across the kitchen floor.

Edwin shifted the rifle back toward Matt. Matt scooted across the room on all fours. He wrenched up Edwin's gun-bearing arm.

Shannon scanned the kitchen, looking for a weapon. Her gaze locked onto the rusty scythe. It scraped the floor with a teeth-jarring sound when she hefted it up. She ran toward the wrestling men.

Another explosion filled the house, plaster and dust falling from the ceiling. A curl of smoke rose from the gun. Shannon stood by with the scythe, ready to use it, but hoping she wouldn't have to.

Her father grinned. An unsettling grin. "You're out of bullets now, old man. Now what are you gonna do?" Matt seized the rifle and flung it aside. Edwin lay back, exhausted. Matt straddled his father's chest.

"Get offa me, you little bastard!"

Her father said nothing. But his smile reminded Shannon of the old man's death grin.

"If thine eye offends thee, pluck it out!" Edwin thrust his thumbs into Matt's eye sockets. Matt shook his head rapidly until the old man's thumbs slipped away.

"Vengeance is mine, sayeth the Lord," countered Matt. His hands closed around the old man's throat, his fingers tightening. Edwin's face reddened. His boots thrashed on the floor, a supine tap dancer. His eyes bulged; Matt released Edwin's throat, pulled his head up by the ears, and slammed it onto the floor.

Shannon forced herself to look away. She didn't know what to do. What to feel. She didn't want her father to murder. Yet, her grandfather deserved to die. She wanted the old man dead. And those feelings filled her with darkness.

"This is for what you did to my daughter and her friend!" screamed her father. "This is for Mary!" He slammed Edwin's head down with each breath he took. "This is for Mom! For me! Even for Peter! All the lives you ruined! Rot in hell!"

When the yelling stopped, Shannon braved a look. Matt sat on top of the old man, his hands again wrapped around Edwin's throat. His breathing wheezed in through his mouth, blasted out from his nose. A bloodstained butterfly spread its wings down the side of his shirt.

The old man lay still. His eyes closed and his mouth gaped open. Yet, Shannon saw his chest moving up and down.

He's still alive. Mixed feelings over the old man's life disturbed her. But she finally allowed herself to relax. Tension fled her. *It's finally over.* She dropped the scythe on the couch. *It's over, my God, it's over.* Retreating to a corner of the room, she crumpled to the floor. She curled up, drawing her knees close to her. Squeezing her eyes shut, she welcomed tears of relief. Cool, life-affirming tears.

The sound of a freight train filled the room, jolting her alert. She held her hands over her ears, praying for a nightmare. Anything but frightening reality.

She watched as her father crashed into the wall above her and slid down to the sofa.

Joshua. Alive and not happy.

Matt had no recollection of the preceding several minutes. Everything had been a blur. Rage had overtaken him with staggering abandon. His vision had slipped out of focus, sharp circles of brightness blinking in and out. The only thing that mattered was protecting his daughter. Like a tiger protecting his cub.

Once his vision cleared, he noticed Shannon holding the scythe, nearly as tall as her. She stared at him, yet she didn't *see* him. He felt this, knew it with sudden lucidity. In her eyes, he witnessed horror. The murder he was going to commit.

Matt relaxed his grip from his father's throat. Sweat loosened the dirt on his face into running streaks of grime. He winced when he touched the bullet wound below his ribs.

The front door cracked open followed by loud, heavy footfalls. A horrible bellow suddenly filled the room. The windowpanes rattled as the primordial roar thundered. Large, filthy hands grabbed Matt off of his father and flung him across the room, his face hitting the wall. Dazed, he heard Shannon yell.

"Joshua! No! He's good! Good!"

Matt turned over onto his back. "Oh, my God." Easily six-and-a-half feet tall and wider than the doorway, Joshua, his brother, loomed over him. Blood stained his t-shirt. Whimpering like a child, he stared at Shannon.

"He's good, Joshua." She'd gotten up and now held the scythe high above her small shoulders. "He's your…brother."

Joshua swiveled toward Matt. His lower lip bobbed. He approached Matt, who lay half-twisted on the sofa, and nudged his curled-up hand in Matt's direction.

"That's right," she said while inching closer behind Joshua. "He's your brother." Blood gushed over one of Matt's eyes, tinting the room with red. He shut the eye and shifted his good one between Shannon and Joshua.

"He's your brother. He's good." Shannon's words remained friendly, but the raised scythe spoke her true intent.

Joshua's half-lucid gaze fell upon Edwin on the floor. Attempting to form words, Joshua's frustrated whimper rose to a shriek. He lunged at Matt. Matt rolled onto the floor while Joshua stumbled into the sofa.

"Joshua! No!" Shannon buried the scythe into Joshua's back. His anguished howl was not human. Shannon struggled to extricate the scythe from him. When her hands slipped off the handle, she fell onto the floor.

Matt pulled his daughter to her feet. His body burned. One eye remained virtually useless, a fiery red eye patch disorienting him. Didn't matter. "Come on!" He thought of the bedroom upstairs he used to share with Peter. They could lock themselves in there until help arrived.

Joshua's moaning followed them to the stairwell. Leaping two stairs at a time, they reached the top.

Oh, God. The lock was on the outside of the door.

Matt kicked the door open just as Joshua entered the stairwell. Matt pulled Shannon into the room and slammed the door. He thrust his hand toward the door lock, finding nothing there, as he feared. He barricaded the door with his back, wedging the heels of his feet against the floor. Joshua pounded up the stairs. He pushed then slammed his fists. Matt nearly fell as Joshua battered the door at his back. *Craaaaack!* The door splintered, but Matt stood firm.

Shannon stood in the center of the room, arms shaking at her sides. The room stank of human waste, decay, and death. She gagged, resisting the urge to heave.

Matt flipped the light switch several times to no effect.

"Shannon. Search the room. A phone…anything." Joshua's attack intensified. Matt felt each thump hammering straight into his throbbing bullet wound.

"Just…a mattress, a bucket…some clothes…"

Matt buckled from another strong thrust. Joshua's unearthly howls continued unabated. Above Matt, a piece of paneling flew into the room. A few more bashes and that would be it. Then the door would fly into pieces.

"Maybe hit him with the bucket?" Shannon's voice remained calm, yet Matt felt her underlying terror.

As he touched his wound again, Matt's hand fell across something in his pocket. *Peter's knife!*

Matt waved the knife at Shannon. "Shannon, when I open the door, distract him."

Shannon crossed the room, stopping in front of the boarded-up window. A tiny sliver of moonlight slipped in behind her, silhouetting her.

"Ready?"

She nodded, ready for battle.

Matt jumped away from the door. He twisted, pressing his back against the wall next to the hinges. The door smashed open, falling to the floor with a *bang.* Joshua, now quiet, stood unmoving in the doorway. Shannon shivered by the window, so tiny, within the large, bare room. Light from the stairwell fell on her, a spotlight capturing her. Joshua's target.

"Joshua? It's me, your friend, Shannon."

Joshua took a step forward. His shadow filled the rectangle of light on the floor.

"That's right, Joshua. Shannon. Joshua, your father's alive."

Joshua took several lumbering steps in and then stopped. The light behind Joshua glinted off the scythe planted in his back.

"Yes, Joshua. He's alive."

Matt pushed off the wall and drove the knife into Joshua's chest. Joshua's mouth dropped open as he stumbled backward. Joshua grabbed the knife handle, swinging his other fist at Matt. Matt sidestepped the blow. He jammed the knife in deeper. Joshua swatted at Matt, this time connecting. Matt crashed to the floor. Joshua yanked out the blade; blood spurted from the wound and spilled onto the floor. He raised the knife over Matt, roaring, ready to strike.

"No, Joshua!" Shannon ran toward the behemoth, barreling into him. She bounced off, dropping next to Matt. Joshua staggered, teetering in the open doorway. Another step backward, and he tumbled loudly down the stairwell.

Matt crawled to the doorway and peered over the top step. Joshua lay splayed at the bottom of the stairs, one leg twisted unnaturally. The scythe, pitching a tent beneath him, raised his chest. Blood pooled onto the floor.

And still, he moaned.

Matt found the bloody knife and grabbed it tightly. He crawled back to his daughter and draped his arm around her shoulders. They huddled together, sobbing, waiting. Joshua's groans continued, crawling up the stairs toward them. Matt discerned a repeated pattern in his grotesque vocals. After a while, it came clear to Matt's ears.

"Daddy. Daddy. No. Daddy," Joshua seemed to be saying.

Shannon cupped her hands over her ears. Joshua's mewling sounded like a sick baby crying for his mother. She felt a heavy sadness and empathy for Joshua. An innocent corrupted by his sick father.

"Dad? We've got to help him." She was realistic, starkly so. Joshua's life couldn't be saved, not with the injuries he sustained. But she didn't want him to suffer. Not any more than he already had.

Her father winced when he swallowed. "You're right." With great effort, he pulled himself to his feet. "I'll help him." Three words of mercy. They both understood.

He shuffled out the door, falling into the jamb before righting himself. The stairwell light fell upon his once-white shirt, now nearly completely red.

Shannon hugged her knees tighter and listened. She heard a clump. Did he fall? "Dad?"

"I'm okay, honey…just gonna take me a while to get…down the steps." His voice sounded weak, Joshua's cries drowning him out.

Another series of clumps followed. Not footsteps. Sliding down the steps on his rear end.

Joshua's moaning finally stopped. No death rattle. Nothing anti-climactic. It just stopped.

"Shannon?" His voice sounded a mile away.

Shannon ran to the top step. Her father sat next to Joshua's still body. "It's okay, now, honey. Joshua's no longer suffering."

She bit down on her knuckles, tired of crying. But she wanted to cry for Joshua. In his own way, he was as much a victim as she was. Or Lindsay. She let it out. To her ears, her sobbing sounded strangely reminiscent of Joshua's moans. They were family, after all.

"Honey? You okay? Shannon? I don't think I can make it up the… stairs again. But…it's safe for you to come down."

Shannon didn't want to look. She really didn't. But she stole a glance anyway. Joshua's dead eyes were open. She imagined him staring up at her. One leg folded impossibly behind him. A red smile opened up his throat, spilling blood everywhere. Impaled into the floor next to him was the knife. Shannon sprang over his body, her stomach hopscotching after her. After a few false starts, her father climbed to his feet.

From the living room, she heard a wheezing sound. An unhealthy sound. She peeked into the room.

"You…son-of-a-bitch. Gonna…kill you." Edwin's arms lay still as his shoulders rocked back and forth with each breath. Even though his words were threatening, he wouldn't bother them anymore. He just didn't know it yet.

Matt glowered at the old man. "Shannon, go to the bedroom and call nine-one-one. The farm's address should be on the mail by the phone, and don't come out 'til I tell you to."

"No…good…ingrate…" The old man coughed.

"Go, Shannon. I have unfinished business." She knew what he was going to do. And it filled her with immense satisfaction.

Matt picked up a sofa pillow and sat down upon his father's chest. The vile, evil monster's chest.

He ruined every life he touched. In fact, had it not been for his father, Matt wouldn't have been a killer. But now he was a murderer. Simply put, Edwin didn't deserve to live.

Matt looked into his father's hate-filled eyes one final time. He pressed the pillow down onto his face. Matt felt the life leave his father just like he'd felt that of the poor dog earlier. And he felt much more empathy—compassion, even—for the dog.

But he had one last thing he wanted to say to Edwin. Matt pulled the pillow away and leaned close to his father's ear.

"By the way, Dad," Matt whispered, "I'm a goddamned faggot." Matt sat up to gauge Edwin's reaction. His eyes bulged in horror. His tongue licked at the air, gasping for oxygen. Matt smiled. He replaced the pillow and finished the job. "Welcome to Godland, Dad."

Then he lost consciousness.

Chapter Fifteen

Matt woke up in a hospital bed, tubes running out his nose and an IV drip attached to his arm. A mound of bandages covered his side. His mouth tasted like dirt. He felt weak and disoriented. But *alive*. Something that had seemed out of the realm of possibility a short time ago.

Shafts of sunlight spiked into the room through Venetian blinds. Dust danced and swirled in the sun's rays. It seemed an age since he'd last seen sunlight.

Looking around for evidence of visitors, he saw only medical equipment. No flowers, no cards. No purses abandoned for a coffee run. Disappointment set in. He'd hoped Shannon would be here. But he was alone, just as isolated as he'd felt through most of the previous night.

And what about Jason? Had anyone bothered calling him? He was probably frantic by now.

Matt fumbled for the call button and pressed it. After a few minutes, a serious-faced woman entered the room.

"I see you're awake, Mister Strothers," she huffed. She strode across the room and pulled the tube out of Matt's nose.

"Water? Ice chips?" Matt didn't recognize his own voice. A stranger in an even stranger land.

"Certainly. You've had quite a night." The nurse didn't smile. Her usual demeanor, he wondered, or was there something more to it?

"Where am I?"

"Karlin Memorial Hospital." She checked his IV. "You're lucky. The bullet entered and exited your body without hitting any organs." She handed Matt a paper cup full of ice chips. He devoured them greedily. "Someone's been very anxious to speak to you." With a squeak, she turned on her white sneakers and left the room.

Matt tried to sit up but lost the battle. He flopped back into bed but was fully inflated with hope.

Shannon, maybe. Or did they get hold of Jason?

A tall, elderly man with a long face sauntered in. He took off his sheriff's hat and held it reverentially in front of him.

"Mister Strothers? I'm Karlin Sheriff, James Tewkesbury."

Matt nodded. Not the company he had hoped for. He really wanted—*needed*—to see Shannon. She probably didn't want to see him, though. He imagined Shannon viewed him as nothing but a painful reminder of his abandonment and the previous night's horrors.

The sheriff gave Matt a half-cocked grin. He cast his eyes about the room, exhaling deeply before speaking. "So, just what in the hell happened last night?"

Matt wondered the same thing. Just what in hell had happened? How had he found himself in such a surrealistic nightmare? Now, within the safe confines of a hospital bed, it seemed so distant, a half-remembered fever dream. Matt opened his mouth to speak but found no words. He lay there gasping before the tears started.

"Uh, I'll come back after you're better rested, Mister Strothers." The sheriff hurried out the door.

Matt cried himself to sleep.

True to his word, the sheriff returned several hours later. Matt had taken advantage of the break to marshal his thoughts. Should he sugarcoat his involvement in the deaths of his family? No. Best to tell the truth. At least, as much as he understood.

"How about the girl, Sheriff?" Matt asked. "Lindsay? Is she okay?"

"I'm afraid she passed away last night, Mister Strothers." The sheriff shook his head. "It was touch and go for a while there, but she eventually lost the fight."

Matt swallowed, his throat on fire. The death toll had risen again. "Is my daughter okay?"

"Yep, nothing more than bruises, scratches, and cuts. And, of course, she's shook up." He paused and frowned. "I'm having a real hard time putting together what went on last night, Mister Strothers." He sat next to Matt, scribbling on a yellow legal tablet.

"I'll help as much as I can." Matt told the sheriff everything he could remember from when the Kansas City detective visited him until he killed his father. He told him how he went to Godwin to save his daughter and ended up killing four people and a dog. Matt surprised himself by how cavalierly he described the murders. He spoke of the bag of money that, to his knowledge, still sat in the farmhouse. He held back nothing, made no excuses. Didn't even proclaim self-defense. No more running and hiding. He would accept the consequences.

"Good Lord," the sheriff said quietly. He stared at Matt, waiting for some form of corroboration. Matt remained silent. "That's some family you have, Mister Strothers."

"Had," responded Matt.

"Excuse me?"

"*Had.* That's some family you *had,* Mister Strothers."

"Yes, well…" The sheriff stood up and stretched. "At least you've been more helpful than your brother. He hasn't said diddly squat."

"What?"

"Your brother, Peter Brookes," said the sheriff, consulting his legal pad.

"He's *alive?*"

"Yep. Hard to believe, ain't it?"

Matt closed his eyes, stunned. "I have to see him."

Peter rolled over in bed, staring at his bandaged hand. The doctors told him they were unable to reattach the two fingers the damned pigs didn't devour. If he'd gone to a real hospital, in a real city, he'd be plus two digits again.

Shitty hospital run by rednecks and hicks can't cure a common cold.

Frankly, he shouldn't be alive at all. The last thing he remembered was trying to drive his car out of the driveway. A vague recollection, at best. When he came to in the hospital bed, the previous night had seemed like a dream. Until he saw his bandaged hand. Everything looked quite a bit different now after wallowing in a pigsty at night, fighting his brother for his life.

Upon awakening, his first visitor had been the county sheriff. Peter couldn't think straight enough at the time to cover his tracks, so he kept his mouth shut. He needed time to concoct a story. Prison, simply, was not an option. He'd grown up in a veritable prison. From those ashes, he had built a good life for himself, free to do whatever he pleased. He wouldn't forego that freedom. At any cost. He just couldn't live that way.

And really, he wondered, what *could* they pin on him? It probably depended on who survived the night. If no one lived, he could easily lie his way out of his involvement. He hadn't killed anyone, after all. His best interests lay in saying nothing until he found out what happened to everyone else. He'd fake a PTSD scenario until the full story emerged.

The more the sheriff probed, though, the more it became clear that Matt and his daughter were still alive. His chances of freedom seemed slim. Would Matt be open to coercion? They could easily blame this all on Edwin. Peter chuckled at his own naivety. Altar boy Mattie would never go for it.

The fact he had more money than practically anyone worked in his favor. Gave him a comfort margin. Surely, he could buy a fleet of top-notch lawyers. Get off on a technicality perpetuated by the expensive shysters he owned. It'd be a walk in the park to rip apart the prosecuting attorneys in this shithole town. His best shot.

Barring this, Peter decided he would take his own life. Suicide seemed preferable over an existence in prison.

Peter let out a long sigh. How unfair that his milquetoast, weakling brother brought him down. Peter had conquered financial empires, bedded unattainable starlets, ate the finest foods, and purchased the most expensive automobiles available. And his mild, meek brother brought him down with a lucky swing of a scythe. The same brother he tried to help, teach, and even protect. The brother to whom he once—a lifetime ago—professed his love.

The sheriff appeared initially reluctant to let Matt visit Peter but finally relented under the stipulation a police officer would be present. Matt told the sheriff it was just fine by him.

Before Matt saw Peter, he called Jason. As expected, Jay had worked himself up into a frenzy. Matt pleaded with him to stay home, but he wouldn't take no for an answer. As soon as their conversation had ended, Jay hit the road. Matt deliberately downplayed his role in the carnage. He didn't want Jason thinking differently of him. He worried Jason might leave him once the entire story came out.

Matt felt numb. He suffered no guilt. Maybe the full realization of what he did would strike him later. Or had he become immune to feeling any-thing after his ordeal?

But Matt would do it all over again if it meant saving his daughter's life.

Goddamn straight.

The dour nurse helped Matt get into a wheelchair. In the hallway, an armed police officer sat outside his room, tilted back in a chair. On the third floor, another officer stood by a closed door.

"I'll take it from here, nurse." The police officer dismissed her with a wave of his hand.

"Fine," she said. "But you ring me when he's ready to go back to his room."

The officer nodded and held open the door, and the nurse wheeled

Matt in. Peter lay in bed, facing the window.

Matt took in a deep breath. "Peter."

Peter rolled over. His eyes were glassy as if he hadn't slept in days, his face haggard. "Matt."

"I'm surprised you're alive."

"I am, too." He held up his bandaged hand. "But three-fingers-less alive."

"You deserve worse than that. What kind of fair world is it that you survived and Lindsay died?"

Peter chuckled, mirthless and world-weary. "Mattie…Matt, how can you still think it's a 'fair' world?"

"I guess I don't. Not anymore. You pretty much saw to that, didn't you?"

Peter shot him a glare. "No, big brother. I'm not responsible for your beliefs. Never have been, never will be."

"Peter, I asked you this before, but you didn't give me an answer. Why? Why'd you do it?"

Peter fell silent before answering. "I did it for the thrill, Matt. The absolute thrill of the ultimate hunt. I wanted to experience the power of taking a human life." He waved his intact hand. "But that all changed. I suppose if you need a reason, I don't know. Chalk it up to fate, I guess."

"Fate," repeated Matt.

"Fate. How else can you explain why we all ended up there last night? One big, unhappy, dysfunctional family gathered one last time to hunt one another? Or do you still believe in God, Matt? Do you think God gathered us all together?"

"I don't know what I believe anymore. Maybe it was God. Maybe God sent me there to do what I had to do—to protect my daughter."

"Oh, and what kind of God would do that, Matt? A kind and loving God? A God that would allow so much unhappiness and death?"

They both sat quietly until the police officer cleared his throat, reigniting their uncomfortable reunion.

"Peter? Do you feel any remorse? Any whatsoever?" asked Matt.

"No, not really. I didn't kill anyone."

Matt said nothing. His brother's words pierced like a knife to the heart.

Yet, Matt felt great relief. Unlike his brother, he *did* feel remorse. Nearly human again.

"How's your daughter, Matt?"

"I've been told she's fine."

"That's good. I really didn't want her involved in this."

"But you did involve her, you bastard!" The officer jolted to attention, placing his hand on his holstered pistol. "You meant to kill her."

"Yes, well." Peter furrowed his brow as if weighing the previous night's events. "Tell me, Matt, what *did* happen to dear, old father?"

"I killed him."

"Good for you, Mattie. I'm actually surprised—and *proud* of you." For a brief instant, Matt remembered the caring brother who had helped him years ago when his father abused him. The brother who had once inspired him to better himself. But the moment faded like mist.

"I'm not. I'm not proud of myself."

"You know he made me the way I am, don't you?" asked Peter.

"That's bullshit, Peter. He was a horrible person, and he tainted everyone around him. But I'm not like you. I refuse to let him ruin me. You need to accept responsibility for your actions. You said you're not responsible for my beliefs, so don't throw blame on that old bastard either. We choose who we are."

"Oh, I'm beginning to think you're more like me than you realize."

"We're done here." Matt wheeled around. "Officer, would you get the door for me, please?"

The officer held the door open as Matt rolled away.

"I *am* proud of you, Matt," repeated Peter.

Matt stopped at the door. "Rot in hell, Peter."

As Matt left, he heard his brother mutter under his breath, "Yeah, I suppose I will."

Shannon sat on the empty hospital bed, dreading the impending encounter. She thought she'd feel more satisfaction. It had been a long time coming, after all. Instead, anxiety washed over her. But there was no backing down now. She deserved answers. She had *earned* them. She had suffered a childhood filled with self-doubt, loathing, and anger. Why?

Her father needed to accept accountability for his actions. Yet, she felt physically and mentally drained, unsure if she was up to the challenge.

Last night, after Shannon called 9-1-1, she had returned to the living room. Her father lay unmoving next to Edwin's dead body. Racing to his side, she shook him. She found a faint pulse. Barely there.

Unable to stay in the nightmarish house, she snagged the knife by Joshua's body and waited outdoors. Freezing and miserable, yet *free*. Freedom tasted sweet.

She checked her father every five minutes until the ambulances showed up.

Flashing red lights brightened the driveway. She ran out to meet them, waving the knife above her head. A patrol officer jumped out of his car and yelled, "Drop it!" She released the knife and threw her arms around the officer's neck, blubbering incoherently about dead people and murderers.

The medics carted her father off on a stretcher. The police asked Shannon incessant questions, but she didn't hear them, not really. At first, when she demanded to ride in the ambulance with her father, they nixed the idea. But after what she'd been through, it was a minor battle, nothing she couldn't handle. On the way to the hospital, she'd held his hand, squeezing it, willing life into him.

Shannon asked the paramedic about Lindsay. He assured her he knew nothing but would call. After a hushed radio conversation, he told Shannon she was still in surgery. But the look on the paramedic's face told her a different story. She fell back, crying, calling out Lindsay's name.

At the hospital, Shannon stumbled out of the ambulance into the waiting arms of a nurse, who assisted her into a wheelchair.

"Dad!" She fought the nurse who tried to restrain her.

"Shhh, honey," said the nurse, "we're going to take good care of him."

Shannon had another half-memory of a police officer badgering her, but she couldn't speak, couldn't think. Attempting to patch together the night's events proved an impossible task. The endless circus of police officers, nurses, and paramedics swirled into vague impressions, blending into a homogenous mess. Before Shannon finally gave in to the night, she remembered telling a policewoman about Gavin, the sweet boy in Barton, Kansas.

When she woke up the following morning, her mother sat next to her. She hugged Shannon too tightly, applying loving pressure to her bruises and cuts. Her mother verified what Shannon already knew about Lindsay. Shannon fell into another crying fit, unable to stop. Her friend—the only person who'd made the last eight miserable years of her life better—was gone, forever.

Shannon's mother kept the police at bay. When they pushed harder, her mother demanded the doctor order the police away. They weren't the only ones Shannon's mother forbade her to see.

"How's my dad?"

"He's going to live, if that's what you mean."

"Mom, I know you're not going to like this—"

"Yes?"

"I need to talk to him. To Dad."

Shannon's mother ran her fingers over the bed's railing, averting her gaze.

"I just want to get some answers, Mom. Some closure—"

"I'd prefer it if you didn't."

"I'm sorry, but I have to." Shannon could be a bulldog as well. She *wasn't* backing down.

Her mother's eyes moistened. "I suppose there's no stopping you."

"No."

"Just don't say I didn't warn you. You might not like what you hear."

Her mother's words filled her with an unexpected dread, nearly as frightening as the night before.

"Fine." *Bring it,* she wanted to add but didn't.

"You have another visitor, Mister Strothers," said the nurse. Matt knew Jason couldn't have traveled that fast.

Upon rolling into his room, he saw Shannon sitting on his bed, hands folded in her lap.

"Dad?" She wore fresh clothing, but her glasses were still missing. Bandages lined her arms, and scrapes blemished her face.

Matt extended his arms toward her. She pulled away.

"You know how happy I am to see you?" Matt's voice cracked, another welcome thawing of his emotions. "I would've thought you'd be back in Kansas City by now."

"Mom didn't want me to see you, but…it's like you said last night. I have unfinished business."

Matt didn't remember saying it at first. Then it hit him. When he killed Edwin. "Okay. Listen, Shannon—"

"What?"

"I'm truly sorry about your friend, Lindsay." Again, Matt reached out for her.

She knocked his hands away with a sweep of her arm. "Lindsay," she sobbed, rocking herself. Matt watched, not knowing what to do.

"Why did you abandon me, Dad?" she asked quietly.

"I…I didn't abandon you, Shannon—"

"Yes, you did. You totally did." She shook her fists at him. "I was eight years old. Eight years old! For the last eight years, I didn't hear a word from you." Tears traveled down her scratched cheeks. "Mom said you didn't want me anymore."

"That's not true, Shannon." But Matt knew—even if not by choice—he *had* abandoned her. He hadn't fought to keep her in his life. "I've always wanted you in my life. I've never stopped caring about you—"

"Helluva funny way of showing it."

"Shannon, I was weak. I admit that. I had some…emotional issues… some problems. Your mother got a restraining order against me to stop me from seeing you. I didn't have a choice."

"Bullshit. You always have choices. You need to accept responsibility."

Startled by the similarity to the conversation he'd just had with Peter, Matt knew she was right. Absolutely right.

"I agree, Shannon. I'm sorry. It was wrong of me. I should've fought tooth and nail to see you. It's just that, at the time—" Matt stopped himself before he could hide behind another excuse. "I'm sorry."

"Was it me? Was it something I did? Did you…not love me?" The words crushed Matt. His daughter—so strong, so brave last night—retreated into herself.

"No. Of course not." He wheeled himself closer. Hesitantly, he reached out a hand to her shoulder. This time she didn't pull away. Crying, she hid her face in her hands. "I've always loved you, Shannon. Always will. My biggest regret is that I missed out on those eight years of your life."

"I've always wondered if it was me."

"Of course it wasn't you." Matt unleashed the tears he held back. He pulled her close into an embrace. "I love you…always."

"Is it true?" She pushed him away to look into his eyes. "Did you leave us for another woman?"

Matt's eyes widened even while resisting a chuckle. Probably not the best response. "Um, no, not exactly. No, I didn't leave your mother…well… for anyone." Shannon eyed him suspiciously. Obviously, Cheryl had never told their daughter he was gay. Cheryl must have viewed the shame in having a gay husband far worse than their daughter blaming herself for their destroyed marriage.

"Your mother and I were unhappy together. You must have seen it when you were younger."

"Yes."

"When you reached sixteen, I was going to try and establish a relationship with you again. When I could. I just never thought it would've happened like it did last night."

"Yeah, that wasn't an ideal father–daughter reunion." To Matt's surprise, Shannon flashed a heart-melting smile.

"No, it wasn't." They shared a cathartic laugh.

"I do truly, truly apologize, Shannon. It was wrong. I know I can't make it up to you, but can we start over? Can we *try?*"

Shannon sat quietly.

"Give me one more chance. Please. I love you."

"Okay." She buried her face in her father's chest. "I love you, too."

ABOUT THE AUTHOR

Stuart R. West is a lifelong resident of Kansas, which he considers both a curse and a blessing. It's a curse because…well, it's Kansas. But it's great because… well, it's Kansas. Lots of cool, strange and creepy things happen in the Midwest, and Stuart takes advantage of them in his work. Call it "Kansas Noir." Stuart writes thrillers tinged with horror and horror tinged with thrillers, both for adult and young adult audiences. He writes at the crossroads of horror and sneaky humor. *Godland* is Stuart's sixth book with Grinning Skull Press. Stuart spent twenty-five years in the corporate sector and now writes full time. He's married to a professor of pharmacy (who greatly appreciates the fact he cooks dinner for her every night) and has a twenty-seven-year-old daughter who's still deciding what to do with her life. But that's okay. It took him twenty-five years to figure that out.

Stuart's blog can be found at http://stuartrwest.blogspot.com/

Drop in on him at Facebook at: https://www.facebook.com/stuartrwestwriter

"Heart-stopping horror infused with page turning suspense."
--Russell James, author of Dark Inspiration and Q Island
DREAD AND BREAKFAST
Stuart R. West

Chapter One

"*Why* are you *doing* this?" The chains binding her wrists drew taut as she lurched forward. Her chin cracked down onto cement, triggering her bladder. Urine warmed her legs. Dignity didn't matter, not anymore. Nothing made sense. As she dragged her locked hands toward her, she pushed up on her knees. Pleading, her last hope. "*Please* don't do this, oh God, please don't hurt me. Just … tell me *why*."

Two figures stepped in front of the floodlight. Joined at the hip, hands entwined like lovers on a stroll.

A dry voice, crisper than crackers, said, "Why? Because it's date night."

The hatchet swung down, delivering date night's goodnight kiss.

❇ ❇ ❇

Snow swirled in the wind, dropping like feathers. Rebecca knew a storm had been forecast, hardly good driving weather. But she wasn't about to let up. Not 'til she put Hollington far behind her and then some. Dangerous? Absolutely. But navigating through a snowstorm sure as hell felt a lot safer than what she'd left behind.

The wipers beat the windshield, struggling to clear it. Snow piled on the hood. Rebecca brushed a hand through the condensation and hunkered down to peer out the narrow opening. She cursed herself for not getting the Chevy's defrost fixed; it never had worked worth a damn. Of course, she also didn't think she'd be fleeing for her life during what one weatherman had gleefully called "the Storm of the Century." Maybe she should've thought this out better. Should've, would've, could've; the old game she'd been playing a lot lately.

She glanced at Kyra, sound asleep. The seatbelt looked tight, confining her daughter's small frame. Kyra's stuffed dog rode with her, the safety belt covering its mouth, its eyes: say nothing, see nothing. The way Rebecca had lived the past ten years of her life.

But enough.

Rebecca had thought—if not accepted, exactly—she understood Brad's violent streak. It didn't happen often, but when he hit her, it hurt. Not so much physically; she'd developed a surprising tolerance to the pain. Emotionally, though, it pummeled her worse than fists. Yet she accepted it, justified it as the norm. After all, her daddy treated her mother the same way. And, as Brad often told her, his job weighed heavily on him, the stress too much. "Being a police detective is a load-and-a-half for any good man," he'd said before punctuating his insight with a blow to her cheek. Now Rebecca thought it nothing more than a load of shit.

Was Brad a good man? At one time she'd thought so. But when he hit their daughter last night, her perception, her entire world, changed.

Enough.

Kyra had sought safety in Rebecca's arms, crying, asking

why Daddy hated her. The breaking point. And Rebecca hated herself for not having made the decision long ago. She knew then, absolutely knew, she and Kyra would leave in the morning. After Brad went to work.

Right now, he probably just arrived home and found her note. Then flew into a rage. Fine. Let him find a new punching bag.

As Rebecca tapped the brakes, the car swerved, the back tire edging toward the ditch. Finally, the car shuddered to a stop, Rebecca's heart threatening to stop as well. With white knuckles over the steering wheel, she blew out a deep breath, staring into the storm. Nothing but endless snow, drifting into dunes along the road. Fear fueled her; not just fear of the storm, but fear of the future, the unknown. Starting over at the age of 32, no college degree, no practical work experience. All very scary. But she still had her life. And Kyra's. This time she'd make it count.

Last night, after Brad had struck Kyra, things turned even worse. She knew Brad wouldn't let her leave, so she suffered in silence one last time. She'd consoled Kyra the best she could, even though she'd lied through her teeth. Hanging a pretty picture on abuse isn't easy. After Kyra had settled down, Rebecca dragged herself up to the bedroom, dreading what she knew awaited her. Five minutes later, Brad was pawing at her, acting like he hadn't hit their daughter. As if his abuse had turned him on. Business as usual, Rebecca a sex object purely for Brad's pleasure.

It felt like rape, torture of body and mind.

Enough.

Once the tears started, she couldn't stop them. Ten years' worth of bottled-up sorrow finally spilled. She covered her mouth with an arm, muffling her sobs. A small whimper birthed in her chest, a sad, little thing that matured into a growl.

That bastard. That miserable bastard. And I took it.

"Mommy?" Kyra yawned, staring at her. "Why're you crying?"

"Shh, honey, it's okay. Mommy's just tired, that's all. Everything's fine." Rebecca wiped away the tears and erased all thoughts of Brad. Time to pull it together. Kyra counted on her.

"Where are we?" Kyra leaned forward, wiping a viewing space through the windshield.

"I think … the sign said Hilston, Missouri." A place she'd never been, nor ever heard of before. Not that that was uncommon. Brad never took her out of Hollington, Kansas. Her entire life she'd been trapped in a lousy Kansas City suburb, her prison.

"Is this where we're going?"

"No, honey. We're going to stay with Aunt Jill and her family for a while. Like we discussed."

"And Daddy's not coming?"

"No, he's not."

Kyra said nothing, reacted indifferently. But a barely audible sigh escaped from her, one possibly of relief. Of course, Kyra loved her dad, warts and all. Yet she wasn't blind. She'd seen Brad at his worst. But he'd never hit Kyra before. It'd been foolish thinking he never would either. Brad was a ticking time bomb more often than not. Hell, she may as well have triggered the bomb herself. She should never have kept Kyra in that situation. Not for six years. *Shoulda', woulda', coulda'.*

"Mommy, I'm sorry I knocked over Daddy's beer. It was an accident. I'll never do it again." She blinked at Rebecca, sincerity sparkling in her eyes.

"I know, honey. Accidents happen." Slowly, Rebecca backed the car up and straightened it out; she noticed the snow was already covering her tracks. Nice and steady, twenty miles per hour. Maddening, like her life, steadily going nowhere.

But not any longer.

"That's why Daddy hit me, isn't it?"

Again, Rebecca felt an emotional punch to the stomach. She couldn't have Kyra accepting Brad's abuse as just punishment. Not the way Rebecca had. "Kyra, Daddy's sick. He doesn't—"

"Is he dying?"

I wish. "No, honey, he's not sick like that. He…he has something wrong in his head. Something that makes him do bad things. Like hitting you. He can't help it. It has nothing to do with his feelings for you. He loves you. But he should never have hit you. And I don't want you blaming yourself. You understand?" Rebecca watched Kyra carefully, ensuring the message took.

Kyra nodded. "Daddy's sick." A simple reiteration, but delivered with firm resolve. Relief coursed through Rebecca, a realization that Kyra would survive to live a healthy life. She marveled at her daughter's resilience, the kind children uncannily possess.

Rebecca reached over and dropped her hand over her daughters'. "Love you."

"Love you…*Mommy, look out!*"

She had only taken her hand off the steering wheel for a few seconds. Not that it really mattered. The car took on a life of its own, angrily determined for the ditch. Rebecca tromped on the brakes. The car fishtailed, the back end sliding. In a panic, Rebecca cranked the steering wheel, forgetting to steer opposite in the snow. Kyra screamed. A complete 180 tossed Rebecca's stomach, then they twisted into a second loop. Closer, closer to the edge of the road. Snow sprayed from the drift they plowed through. The front of the Chevy lowered into the ditch, the back two tires banging down. Trees rushed up. Rebecca flung an arm over Kyra's chest, an impotent shield. Metal roared as they smashed into the tree. Rebecca flew against the steering wheel, sharp pain jagging into her chest. Glass tinkled, something hissed.

She held onto the wheel for another few seconds, uncertain their wild ride had ended. Smoke drifted up from beneath the sprung hood.

"Kyra, you okay?"

Kyra clutched her stuffed dog to her chest, eyes wide. She nodded, not reassuring enough for Rebecca.

"*Say* something, Kyra. You okay?"

"I think so. Gotta potty."

The damage to the Chevy appeared extensive. The front end resembled an accordion, a web-like vein crossed the windshield. A heavy tree limb lay over the hood. No signal on her cell phone. And the snow kept falling, God's frozen tears.

Rebecca wanted to cry. But she didn't. Instead, she laughed. Just a little at first, then it swelled, nearing hysteria. Nothing else seemed appropriate. Kyra joined her, a nervous titter.

Welcome to the first day of my new life.

❄ ❄ ❄

Harold really shouldn't have done it, pretty much a no-brainer. Betraying the Kansas City mob is hardly the smartest career move. But money can be a strong motivator. Over the last several years, Harold had managed (or "mismanaged" might be more apt) Vincent Domenick's books and financial affairs, skimming a few tips off the top for his hard work. It's not like Domenick would miss a few bucks; the man had more money than several countries combined. Besides, the money had blood all over it, supposedly the net gains from Domenick's trucking company. But Harold knew better, knew where the cash really came from. Not exactly stealing from charity.

Things had heated up, though. Fast. Men wearing dull

suits and flashing shiny badges had taken a sudden interest in Mr. Domenick's affairs, poring over his financial records and asking Harold uncomfortable questions. They had instructed Harold to keep Mr. Domenick blissfully unaware. No problem, he could live with that. But what really sealed Harold's bold career move was when one of the feds flat out stated that ignorance of Domenick's crimes wasn't a valid legal defense. He said it with a shit-eating smirk, as if he enjoyed watching Harold squirm. Harold received the message loud and clear: once Domenick goes down, Harold would be dragged to prison along with him. No thanks.

After Domenick's goon dropped off the monthly briefcase of cash that morning, it practically beckoned to Harold, screaming like a wild lover, "Take me, Harold, take me!" He would've been a fool to turn a deaf ear on such wanton lust. The time felt right to get out of town, his start-up funds handed to him in an easy-to-take briefcase, perfect for the man on the go. He'd always wanted to visit the Caribbean, never thought he'd live there. Life is sweet.

By now, Dominick had probably realized his money had vanished. Then again, maybe not. The man never did have an eye for numbers. Still, jumping on the first available plane seemed risky, too easily traced. And Harold swore he had spotted several suits following him over the last week. Pretty damn lousy at their jobs if an accountant could sniff out the feds. On the other hand, it could've been his imagination. Seven hundred thousand dollars' worth of hot can make a guy paranoid. But he hadn't seen anyone on his tail over the last couple of hours. Hell, in this weather, even the feds must've called in for a snow day.

He had a plan. As far as winging it goes, a pretty decent plan—catch a flight out from Los Angeles. Dominick's reach didn't extend to the west coast. But first Harold had to get there. And the damn snow didn't make it easy.

Married to his work, as they say, he had no real good-byes to make. He could always call his ex-wife from the Caribbean, rub it in her nose a little. She'd always wanted to go there. A smile crossed his lips as he planned what he'd say to her: *Eat it, Barb.*

But now he needed sleep. Absconding with mob money wears a man out. He couldn't get very far in the storm anyway. The sign he'd just passed had read, "Welcome to Hilston, Missouri. A lovely place to antique."

Of course, the sentiment made him gag. Pretty twee using "antique" as a verb, not to mention bragging about it. And he really hated "antiquing." Barb had forced him to join her on some of her expeditions, wasting numerous hours in musty shops full of crap the owners tried to pass off as collectibles. But Hilston was the closest place to stop. Surely he could stomach it for one night.

He followed a sign pointing toward the downtown district. Downtown amounted to basically one block lined with antique shops. At a stoplight, he stepped out onto the empty street. Snow buried his shoes. Squinting from the blizzard, he looked beyond the one-storied shops, searching for a tall building along the skyline. Nothing. Crummy little town didn't even have a single hotel. But he knew there'd be a bed and breakfast, possibly several, a mainstay for those foolish people who just can't get enough "antiquing" done in one day.

Several blocks over, on a hilly street so narrow only one car could safely drive down it at a time, he spotted his destination. His tires lost traction, plunging him into sickening helplessness. At the bottom of the hill, the car slowed, then popped up on a curb, delivering him in front of the "Dandy Drop Inn." Even the name nearly made him wretch. Everything in this damned town wanted to be "cute." "Cute" was about as relevant to him as nipples on men. But the inn promised a bed, and what the hell, breakfast to boot.

❄ ❄ ❄

"Got his location, boss."

"You gonna give it to me or have I gotta guess?" Winston's patience had run thin. Not only did he despise driving in the snow, but talking on the phone while driving was something he rarely did. Just not safe; kinda stupid, really. But tonight it couldn't be helped. He wanted to get the job done, get out of the storm, get back to Julie and the kids. Tonight, multi-tasking trumped safety.

"Sorry. You're never gonna believe it …" The kid paused, still forcing Winston to play "Twenty Questions." Yep, patience had about run its course. Still, in Winston's line of work, patience is a virtue.

"For Christ's sake, just tell me, Lenny."

"Yeah, uh, sorry, boss. The accountant's holed up at a bed and breakfast. In some shithole called…let's see…Hilston, Missouri. Want the address?"

"No, I'll just read your mind. Yes, *give* me the damn address." He really shouldn't snap at Lenny; the kid had proven himself time and again with his crazy computer and hacking skills. If he wanted to find anything or anybody, Lenny was his go-to guy. When you're in the "security consulting" business, assets like him are invaluable. Sometimes he wondered how people in his line of work made do before the advent of computers. Didn't matter. Lenny'd sussed out the missing accountant's location in no time at all. The accountant may be a whiz with numbers, but apparently didn't know jack about technology. The fool didn't realize his cell phone could be triangulated. Gotta love progress.

"Okay, got it." Winston pulled over, then entered the address into his G.P.S. Quickly, he switched the "creepy man's" voice his kids delighted in to a British woman's voice. On a night like this, Mr. Creepy made a lousy traveling companion. "Thanks, Lenny. We'll talk soon."

Hilston, Missouri. *Crap.* Another forty miles or so. Since he'd only been able to travel about fifteen miles over the past hour, he still had a good three-hour trip ahead of him. Long night. Better call home.

"Hey, Julie, it's me."

She laughed as she always did when he identified himself. Old habits and all. "I know, Win, we have Caller I.D."

"Yeah, yeah, right. Hey, the storm's not letting up, and I'm still trying to get home. I'd better find a spot to hole up for the night. It's coming down like…I dunno, blankets. It's bad."

"Blankets, huh? Lame metaphor, hon."

"Hey, a poet, I ain't."

"Just be careful, 'kay? Promise?"

"Promise. Love you, honey. Kiss the kids good night for me."

"Will do. Love you back."

Spending nights away was a necessary evil in the security field. Lousy beds, paper-thin walls, diner food that could start a grease fire in your belly. But, mostly, Winston hated being away from his family. He lived for his wife and two daughters, pretty much the reason he extended his field of expertise in the security industry.

Of course, he'd been hesitant at first. Ever since childhood, he'd never had a stomach for violence, always preferring to talk his way out of a bad situation if possible. But Mr. Dominick had planted the idea in his head. Just a small seedling at first, but it blossomed, watered by Dominick's pushing.

And, frankly, when Winston looked at the resources he had available—the entirety of his company, "Ashford Security Solutions" (unfortunate acronym and all)—pushing "Security Consultant" to the next level seemed like a natural step. Via Lenny, he could access anyone's personal accounts and files; false identities and papers were a snap to acquire; and, of course, his business led him to people who had no qualms about securing untraceable weapons for him. Sure, his company was profitable, but just not quite enough. When he considered his house mortgage and his daughters' costly private school tuition, well, pulling the first trigger wasn't so bad after all. Just as long as he never made it personal.

Family came first, though, one hundred percent. Several years ago, when he had first started taking on out-of-town assignments, Julie had grown aloof, her frustration evident in her uncommon silence. Once—and only once—she'd straight out asked him, "Are you having an affair?" Her lower lip had trembled, obviously dreading—yet anticipating—his answer.

He swept her up in his arms with an amazed chuckle. "No, Julie, I swear to you I'm not. I never would and never will." Within his hug, he felt her physically lighten, her tense shoulders relaxing.

"I know, Winston. I'm just being silly. Forget I said anything."

And they both had. She never questioned him again. He told her about the more mundane details of his workload, the majority of it. But he never mentioned anything about his extra duties for Domenick. If she suspected, she never let on. Sure, guilt gnawed at him from time to time for withholding the complete truth, but he didn't outright lie. He reasoned it was for her benefit. What she didn't know wouldn't hurt her.

He glanced at the glove box where he stored his gun on road trips. The .22 LR handgun was small enough to conceal, yet packed a punch like a charging rhino. It hadn't let him down once.

Yet he dreaded using it. Sometimes completing duties for Domenick left a sour taste in his mouth. Especially when the assignments pleaded for their lives. Usually why he liked to take them out without any personal contact. Never put a story to the face. It helped him sleep at night.

How this job was shaping up worried him. He couldn't very well sleep in his car, not in this storm. And there didn't appear to be a motel in Hilston, not according to his phone. Against his better judgment, he'd probably have to stay at the bed and breakfast until the storm blew over. Then he'd make his move.

As his car crunched over the snow-packed highway, he flipped the visor down, kissed his fingers, and tapped the photo of his family. *This one's for you.* Then he drove on into Hilston.

❄ ❄ ❄

From an early age, Heather Peterson knew she was different. She just couldn't quite put a finger on how. Her schoolmates had shunned her, running in exclusive packs, which suited Heather just fine. She had other interests; not the typical sort either, the ones the silly girls thrived on. Growing up on a farm enabled her to pursue her new-found hobby. But she'd longed to share her passion with somebody, something that seemed out of the realm of possibility.

Until God, in His kind and gracious manner, led her to Tommy. Or rather, led Tommy to her. Miracle of all miracles, Tommy had strolled up to her at her first Young Christians meeting, drawn to her inner light, and boldly stuck his hand out. Handsome, and with more confidence than a movie star,

Tommy Goodenow regaled her with tales of his accomplishments. Heather had listened with rapt attention, drowning in his blue eyes, and swimming in his deep, soothing voice. Smitten like a silly schoolgirl—which, she supposed, she was—Heather knew Tommy was the man for her. Knew it as sure as she knew God had gifted Tommy to her. Once the meeting had ended, Tommy asked her out. Her hopes soared, then crashed back down to earth. What if he found her strange like the other students did? What if he found her impossible to love, the way her parents had?

But she should have had faith in God. Things worked out better than she dared hope.

Holding her ring up next to the car window, a street lamp caught a glint of diamond. Her smile stretched, grew even wider when she looked at her new husband behind the steering wheel.

Mrs. Tommy Goodenow. Heather Goodenow. She couldn't believe she was now a married woman. Something she had only dreamed of before.

Tommy must've sensed her thoughts, the way he innately knew so many things about her. He swept his brown hair out of his eyes and flashed his killer smile, incredibly toothy and white. "Penny for your thoughts, Missus Goodenow?"

"Why, Mister Goodenow, a girl has to keep some secrets." Truly a miracle how he brought out her playfulness, a daring flirtiness. Still, she didn't want to tell him what really bothered her, something that caused butterflies to swarm in her stomach. While her newlywed status thrilled her, to be frank, the inevitable consummation terrified her. Momma'd never been much help in such matters, never taking the time to explain things. Heather'd pieced things together as well as she could from stories overheard in the high school locker room. She thought she knew what to expect. But did she truly? Was it possible to be petrified and exhilarated at the same time? Something burned in her lower regions, a warmth that spread throughout her body and spiked in her brain. Her mind toyed with her, teetering on the verge of unlocking the secrets of the human body. All led there by God, of course. She turned toward the window, hiding, but not out of shame, never shame. Rather, she didn't want Tommy to see her surely pale complexion. Fear of consummating their love. *Sex*. There she said it; well, not out loud, but she put a label to the act. And it didn't sound dirty at all, not really.

Tommy's hand crawled on top of hers. "We'll be there soon, babe." Always so darn self-assured, Tommy had enough confidence for both of them, and then some.

"Both hands back on the wheel," she chided. "With this crazy storm, you'll need all your attention on the road." She swept back a lock of her blond hair and tucked it behind an ear. "You'll have all the time in the world later to attend to me." Had she just said that? She couldn't believe her audacity. Tommy had that effect on her.

She'd told Tommy she was a "V." Honestly, she'd never even had a boyfriend until him. Sure, she kissed a few frogs, stupid boys hopping around on the playground. But never one like Tommy. And he'd handled the news of her virginity like a true Christian gentleman. He didn't laugh, as she suspected he might. He didn't ridicule. Instead, he'd seized her hand within his, held it to his heart, and said, "Then we're meant to be together. I've been saving myself for marriage."

Which totally blew Heather away. How in Heaven could a boy this gorgeous have gone untouched? She pretty much assumed Tommy had indulged in "lighter" petting, making out, who knew what. Part of being a boy. But she never asked, he never volunteered. Some things are better left unknown.

God had smiled down upon them both that fateful day.

And they had agreed to help others see the light as well. Spreading the wealth of God.

As they approached a traffic light, Tommy tapped the brakes. The car slid a few feet into the intersection before crunching to a halt.

"My goodness." Heather fanned herself with a hand. Mostly to calm herself from the slight scare, maybe to cool herself down for more intimate reasons. "Be careful, babe." Funny how comfortable she'd become calling her new husband "babe." Before, she would've thought it juvenile, vulgar even. Now it sounded daring, liberating.

"Always with you, babe. I'd never put you at risk." Again he patted her hand. This time she allowed it since they were stopped. "We're almost there." Another knowing grin. "G.P.S. says just a few more blocks."

Anticipation crawled inside her, an uncomfortable scratching at her private parts. Only several blocks separated them from their marital bed. How far they'd come along God's path, all building to this moment. "Can't wait," she said quietly.

After months of chaste dating, she had expressed her innermost feelings to Tommy, told him of her unusual passion. Bravely, she'd demonstrated her hobby, leaving any judgment in God's hands. At first, he'd watched slack-jawed, an uncommon look for him. Nothing ever seemed to faze him. When she finished, she stood up, looking at him in silence. Waiting. Finally, his grin fell back into place. He strutted forward, the cock in the henhouse, and kissed her. Then, dropping to his knees, he picked up where she left off. Finished the job and followed it with another kiss, full-on, sensual, exciting. *Forbidden.*

She closed her eyes, basking in the blissful memory, and silently prayed: *Thank you, God, for leading us to one another.*

Tommy jarred her out of her reverie, concern tightening

his handsome features. "Okay, babe?"

She nodded. "Never been better. Just … praying. I'm thankful for us and wanted to let God know."

"Amen," he said.

The wedding had been a small, slap-dash affair. With no friends to speak of, Heather's side of the church had been fairly barren, occupied by a few relatives she didn't really know. Tommy, on the other hand, had invited a raucous group of male friends who laughed and hooted throughout the ceremony. Since Tommy had graduated a year before her, she didn't really know them either. To be honest, based on their childish actions, she didn't think she wanted to get to know them. The louder they carried on, the redder Reverend Paxton burned. Not nearly as bad as her father, though. He sat in the front row, red as dawn, ears on fire from a head full of hate. He had been dead set against the wedding, actually believing it to have been a "shot gun" affair. *Hardly.*

After the glorious event, they stopped by home to say goodbye to her parents. Her father had grown even more sullen, falling into a whiskey fit. And he hadn't even blessed them with a wedding gift.

But that was okay, though; turn the other cheek as the Good Book says. Heather and Tommy had left her parents with the ultimate gift, the true Christian thing to do.

Heather smiled at the memory, warm in the afterglow.

Close-set, quaint houses and trees lined the street. Heather's heart knocked, practically jumping up the hill ahead of them. Ready for the final mystery to be unwrapped. She swallowed, an audible dry click.

The car hurtled down the hill, Tommy grinning behind the wheel, letting gravity take over. At the bottom of the hill, he pumped the brakes, *thunk, thunk, thunk, hiss.* The car slalomed to a stop, deep tire grooves in the snow-laid street behind them. Wind rattled the chains on a sign reading, "Dandy Drop Inn."

"We're here, babe." Tommy leaned over and kissed Heather. His tongue darted into her mouth, a hand gently caressing her breast. His reward for having conquered the snow storm.

"Tommy!" Heather pushed him back, not too much. She couldn't resist a smile, giving away her true desire. "Not in public!"

Tommy looked around, seriously puzzled and nearly comical. "This ain't exactly public. No one out on a night like this but us."

"I'm no slut, Tommy Goodenow, to be pawed on the street. You just wait."

"Reckon I can, at that. Reckon I will. Lookin' forward to it."

"Me, too." She tossed her arms around his neck and gave him a quick peck. Just a tease, enough to titillate, not enough to ignite his male hormones again.

"Okay. Ready?"

Not really. "I suppose. As long as you're gentle," she whispered.

"Always, babe. Always."

They stepped out into the snow. Heather cinched her coat beneath her chin against a sudden, brutal gust. Snow blew into her face, biting cold. "*Oh.* Don't forget the knives."

"Right, babe." Tommy pulled open the car door, reaching into the back seat. He gripped the knife sleeve, waving it as validation. "Can't forget God's work."

The wind seized and conquered his words, everything except for "God." But she intuited what he'd said. With her gloved hand coiled around the crook of Tommy's arm, he escorted her down the sidewalk to their honeymoon abode.

Stuart R. West

Author of Dread and Breakfast

GHOSTS OF CANNAWAY

Chapter One

1929...

Something looked off about Karl, no doubt about it. Tommy Donnelly saw it in Karl's eyes the minute they got in line. Not the usual red-eyed glassiness that accompanies miners' fondness for moonshine, either. Karl's gaze flicked back and forth, unfocused and yellow, like a desert lizard's eyes.

Tommy didn't know Karl well. Just by reputation and his daddy's mining tales. An old-time roof-trimmer, Karl's responsibilities included clearing loose rocks, making the mines safe for the other men. Apparently, he'd been in the mines since before the turn of the century. But on this gray Kansas morning, Karl stayed to himself, mumbling. He stared into the dirt like he was prospecting for gold. Hardly in keeping with what Tommy'd heard about this legendary miner.

Truth to tell, though, as it was Tommy's first day in the mines, Karl's odd behavior just set him more on edge.

Big Ed took it all in stride, of course, as he did everything. He chuckled deep within his formidable belly. "Kid, first-day jitters? Stay by my side and you'll be fine."

"Thanks, Ed. Guess I'm just gettin' my feet underneath me."

"That so?"

"That's so." Tommy forced a weak smile. It didn't make him feel much better, but the fact Big Ed had taken him under his wing gave him a small cushion of comfort. Tommy's daddy would've wanted it that way. It bothered him no end that Big Ed didn't think Karl's behavior seemed peculiar. But maybe that's the way Karl always acted.

The line of denim-clad, ruddy-faced men snaked across the grounds. The closer Tommy came to the pull derrick, the more his stomach flip-flopped. Watching the men disappear into the earth in a large bucket increased his anxiety.

Big Ed picked at his teeth with a dirty fingernail. "*Pfft, pfft, pfft!*" Big Ed launched his excavated oral debris onto the ground.

"Tommy, you're gonna start as a dummy. I talked to the ground boss, told him I want you. You'll carry my drill bits. You do good, show you're a man who ain't afraid to work, you'll move up to mucker in no time."

Karl lifted an eyebrow, appraising Tommy as if seeing him for the first time. "They're down there. Told me what I gotta do." He stared at Tommy, waiting for a response.

Big Ed ignored him. Tommy followed Ed's lead.

"All greenhorns gotta start somewhere, kid." Ed raised his voice to be heard over Karl's muttering.

"They come to me, no matter the time, day or night, they talk to me, tell me what I gotta do…"

They were next. Tommy hoped Karl would go down in the bucket in a different grouping. No such luck. Luck wasn't on his side today. Never a good thing for miners.

Jim Reaper, a particularly taciturn man who lived up to his name, was hoister man today. The empty bucket clanged down in the shaft as Jim cranked the hoist handle. Every time the bucket banged into the shaft's wooden walls, Tommy's heart jumped right along with it.

Big Ed let out a long sigh and climbed the platform. The boards creaked beneath his weight with every step. He grabbed the cable and swung a leg up and over the bucket's rim. "Come on, kid." He jerked his chin toward Tommy.

Tommy stepped up onto the platform. Karl followed behind him. *Closely.* So close Tommy felt Karl's breath on the back of his neck. Ed reached out a helping hand, and Tommy hopped in. Karl gripped the bucket's rim and gave it a spin.

"Come on, Karl," said Ed. "Quit horsin' around. Time to get into the mines."

Karl's lips pulled back, showcasing his yellow-toothed smile. He looked around at his surroundings, lost, a man awakened from a dream. It rattled Tommy, but at least Karl had stopped babbling.

Didn't take long, though, for Karl to shrug off sanity and resume his ongoing private conversation. He turned, asked a question of someone not there, laughed at an unheard response. Finally, he hopped into the bucket, his long legs neatly clearing the rim.

The bucket rocked back and forth over the shaft's collar. The bail holding the cable hook above them groaned. The gaping opening sat at about 12 feet wide by 12 feet across. The darkness reminded Tommy of the hole in the ground they put his daddy in when he passed. Miners work underground, die underground, get put back there again when all's said and done.

"All right," said Jim. It was more a declaration than a question, but Big Ed nodded anyway. Tommy grabbed the cable, a tenuous lifeline at best.

Karl stared at Tommy, his eyes dull. Rather, he looked right through him. "They won't let me rest, gotta do what they say…"

"God damn, Karl!" said Ed. "You liquored up or the devil on fire inside your belly?"

Karl didn't answer. He just gave a lopsided, lazy man's grin.

The square of skylight shrank as they lowered into the ground. A few torches lit up the shaft wall's cribbing of strategically placed 2" x 6' timbers.

The light played across Karl's face, shadows obscuring his eyes. Ed hummed a mostly melody-free ditty, something Tommy didn't recognize. When Karl fell silent again, Tommy couldn't help but steal glances at him. His stillness unsettled Tommy more than the constant mumbling.

Karl's arms shot up. He lurched toward Tommy. The bucket rocked, bashed into the walls. Tommy stumbled, his back against the bucket's rim.

"Karl!" Ed roared. "Jesus Christ!"

Karl shot Ed a puzzled look, then reached a trembling hand toward Tommy. He stroked Tommy's shoulder like petting a mining mule. "It ain't time yet," Karl said. "Not yet, they tol' me…"

"Sorry, kid," said Ed. He glared at Karl. "He ain't usually like this."

Echoes rose above and sank below as the bucket landed on a wooden platform four hundred feet below ground. Water bubbled and churned below the wood planks. Tommy couldn't distinguish the sump-pump from the pulse pounding in his ears.

Tommy hopped out of the bucket first. He didn't want to spend any more time with Karl than he had to. Ed must've had the same thought. He hefted himself out with surprising speed for a man his size. Karl dawdled behind as Tommy and Ed walked down the drift.

Ed clapped a hand on Tommy's back. "Time to light 'em up." He struck a long wooden match and held it to the lamp on Tommy's helmet. "Gotta be careful with fire down here, kid." The welcome light illuminated the dark drift. The match hissed out in a puddle at Ed's feet. "You're lucky, boy. Wasn't too long ago we made do with cloth helmets. Didn't protect us worth nothin'.

Damn Gannaway was one of the last mine owners in the tri-state area to give us hard helmets."

Their boots squelched through the water. Using the steel rails as guides, they walked toward the light. After three hundred feet or so, the drift opened into a large stope, already mined and hollowed out for the most part. Artificial orange lantern light painted the cavern's walls. Carefully chiseled pillars of unmined rock braced the cavern roof for support. Nothing looked particularly steady. Boisterous voices greeted them.

"Big Ed! Who's the dummy with you?"

"Is he outta his momma's diapers yet?"

"Ground Boss," said Ed, to a sweaty, short, round man, "this is Tommy, my new dummy. Matthew's boy."

The man's eyes brightened. "Matthew was a good man and a better miner. If you're half the miner he was, son, you'll do just fine down here. Call me Ground Boss. Or sir."

"Yes, sir."

Against the wall, a man stood on a tall ladder, twenty-five feet above the cavern floor. Two miners pulled attached guide ropes taut. The ladder man stabbed a ten-foot-long spear into the rock above him. "Look out below!" he yelled. *Clump.* Loose rocks rained down from the ceiling.

"They tell me what to do…" Karl brushed past them, drowning out the Ground Boss's instructions. Karl walked toward the men steering the roof trimmer on the ladder, purpose in his stride.

A mule brayed once, then again.

Water around Tommy's feet bubbled. Invisible raindrops pelleted down, circular ripples spreading outward. The ground trembled. A hush fell over the miners. Big Ed looked puzzled. Worse, he looked *worried.*

The ground shook again. A roar ripped through the cavern walls. Not a horn exactly. Something deeper, more resonant. An inhuman moan, far away and all around them at the same time. A one-note, unending blast from the bowels of the earth.

Tommy felt the vibrations in his legs first. Then it traveled up into his chest, rattling his ribcage.

"Cave in!"

Panic. Water splashed, churned by fleeing feet. Miners dashed by Tommy, running toward the bucket.

Big Ed held his own, solemnly shook his head. "Nope. This ain't no cave-in. Nothin' like one I never heard."

Screams erupted by the ladder.

"What in *God's* name?"

A pickaxe dangled in Karl's hand, a skull-faced grin on his face. A man lay crumpled at his feet. The other rope-holder lunged at Karl. Karl sidestepped and the man went head first into the wall. With the grace of a dancer, Karl swung around and brought the pickaxe down onto the man's head.

A man on the ladder scrambled down. Karl kicked at the bottom rungs. The man flailed his arms about as if trying to sprout wings. The ladder slowly teetered, then crashed onto an outcropping of rock. The miner's eyes popped clean out of his head. His teeth shattered, spreading small white gems out on the rocks.

"God *damn!*" said Big Ed.

Karl propped a boot onto the dead man and yanked out the pickaxe. He licked the tip. Lovingly, almost. He opened his mouth, his smile crimson. Karl snatched the spear from off the ground. Then he raced straight for Tommy.

Tommy froze, standing still as miners rushed past him. The bellowing sound churned his innards, filled his bladder.

Without breaking stride, Karl ran the spear through another man's stomach. The tip poked out the man's back. He gave it a twist and withdrew the weapon as smoothly as a knife slicing through butter. Intestines slithered to the ground, smooth as a snake over a rock.

A bear of a miner tossed his arms around Karl's neck. Karl thrust the pickaxe into the man's neck repeatedly, missing his own face by inches. He studied the pickaxe, then dropped it.

"Good God in heaven!" the Ground Boss moaned.

"Come on! We gotta get outta here!" Ed yanked Tommy's arm. *"Tommy!"*

Karl dug through his newest victim's burlap bag and pulled out a handful of cylindrical-shaped objects.

Dynamite.

The hellish moaning loosened rock from the ceiling. Small pebbles at first, then a thunderstorm of larger debris. Ground-water danced, shimmied, and rippled.

Karl struck a match, held it to the wick of a dynamite stick. *Fssst.* He dropped the dead match, grabbed for another.

Something struck Tommy's cheek, pulling him out of his horrified stupor. Big Ed had his hand pulled back, preparing for another slap.

"Oh…lord," said Tommy, tears stinging his eyes.

"Let's *go,* goddammit!" Ed clamped down on Tommy's arm, nearly pulling him off his feet.

Karl chased after them, cradling the dynamite to his chest while he swung his spear.

They stormed down the drift. Tommy stumbled, his shoulder catching against the wall. The Ground Boss struggled to keep up, his panting loud in the drift. Tommy risked a glimpse back. Karl stood at the drift's entryway. Singing in an eerie, high-pitched tone.

A gospel song.

"If you could see inside insteaddd, you'd see a brand new mannn…"

The bucket had vanished. There was no way out.

From somewhere far away, a mule whinnied, mocking them.

Hysterical shouts echoed down the shaft. The bucket

crashed in front of them. The bottom flipped out like an open can of beans. Its broken cable swished back and forth above it like a horse's tail swatting flies.

"Jesus God!"

"…'cause the old man is deaddd…"

Karl walked slowly down the drift, three sticks of dynamite tucked under his arm. He scrabbled at a matchbox. He struck a match against the rock wall. It snapped in half.

"Go!" Tommy pointed at the swinging cable. "Our only chance! God, it's our only chance! *Go! Now!*"

The Ground Boss grabbed hold of the cable, his knees and ankles entwining around the line. He scurried up inch by inch.

"You would see a brand new man…"

"Ed! Go!"

Ed shook his head. "You go, boy. Your daddy'd never forgive me if I left you down here."

"But I'll be *faster!*"

"More the reason for you to go, kid! *Dammit* all to hell, now *get!*"

As soon as the Ground Boss cleared the top, Tommy jumped onto the cable. Hand over hand, he scrambled up quickly. Faces peered down the hole. The skidoo bell warning clanged.

And over it all, Tommy heard Karl's death dirge.

"… 'Cause the old man is deaddd!"

Tommy looked down. Ed steadied the cable with one hand, his other held out, warding off Karl.

Karl's singing dried up. The loud thrumming noise diminished. Silence. Except for the scritch-scratching of a match head.

Halfway up the shaft, Tommy spotted a niche carved out of the rock. A hole for the workers who laid down the cribbing along the shaft walls.

Tommy knew Ed couldn't make it to the top. Not before Karl lit his dynamite. Tommy swung toward the niche. His arm and leg took hold, and he crawled in.

Tommy heard Ed talking quietly to Karl.

"Ed! Come on! *Move* it!"

Ed squinted toward Karl before hopping onto the cable. With a grunt, he inched his way up. His weight tugged at the cable Tommy held, burning his hands.

Karl shoved the ruined bucket off the platform. He crawled on top and sat down. By all appearances, he didn't have a care in the world. He chuckled and scratched a match.

Ed struggled hard. For every five feet he climbed, he had to pause to catch his breath.

"Just get to me, Ed!" Tommy leaned out of the niche, extending his hand toward Ed, straining so hard his muscles shook. Willing Ed to keep going.

Ed climbed and clawed, gasping for air.

A tiny spark of light flashed at the bottom of the shaft. Karl stared into the match's flame. Then he wedged a stick of dynamite into his mouth. The fuse caught, sparkled, brightened, then continued on its trail to destruction.

"Oh sweet Lord, Ed, hurry! Hurry!"

Ed surged forward, using every bit of energy he had.

Karl lit the other two sticks of dynamite. Then he lay down like Jesus on the cross, arms outstretched, the lit dynamite in his hands.

Tommy's fingers swept the tip of Ed's outreached hand. *Missed.* Ed jumped up an inch and grasped Tommy's hand. Tommy pulled, throwing himself back. His backside scraped along the rock toward the shaft, Ed's weight dragging him out. He anchored his feet against the niche's edges, slowing himself. But not enough.

"Ed! Climb! You gotta climb more! I can't pull you in!"

Ed clawed a foothold into the niche and rolled in on top of Tommy.

The first explosion ripped through the shaft, followed by two more. Wood-reinforced walls shook. Rock crumbled. Fire roared up the shaft, bathing them in blistering heat. A cloud of black smoke roiled up and out into the open air above. Tommy and Ed clung to one another like early morning lovers.

The flood of falling rocks dwindled, became a rare pebble. The dead quiet after the chaos should have been comforting. Instead, it seemed an additional threat, devouring Tommy with false hope.

The smoke cleared, and Ed and Tommy separated. Tommy had soiled his pants. Ed wouldn't hold it against him, though. Or say anything about it. Ever. He'd done the same thing.

Chapter Two

1969...

The music stuttered, stopped, sped up. Then it faded out.

"Damn it." Dennis pulled the van onto the shoulder of US69. He reached down and tugged at the eight-track cartridge. Wrinkled tape trailed from the player like ribbon on a gift.

The one concession Dennis had asked Meyers for was an eight-track player installed in the research van. He knew Kansas radio would be hellish. Especially out in the boonies. Nothing but country music and preachers ranting about saving souls from damnation.

It didn't matter much, not really. Just moving on and doing something different renewed him with a vigor he hadn't experienced in a very long time. Getting away from Los Angeles, at least if for a while.

Meyers had seemed reluctant to send Dennis to Gannaway, Kansas. He'd never given a reason. But he saw it in Meyer's distrusting look. A look filled with pity and doubt. Obviously, Meyers didn't feel Dennis was emotionally up to the task.

But Dennis needed the job. Anything to take his mind off what had happened six months ago.

A flash of movement caught Dennis's eye. An American Indian man stood just off the highway, knee-deep in dried bushes and weeds. He looked as startled as Dennis, but recovered with ease and tipped his fedora. Dennis nodded a greeting. The man dropped a potato bag and spread his hands in a "what the hell" manner. Then he pointed across the two-lane highway.

A modest home sat on the other side of the highway, nothing memorable. But the yard burst with a carnival of color. A white-painted garden jockey statue guarded the graveled drive-way. Psychedelically colored birdbaths decorated the yard, a pop-art fever dream. Metallic pipes and rods clung to one another, pitched somewhere between sculptures and warnings. A giant peace sign covered the garage door. Above it hung a basketball hoop, wind chimes replacing the net.

The man pointed inside the van, and his lips moved. Appearing frustrated, he cranked his hand around like an organ grinder. Dennis scooted across the bench seat and rolled down the window.

The Indian leaned over the sill and Dennis extended his hand. The man surprised Dennis by foregoing the traditional handshake and offering his thumb instead of his hand. Their thumbs entwined in a soul handshake.

"Peace, brother." He gestured toward the ruined cartridge Dennis held onto. "Can I have that?"

"Sure. You know it's no good anymore, right?"

"Can see that."

Dennis shrugged and handed over the tape. The man cradled

the draping tape as tenderly as a gardener would an uprooted plant. He eyed the tape's label. "Good band."

"Yeah, real rock and roll."

The man's smile burned warm and brilliant, his teeth dazzlingly white against his sun-drenched skin. "Come back some time and see what I do with it."

"I might just do that. Peace."

Dennis looked back in his rearview mirror as he ambled on down the highway. The Indian flashed the two-fingered peace sign. Dennis stuck his hand out the window and returned the gesture.

He thought he might enjoy the people of Kansas.

Judging by the desolate surroundings, Dennis knew he didn't have much farther to go. The trees lining the highway were barren. Permanently bowed, the dead ushers pointed the way to Gannaway. Tornado devastation had splintered and weathered the roadside signs, but they were still legible. Competing chicken restaurants battled for the traveler's taste buds and cash. Chicken Rosie's, Chicken Greta's, and the under-achiever of the bunch, Lazy Harry's OK Chicken. The board demanding passersby to *Cherish God's Gift* seemed miraculously untouched, probably not too much comfort to Gannaway's past residents now.

Hawks nested on sagging power lines, heads craning, watching Dennis's progress. The only sign of life he'd seen for a while.

Dennis nearly missed the faded "Welcome To Gannaway—A Perfect Piece Of Heaven" sign. He parked the van in a lot filled with abandoned tires and hopped out. He took in a deep breath as he walked by the remains of a building, now nothing more than a crumbling stone foundation. A sour tang of metal filled his mouth, so overwhelming he could taste it.

Next to the destroyed building rested a small, fence-enclosed graveyard. A defunct electric tower loomed high above the gravestones, a guardian of the dead.

Across the highway, he spotted the Gannaway Mining Museum, or at least its remains. The wrap-around porch slanted like a storm-tossed boat deck, rising and falling by nature's whim. Several of the wood pillars holding the roof over the porch had toppled. The few survivors looked ready to join them.

Dennis's walking tour brought him to the main strip, four stores in a row. What used to be stores, anyway. A bathrobe hung behind a *Closed* sign on the Gannaway General Store's door, the owner's final word on the topic, no doubt. Boxes and a flattened shelving unit spread across the floor. Earl's Machine Shop crumbled to pieces next door, the front window, door, and back wall all blasted out. Graffiti decorated the walls, forgotten artwork for a dead town. The next two establishments were in even worse shape. Impossible to tell what they once were. One block over, the Old Minetown Pharmacy appeared open against all odds, a soda sign lit up in the front window.

Across the two-lane road stood a water tower, ballyhooing the high school's football team: "Gannaway—Home of the Lions Since 1918." Below it, a statue of a lion sat, one paw perched up. Rusted and discolored, it stood proudly amid the devastation like the king of the jungle it once was.

Towering over it all were the chat piles. Man-made anthills hollowed out from below the surface, the earth's unwanted refuge stacked skyhigh. They dotted the horizon. For over forty square miles they covered the landscape, some of them perhaps 300 feet in height.

Alongside them, the remains of mining equipment rusted

away, relics from a different era.

Before he left Gannaway's city limits, Dennis saw the only other open business in town. Durwood Funeral Home. *Telling*.

How could one of the once most thriving mining towns in the country come to this? Once it was proclaimed "A Perfect Piece of Heaven." Now Gannaway felt more like hell on earth.

A knock on the door jolted Dennis awake from his nightmare, the same nightmare that had plagued him for six months. He owed his unexpected visitor his gratitude.

He slipped on his glasses, flipped on the lamp, and checked his watch. Nine-thirty. Early for him to have fallen asleep, too late for a visitor.

"Who is it?"

"County Commissioner."

Dennis opened the door. An overweight man in a sheriff's uniform grimaced at him, toeing at the gravel. The holstered gun at his side weighed down his pants. He constantly hitched them up by the belt loops.

"Um, hi." Dennis rubbed the sleep from his eyes and stuck out his hand. "Sorry, you caught me sleeping."

"You sleep in your clothes?"

"Don't usually. Just wiped out." Dennis stepped back and waved him in. "I'm Dennis Lipstein. What can I do for you?"

The Sheriff waddled in, studying the small motel room's interior. He pulled out the desk chair and fell into it with an exhausted sigh. "I'm Eddie Stokes. County Commissioner and Kwashau, Kansas sheriff. I reckon you can also consider me sheriff of Gannaway, too."

"That's a lotta titles for one man." Dennis sat on the bed.

"I'm a lotta man." Stokes laughed at his own joke, although Dennis thought he just stated the obvious. "Lipstein, huh? You a Jew-boy?"

Dennis blinked, unsure if he'd heard the man right. "Excuse me?"

"Son, I don't stutter. I asked if you was a Jew-boy?" The chair creaked beneath Stokes as he leaned forward.

"Yes, I am. Not currently practicing. Are you an ignorant bigot?" The instant the words tumbled out of his mouth, he wished he hadn't said them. But Dennis didn't tolerate bigotry easily. Not after growing up with it most of his life.

"Did I hear you right, son?" Stokes patted his chest, then his holster.

"Like you, Sheriff, I don't stutter."

Stokes gave a one-note chuckle. "I reckon not. You got a smart mouth on you, son."

"Sheriff, I'm sorry. I apologize. I shouldn't have said that. You just caught me off-guard. I wasn't expecting—"

"Well, now, you've done gone and gotten on my bad side, Mr. Lipstein."

"Dr. Lipstein."

"Come again?"

"I'm an environmental scientist. Dr. Lipstein."

"Well, hell, now, Mr. Lipstein, if this is your'n way of getting back on my good side, you're sure not very good at it."

Obviously, Sheriff Stokes carried around more than a few chips on his shoulder. But Dennis didn't want to begin his stint in Gannaway with the local law harassing him. "Okay, let's start over." Dennis crossed the room, hand outstretched. "Peace?"

"You a hippie, too, Mr. Lipstein?" Stokes leaned back, relishing his intimidation.

"No, I'm not a hippie."

"Smoke a li'l grass, maybe?" Holding two fingers to his lips,

Stokes made a sucking sound.

"No, I *don't* smoke marijuana."

"With that long hair and that scraggly beard—"

"What can I do for you, Sheriff?"

Stokes's face turned redder than a twelve-hour sunburn. "Well, believe it or not, it's what I'm supposed to do for you."

"I don't follow."

"Mr. Gannaway told me you was coming. Some high muckety-muck from the United States Corps of Engineers."

"That's right. Wouldn't consider myself a high muckety-muck, though."

"From the looks of things, I wouldn't either." Stokes passed a huge hand through the air. "But Mr. Gannaway told me to give you assistance. *Supervised* assistance. Now, I gotta tell ya, folks around these parts don't cotton much to strangers nosin' about their business. Just what is it you're hopin' to achieve, son?"

"We, ah, don't really know yet. That's what I hope my re-search will—"

"And you're a scientist? Back in my school days, I learned science is based on hard facts."

Dennis toyed with the idea of asking him what his education entailed, then common sense prevailed. "Finding the facts is my research."

"And what facts are you lookin' for?"

They could go around and around all night. Dennis cut to the chase. "Gannaway used to be one of the richest mining towns in the tri-state area, if not the wealthiest. The zinc and lead mining industry boomed, particularly in the '20s and '30s."

Stokes seemed disinterested, nodded nonetheless.

"It's a fact the mines under Gannaway have been depleted. Or nearly so. Mr. Gannaway shut down his last mine in 1968 due to lack of minerals. And now the overseas countries have grabbed a large portion of the market."

"Damn commies." Stokes scowled. "Still doesn't tell me what you're doing here."

"There've been reports the water's contaminated in Gannaway. Acid mine water from the minerals. Air contaminants are also a concern. There's—"

Stokes jumped to his feet, faster than Dennis thought possible. He yanked his pants up again. "Son, you *still* ain't told me what you're doing here."

"I'm testing the water and the air. Preliminary investigations. Find out—"

"What's the bottom line?" Stokes wandered off toward Dennis's open suitcase on the floor. He leaned over, one foot off the floor, and peered inside.

"We're going to determine what to do with Gannaway. Make recommendations. Maybe turn it into a wetland."

"You know there's still folks livin' in Gannaway. You gonna take their homes from them because of some scientific nonsense?"

"We'll do what we need to do." Dennis crossed the room and closed his suitcase. "We're trying to save these people's lives. Seems to me there's been plenty of lives lost already in Gannaway."

Stokes prodded a finger into Dennis's chest. "And I'm tellin' you, son, you'd best watch what you look into. It ain't your concern. You may not like what you find." He poked Dennis again before he dropped his rounded shoulders. His face sweetened with a baby's smile. "But I'm here to help you." He tucked a piece of paper into Dennis's shirt pocket. "My number. Mister Gannaway says I should help you. But don't you go off on your own, now, hear me?"

"I hear you."

"Think I can find my way out." Stokes left the door open behind him. Dennis slammed the door and pulled back the curtain. Stokes sat in his Sheriff's car, speaking into a walkie-talkie. He replaced the walkie-talkie with a flashlight and swept the beam across Dennis's window. Dennis jumped back.

He had to reconsider his earlier assessment. Maybe Kansas was going to be a huge bummer.

Press
Presents

And by sure to check out Stuart R. West's
Twisted Tales from Tornado Alley:
A Collection of Short Fiction

www.ingramcontent.com/pod-product-compliance
Lightning Source LLC
Chambersburg PA
CBHW061252210726
48293CB00003B/937